RODRIGO'S TREASURE

A SONORAN BORDERLANDS MYSTERY

VERN LAMPLOT

MORE PRAISE FOR A LINE IN THE SAND

The action plays out on both sides of the border and in the tourist towns along the Sea of Cortez. In a gem of innovation, events are moved forward at a key point by a small but very violent group of indigenous musicians calling themselves the Sand Papagos. Lamplot, the "indie" author, clearly knows the terrain, and his affection for the land and the people is apparent.

— AF L.

Filled with international thrills, "Line in the Sand" features retired homicide detective expat assisting soon-to-be female Mexican sheriff, in an intriguing narco-traffic border tale. Top-notch suspense mixed with evil cartel maneuverings, you'll hope author Vern Lamplot delivers more stories soon.

— SUSAN G.

RODRIGO'S TREASURE

The characters and events portrayed in this book are fictitious. Any similarity to real persons, living or dead, or specific locations is coincidental and not intended by the author.

Copyright © 2021 by Vern Lamplot

❀ Created with Vellum

Always for my wife, Joby, and to our amazing supportive family.

1

THE MOUNTAIN REVEALS A SECRET

R odrigo felt the warm afternoon sun on his back as he lay prone on a ridgeline, Nikon binoculars up to his eyes. It was time. He took deep breath and focused on a spot on the road below. His heartbeat quickened as he waited for the white Toyota, to come into view. This would be his only chance. Right on schedule, the vehicle entered the target zone. Relax, he thought. *Steady.* His finger pressed the button, and the vehicle was gone. He exhaled in relief. The image was saved to his binoculars.

He was perched on the edge of a rocky ledge high on a mountain in southern Arizona that overlooked a state highway leading to Interstate 19, to Tucson and beyond. He heard several scratchy squelch bursts, a coded message on his walkie talkie. The code caused him to stand up and prepare to move his tiny base camp. Moments earlier, he'd signaled "affirmative" after he was sure he captured the photo of the passing Toyota heading toward the interstate.

Rodrigo had been recruited off the streets of the resort town of Puerto Peñasco, Mexico, by the Mexicali Cartel after it pushed out a rival gang. Before he agreed to join, he'd worked part-time, mostly for tips, delivering American-style pizza on his motorbike to the gringos staying weekends in the high-rise towers on Sandy Beach. The pizza franchise required him to wear a company T-shirt and display a logo pennant on his bike when he worked. They were so uncool. He hated them as though the weight of the corporate symbols themselves kept him down. Many American tourists were also condescending and rude, feeling superior to the lowly Mexicans who served them. Gringos, especially the younger ones, were lousy tippers. Some made fun of his lack of English. It was a shitty job but the best he could find. Surviving on free leftover cold pizza got old. He hardly earned enough to live on.

His situation changed when he delivered pizzas to a run-down motel tucked away from the main tourist area. A rough-looking Mexican man met him at the door. Rodrigo could hear scuffling in the room then a sudden thud against the thin motel wall. The man smiled and uttered a short guttural laugh. He took the pizzas and gave Rodrigo a twenty-dollar tip along with his card and phone number. A few weeks later, after a very bad Saturday night when he made barely enough cash to put *gasolina* in his bike, Rodrigo called the number. He recognized the man's humorless laugh on the other end. The man told him that he looked like a kid who could pay attention, follow directions, and keep his mouth shut. If it worked out, Rodrigo could earn a lot more money than selling *pinche* pepperonis to spoiled *gabachos* who squatted on prime Mexican seacoast just to have a good time.

His training was a couple of conversations and driving around Puerto Peñasco with several *sicarios* who told him how to use the binoculars and the radios and what to do if he got caught. When he'd asked for more details, they'd said the fewer details he knew, the better for him.

This Arizona mountaintop was his first assignment as a scout, a *halcón*. The cartel had taken over drug routes between northern Sonora and Arizona, and it was testing him to see if he could follow orders and perform tasks. He knew nothing about the vehicles he recorded—who was driving, what was in them, or where they were going. That wasn't his job. His only task was to monitor traffic at a predetermined spot, avoid detection, and alert his boss when a cartel-identified vehicle moved past his line of sight. What happened after that was not his concern. It was a lonely job, he saw no one, but the cartel provided him with all his supplies—carpeted shoes, a sleeping bag, cold food and water, a pair of high-powered binoculars with a camera and a walkie-talkie for coded communications. Some days, the isolation depressed him. It was like being in solitary confinement but out in the open desert. In many ways it was worse. He had to make his own meals and sleep on the cold ground. He tried to avoid people or attract attention. The possibility of being discovered weighed on him constantly. *If I'm found, who will come—Border Patrol? The cartel?* But he held on to their promise that he would be well paid if he proved himself.

When they recruited him, they'd told him this was the best of the entry-level jobs. Other *halcones*—hawks—had it tougher. They were dropped off in inhospitable desert areas on the reservation or some federal-protected district crawling with law enforcement. Those *cabróns* were marijuana spotters. Not only did they count walkers carrying large backpacks of baled weed through the desert—they had look out for rip crews and alert the smugglers if they saw any threats. It was a more dangerous job. They had to count individual loads as the walkers passed. And the loads were often delayed. Some smugglers were caught by the Border Patrol. Others were slowed by stragglers not used to the heat or terrain. The marijuana *halcones* had no downtime. They were on constant alert. Plus *mierda*, marijuana, was the low end of the drug trade. His handlers called it *negocio tradicional*, old-school drug trade. They said because it was legal in many places, the price had dropped, and so had the profit. But it was steady money with low overhead. Many walkers were indebted to their smugglers for their passage across the border. The cartel extorted some of them into carrying the bales. Neither the smugglers nor the *halcones,* the ones who made it work, were paid much.

The fact that the others had it worse didn't make Rodrigo believe his job was glamorous. He was alone. He watched and recorded vehicles. He knew the traffic that passed before him was much more valuable than marijuana. The cargo was transported on a strict schedule, and it was never on foot, always a car or truck. He had no idea what it was. He told himself that it was nothing to him whatever it was. His boss, Choto, said Rodrigo would get an opportunity to move up in the ranks if he followed instructions, did what he was told and avoided the authorities. Rodrigo never called him by that name. His boss's nickname carried some bad associations. It meant little goat but was street slang for "snitch" as well as "dick." Choto's *sicarios* gossiped—whispering like old hens behind his back—that Choto had a very large penis, *gigante verga,* laughing as they talked, suggesting his nickname was meant ironically, like calling a large man Tiny. The name Choto itself was enough to make Rodrigo afraid. He figured that was the idea. The only time he met Choto, he stuck to calling him Jefe or Patrón.

His *sicario* trainers warned him that US Customs and Border Protection flew a drone that surveilled the area at irregular intervals. You couldn't see or hear it because the aircraft circled so high. At odd times, he would receive an order to move his base camp to avoid detection.

That day, the signal prompted him to return to his camp and pack his few tools and belongings. He walked along a dry, narrow drainage path that ran along the steep rocky ridgeline. As he searched for a new campsite, he made sure that he had a good view of the highway below. Looking ahead for a new location, he sought out some large boulders where he could hide from the direct view of a drone and stash his few things about a kilometer from his present site. The warm March day, the dry weather, and the exertion made him pause, take a sip of water, and enjoy the beautiful horizon-to-horizon views of the valley below. For a time, he could pretend he didn't know the real reason he was here.

After taking up his backpack of supplies, he stepped carefully along the narrow path. Carrying a foam bedroll under one arm as he walked, he felt his right leg give way, causing him to lose his balance. His feet slid out from under him on some loose rocks along the hardpan drainage path. Abruptly, he was on his back, an electric shock of extreme pain at the base of his spine, his bedroll flying, tumbling down the steep hillside. He grabbed at rocks and the scrub plants that clung to the side—anything to break his fall—as he rolled helplessly, gaining speed, unable to recover any equilibrium. The desert and deep-blue sky rotated in front of his eyes as he flopped over and over, pain and fear pulsing through him. A spasm rolled from his lower back up his spine. He felt his left arm smack hard into a pile of rocks stopping his fall. A torturous pain radiated from his shoulder as though someone had yanked it violently from its socket. He almost passed out in agony, or maybe he did for a short time. Rodrigo fought for consciousness, knowing he was alone—there was no one he could count on to help him. He lay motionless in a remote area, injured and in severe pain. His left shoulder felt like a spike had been driven through it. He knew it was dislocated. With the pain in his back, it hurt to breathe.

He lay where he'd come to rest, staring at the sky, and tried to gather himself. *What hurts? Hell, what doesn't?* He had no idea if he'd broken a bone, was bleeding, or had suffered an internal injury. He stared at the deep blue of the *cielo* above him. He could not tell how far he had fallen. He focused on controlling his breathing despite the pain, and as minutes passed, his head began to clear.

Rodrigo brought his right hand up to his face and rubbed his cheeks and chin. His head was bleeding but not heavily. He felt around his scalp and the back of his neck, surveying the rest of his head. It was the only part of his body that didn't hurt. He was grateful his cabeza wasn't smashed in. His left arm was limp, pinned by his body against the large rock that had stopped him from falling farther. He found he could move the fingers of his injured arm. That was good.

After a while, he tried to move the rest of his body. He wiggled his toes then moved his feet. *Slowly. Let's not make anything worse.* But he found he could flex his hands and lift his legs. He observed the area to get a sense of where he was then sat up, despite the back pain, and peered toward the mountain where he'd fallen. His left shoulder screamed in protest. Now that he'd moved, he couldn't catch his breath. He guessed some ribs were bruised if not broken. He sucked in oxygen in quick, short bursts. He guessed he'd rolled about thirty to forty meters or more below the ridge where he had fallen. The hillside where he'd stopped was steep, but the rocky outcropping offered him a narrow, almost level space before it dropped off. Giddy at the thought, he decided that the rocks had saved his life.

Determined to reset his dislocated shoulder, Rodrigo held his left arm at the elbow with his right hand and, after resting it against the large boulder, pushed the arm sharply upward with a quick move. He felt the shoulder pop back into place.

"*Pinche puta madre!*" he screamed at the sudden intense pain. But once the arm fell into its natural place, the extreme pain near his collarbone ceased, replaced by a deep throbbing ache.

He searched the hillside for a possible path to climb back to where he'd fallen. The dark movement of an animal within the brush on the hill higher above him—maybe a dog or a coatimundi—caught his attention out of the corner of his eye. As he focused on the shape, he spotted a small opening about thirty meters above it. He could make out several planks of old lumber resting across it. *Firewood* was his initial thought. Jefe would not like it, but the nights on top of the mountain were still cold, especially for a kid from the beach. A small fire at night, shielded from the road below by large rocks, wouldn't attract any attention, and he could heat his food. No one needed to know. The idea of a warm fire was something for him to think about other than the pain in his shoulder and his aching ribs.

Awkwardly, he rose to his feet. His legs were wobbly—a bit numb—and his back protested the movement. He assumed his legs were scratched under his pants, maybe full of needles from the cactus. He found that his legs worked if the pain in his back would allow them to. He rubbed the lower back muscles above his pelvis with his right hand. That area seemed more bruised than anything else, and it complemented the pain in his ribs.

Slowly, he raised his legs, bringing each one up to knee height. *So far, okay.* He looked about the hillside for his backpack and, after squinting back toward the sun, found it resting against the base of some small gnarled trees above him. His bedroll had opened and was caught on top of a bush and flapping in the wind. He climbed up the hillside to retrieve it, the pain in his back reminding him, with each step, to go slowly. He put his hands to the ground to stabilize himself as he moved stiffly up the slope crawling close to the ground until he reached his backpack. Fortunately, he'd remembered to tie the flap on the pack, and the contents remained inside.

Securing it to his body and careful of his throbbing left shoulder, Rodrigo plotted a pathway in the brush and began the upward trudge to the ridge. But he stopped, reminding himself about the firewood. He changed course to move diagonally across the steep hill until he reached the opening. With his injuries, the climb seemed to take forever. The prize was in sight—four old timbers roughly two meters in length that were nailed across an opening in the mountain.

Obviously, it was the entrance to some old mine shaft. Staring into the retreating sun, he knew it would be dark in a few hours. He still needed to get back to the trail to find another campsite. He didn't feel well enough in his current condition to carry the wood, but he thought he could remove the timbers and stack them to retrieve later. It would be worth it for the warmth. Rusted square-head nails secured the planks to a couple of thicker vertical timbers that framed either side of the hole. Rodrigo pried off the top plank easily and placed it carefully on the ground, trying to minimize his back pain. He chose to ignore the ache in his shoulder, which felt a little better since he'd been using his arms. He pulled on the second board and, once it was free, used it to pry off the remaining two planks, the nails squawking loudly in protest as he shoved against the timbers.

The shaft opening was about a meter and a half high and a bit wider than its height. He couldn't see very far inside. The sunlight began to fade. He knew he should leave and come back for the lumber at another time. But he was curious. Banged up and hurting, he was drawn to going inside. *Who dug the mine? How long ago? Is there anything useful left behind?*

He fished through his backpack for his LED headlamp. He picked up the shortest of the stacked boards and used it to shove aside some of the dirt and rocky debris from the entrance, probing for snakes and other creatures. Then he cleared a space around the opening big enough for him to crawl into the shaft. On his hands and knees, he inched his way into the hole, leaning on his right elbow to relieve the stress on his back.

The mine opening was supported by an irregular series of rough wooden beams that had been wedged tight against a rock ceiling. The rustic supports continued on either side toward a larger, more spacious anteroom that was not quite high enough to stand in. He got to his feet to catch his breath but had to stoop to avoid bumping his head on the stone ceiling. The tiny LED light provided only limited illumination, and it took a few moments for his eyes to adjust to the mine's absence of sunlight. The air inside the mine shaft was so dry, he could almost feel it sucking the moisture from his mouth.

The interior of the anteroom was quiet enough that a person could hear the mountain itself breathe. Rodrigo heard the yipping call of a coyote outside but nearby. *Is this an animal den?* The headlamp projected a short way into the blackness, but he could see enough to know the place had been abandoned long ago. The dust penetrated his nostrils, causing his eyes to water, and he sneezed abruptly, sending another shooting pain up his spine. He covered his face with his right arm and stifled another sneeze. Focusing again, his watery eyes now better adjusted to the low light, he could see more of the wider chamber. He didn't find bones, scat, or den debris to indicate that an animal had inhabited the space. But what was there startled him—a stack of canvas bags about the size of old flour sacks piled closely together on the dry stone floor. The sacks, less than a meter tall each, looked dirty and abandoned. Someone must have set them there a long time ago. Pulling the top of the nearest one, he untied a thin horsehair rope and peered inside.

He shone his light into the bag and was stunned at the sight. The sack contained rough chunks of a gray—but still shiny—metal reflecting the glare from his headlamp. It had to be silver, *plata*. He didn't dare believe it, but what else could it be? He remembered from school, the search for *oro y plata* had brought the Spanish conquistadors to this part of the world.

He tried to move one of the sacks. It was heavy, and he knew he couldn't carry it any distance now. He would have to come back for it later. Until then, he had to go establish his camp and do his job. It would take time for him to recover from his injuries.

During his hike to the ridgeline of the mountain, his thoughts ran like a rare torrent of fresh water. He nearly forgot about his pain except when reminded by a sudden movement. *Silver. A lost treasure. Who put it there? How long ago?*

The canvas and its ropes looked very old. Should he tell Choto? If he kept it for himself, how could he get it off the mountain?

2

CHUY RUIZ ASKS FOR HELP

"We have to meet," he said as soon as she answered her cell phone. No smirking greeting, just Chuy Ruiz's strained request.

He was a local hustler whom Puerto Peñasco Police Chief Antonia Ramirez had coaxed into becoming an informant, reporting on the local activities of drug cartels in the Sonoran resort town. The cartels fought over drug routes into the US, but they remained in the shadows of Chief Ramirez's jurisdiction. She and the mayor were determined to keep it that way. She heard an edge of alarm, or maybe stress, in Chuy's voice. Most of the time, he was not a willing informer. Frequently, she had to track him down to extract what she needed to know, which strained her patience. So Chuy's request for an in-person meeting piqued the new police chief's interest.

"Okay, the usual location in ten," she responded.

Their standard meeting site was a fenced, idle hotel-construction site not far from the beach. The place was unlikely to attract anyone's passing interest. She grabbed her white straw cowboy hat, pocketed her cell phone, and after closing her office door, walked through the day room.

"Luis, don't let anyone commit crimes while I'm out," she said to one of the two young cops sitting at their desks.

Luis was a tall, thin officer with styled side-cropped black hair. His light-blue polo uniform shirt and dark chino pants looked like they belonged to someone weighing about fifteen kilos more. He and his partner Hector—who wore a perpetually perplexed look—were pretending to do paperwork.

"I will do my best, *Sargento*... uh, Chief," Luis said, smiling and looking up from a computer screen as she walked past.

"*Otra ves*, Jefe," said Hector, swirling a flat wooden stick in his coffee mug while focusing on some papers on the desk in front of him. He leaned over them in hard concentration, his shirt bulging over his belt at his ample waist.

She left the station in a police SUV for the short ride to the meeting place. Chuy ran a small but profitable recreational drug business, selling through the resort town's nightclubs. His former supplier, El Jefe, had been the boss of the local cell of the Jalisco Cartel. Sickened by his best friend's murder ordered by El Jefe, Chuy turned on the cartel boss and offered American DEA agents vital details about a large cocaine shipment. His information led to a major drug bust in southern Arizona, where Jalisco Cartel members were captured or killed. Drained of resources, the local cartel cell slipped away only to be replaced by the insurgent Mexicali Cartel from the west.

To maintain some eyes and ears on the Mexicalis, Ramirez and the mayor had installed Chuy as a protected informant. To her, the Jaliscos melting away after the bust felt more like a strategic withdrawal than a defeat. She was prepared for more conflict later. Through it all, Chuy had landed on his Nike-clad *indio* feet. His betrayal remained unknown to all but a very tight circle that included the mayor and her expat mentor, Dave "the Sandman" Sanderson, a retired Phoenix homicide cop.

The Mexicalis had encroached on Jalisco territory and quickly assumed the abandoned smuggling routes through Sonora into Arizona. According to Chuy, the Mexicalis had approached him soon after the bust with an offer to become his new supplier. *Nature and cartels abhor a vacuum,* Ramirez thought. She didn't interfere with Chuy's low-level activity among the tourists. In exchange, the Huichol boy with the electric smile and a smooth patter of bullshit kept her and the mayor informed about any cartel-related criminal activity he'd heard about—when she was able to track him down.

She was more than a little curious about Chuy's sudden desire to communicate. Driving up to the vacant site's construction gate in front of Sandy Beach, she spotted Chuy waiting near his red pickup, parked inside the high tarp-covered fence of the abandoned beachfront. His white smile contrasted with his dark face. Chuy was always smiling. The rusting steel bones of a partially constructed hotel rose out of the sand toward the afternoon sun like the fossil of a prehistoric beast. Building activity had ceased a few years earlier, but the illustrated sign on the fence still proclaimed that the San Carlos Princessa was "COMING SOON." The west side of the property fronted the beach, so the chain-link sections surrounding the hotel footprint were more decorative than secure. But the fence was enough of a deterrent that tourists walking along the sandy shoreline would ignore it.

"Hola," said Ramirez, stepping down from the high-profile police SUV she had parked next to Chuy's red Chevy pickup. "*Qué onda?* What's up? You have something for me?" she asked, standing with her hip cocked.

"*Sí,* Jefe," Chuy said, shaking her hand formally. "Two things actually."

"Okay."

"The first is I have been thinking about expanding."

Ramirez frowned. "I'm not sure that's an acceptable option." Tolerating Chuy's present activity was one thing, but looking the other way while it grew would be a problem. She could hear the mayor squawk as though he was standing next to them.

"No, no. Not my usual business. I am planning to buy a *farmacia*," Chuy said, his smile even bigger than before. "It would allow me to move to a more legal business enterprise. And I would report to you any illegal transactions. You know that the cartel is using legitimate prescription drugs as a cover for drug sales. It would be like a window to look inside."

She'd expected some substantial intel about the cartel rather than a store announcement. "I can see that there might be some advantage, Chuy. I can't stop you from buying it, but I want to talk to the mayor about it. In any case, you wouldn't have *la carretera libre*—free to do whatever you wanted."

"No, of course. I would be transparent to you." He seemed disappointed in her reaction, though the smile on his face never dimmed.

"You could have asked about this on the phone. Why are we here?" She crossed her arms, a bit frustrated.

"It is an odd thing. I'm not sure where to begin." His face screwed into a strained wince.

"Chuy, just tell me." They did not have the typical cop-informant relationship. She treated Chuy more like a stern aunt counseling a younger relative, trying to persuade him avoid more trouble.

"First, let me show you," said Chuy, who pulled his right hand from his pocket and, in opening it, revealed a lump of *plata pura*, pure silver.

It looked like maybe a couple of ounces to her.

She nodded with a light shrug. "*A poco!* It looks like *plata*. Maybe eighty dollars—one hundred dollars US—if that's what it is. You discovered silver in Puerto Peñasco." She made a face. "Really? On the *playa* or in someone's hotel room?" It was the tease of the disapproving *tia*. She smiled sarcastically back at him.

. "It is *plata*. I checked. I got it from a friend," Chuy said, anticipating her next question. He told her that Rodrigo, his amigo he hadn't seen since school days, had brought it to him to turn into cash, knowing that Chuy always seemed to have money. "I gave him some dollars for it. He took less than it was worth because he could be in trouble with our boss, Choto. Rodrigo works for him too."

Choto was the current object of fascination by the Mexican government's multiagency drug task force, which consisted of federal, state, and local cops and officials who met regularly and communicated with US DEA and FBI. After replacing the former chief, Ramirez was a reluctant new participant. She got the same hesitant vibe from other members of the group. Most acknowledged privately the task force was primarily for political show. There was not a lot of trust among the participants. Each member held information close, like sullen students forced to sit quietly until the detention hour passed. The task force was aware that the Mexicalis had moved in, but Ramirez and the mayor didn't share with the group much of what they had learned from Chuy, fearing that leaks from within the task force would put him in danger as a confidential source.

Chuy repeated that he hadn't seen Rodrigo since high school. Then, the previous day, Rodrigo had shown up at a club while Chuy was working and confessed to him that he was a drug scout and needed money. Chuy had said he was shocked to hear it.

Ramirez tried hard to imagine a scale that could measure Chuy's capacity to be shocked. Chuy told her that he wasn't close with Rodrigo and people changed. Rodrigo had told him that he'd been sent to Arizona to monitor drug shipments that passed through the town of Arivaca.

"Chuy, why are you telling me this?" Ramirez was impatient with the pace of Chuy's storytelling. She was about to give him a lecture about the duties of a confidential informant, but he interrupted.

"I'm hiding him, but I don't know what else I can do," he sputtered. "I'm sure Rodrigo is in danger."

"I'm trying to figure out what's in it for you. Unless you think he's found something."

"You know the cartel has eyes everywhere. I've already lost my best friend to them."

Ramirez read the real concern behind Chuy's relentless smile. "Get him to the police station, and if he has information about the cartel, I can help him through the drug task force."

"Big *problema*, Jefe," said Chuy, the smile disappearing. "I don't think it is wise for him to go to the *policía*. It's about the *plata*. Rodrigo says he found a lot of it hidden in a mine."

Ramirez raised the brim of her white cowboy hat. Her dark hair, which was stuffed inside, fell against her cheeks. *Lost treasure? What next? Did Pancho Villa's ghost appear at Rodrigo's camp and say he's getting the band back together?*

She wiped her forehead with the back of her hand. The March sun suddenly felt hot. "How much is 'a lot'?" So far, Rodrigo had produced one small lump of *plata*. It could have come from any place, including his cartel bosses planting it to divert attention from something else.

"I have not seen it myself, but he says a large *bolsa*," Chuy answered, holding his hands in front of him with top and bottom about two feet apart.

Air rushed from Ramirez's lips. "Where did he say he got it?"

"He tole me he slipped and fell into a crevice and when he got up, he saw the mine opening. He said there was bags and bags of *plata* like this," Chuy said, once again opening his hand and showing the silver. "Very old."

Buried treasure. Colonial mines. It was like the plot of an old Cantinflas comedy with Rodrigo as the hapless sidekick. Only this wasn't funny.

"Take me where you've stashed Rodrigo now, before this whole *chingada* blows up in everyone's faces."

3

CHIEF RAMIREZ WANTS INFORMATION

"Teagarden and Associates," said Will, answering his phone at his rented office near the Rillito Park Race Track and sports facility in Tucson.

There was a Teagarden—himself. But Associates was merely the name of the LLC. He was a one-man band, a sole practitioner. Will had worked as a legal assistant at a large law firm before he figured he could set his own fees and hours if he started his own business. He specialized in legal and court-related research outsourced to him by a small group of law firms. Legal work kept the lights on, but sometimes the work veered into "other" areas. He had recently gotten an Arizona investigator's license. His clients were mostly attorneys, but for his nonlegal clients, he kept a lawyer on retainer to give them a cover of attorney-client privilege. Whenever the investigative work swerved in a different direction, the clients had a legal fig leaf and could argue that their research results were confidential.

"This is Antonia Ramirez in Puerto Peñasco," said the cop. "How are you, Will?"

"Chief, qué pasa? How's the Sandman and Speed?" Will and his girlfriend, *Tucson Daily Mirror* reporter JD Guzman, had helped Ramirez and her mentor, the Sandman—an expat detective—during a recent investigation into the death of a Tucson college student in Puerto Peñasco. The Mexican resort, about four and a half hours from Tucson, was a popular oceanfront destination, particularly for middle-class families in Arizona and New Mexico. It was also party central for university students looking for a safe but foreign spring-break experience or graduation trip. The town's bars and clubs catered to Americans and were hopping until the early-morning hours during all but the hottest times of the year. Will and JD had vacationed there several times.

Will asked Ramirez about her sister and her niece and nephew. After those pleasantries, she got to the point. "Is it possible that you could make a discreet inquiry for me?"

Will smiled, remembering her directness. "How can I help?"

"I hope this is a good time for you. I wonder if you could search some historical information about lost silver mines and buried treasure in southern Arizona, specifically near Arivaca. I am concerned enough about leaks that I don't want to do it from here."

"Sure, sounds like a fun project. Give me a couple of hours, and I'll get back to you."

"Gracias. I wish it was fun," she said. "I hope to prevent a crime before it occurs. I need to protect someone."

Will frowned. "Sounds serious. Let me get on it."

"It could be. That's why I need the research. Please keep this between us. Gracias, Will. You can call me at this number anytime."

Will was working on a report with heavy legal citations, for an attorney client, and the urgency in Ramirez's voice pushed him to finish the job quickly. Silver—the stuff of legends featuring Spanish conquistadors, miners, cowboys, outlaws, soldiers, Native Americans, politicians, and yes, lawyers. He couldn't wait to dive into her request.

Finally, he wrapped up his work, and satisfied with the results, he placed the encrypted digital report in the client law firm's proprietary Dropbox account and started the project for Chief Ramirez. Despite the chief's anxious mood on the phone, Will enjoyed the search, which involved stories of the old West. The search engine flagged pages of references to lost mines, Jesuit priests, Indian legends, Mexican miners. He tagged groups of references and sorted them into categories, creating a list. Reading through them, looking for commonalities, he edited the collection down to a manageable number of threads. There were plenty to choose from. The Arizona State mine inspector's office estimated that there were at least one hundred thousand abandoned mines in the state. *An astounding number if you think about it*, Will mused. The Arivaca area had its share.

After grabbing an afternoon coffee, he called Ramirez back. "I'm not sure exactly what you're looking for, but I have a list. Would you like me to send it to your phone?"

"*Sí*, that would helpful. Gracias."

"Just so you know, the subject of gold and silver mines is a tangle of myths, fantasy, and outright lies. There really is no way to know where the tall tales end and the truth begins. If you have time, I'll tell give you several examples."

"*Sí*, por favor," she said. "I'm not so much concerned about the truth of the stories as I am about what kind of information exists. I need some background on this."

"Okay, then. One example is The Treasure of Tumacacori. That's an old mission in Arizona, south of Tubac near Nogales. It's now a national monument. In the nineteenth century, priests supposedly mined the area for gold and silver, hiding the treasure from both the King of Spain and the Apache that attacked the churches. The legend is that the treasure is still beneath the mission. Now it belongs to the federal government, which enables fantasists to keep the story alive because no one is permitted to dig on federal property. The park employees say there has never been any evidence of gold or silver at the mission."

Will paused and took a breath. "There is another mission tale. This one claims that during the Pima Indian uprising, priests fled the mission with wagons full of silver and gold. The story goes that they buried the treasure in an old silver mine in the mountains north of Nogales. It's said the mine entrance is protected by a heavy wooden door. Both tales rest on the idea that missionaries spent much of their time overseeing the mines worked by their tribal flock rather than teaching them the word of God. Most historians discount this idea. They say it's likely that neither the Jesuits nor the Franciscans were involved in mining at all. But a few contrarians argue the opposite. I've been to Tumacacori. It's a tourist attraction, and I can tell you, nothing suggests it was ever a wealthy church. You see what I'm getting at. Many stories are backed by no real evidence. Is this helpful?"

"I'm familiar with the area, but I have never heard these stories," said Ramirez.

"Maybe a bit more plausible, and only by degree, is the Black Princess Lost Mine, where two brothers dug gold out of the Cerro Colorado Mountains in the 1800s. People say the brothers died rich. If they did, they took the secret of the mine to their graves. No one's found it. Supposedly, it still out there waiting to be discovered… or not. There's the Lost Sopori Mine, which may be the same as the Black Princess but by another name. Some say that's the mine the two brothers found. Another tale claims early Spaniards worked it and later Jesuit priests and still later the owners of the Sopori Ranch. People say it somewhere in those same Cerro Colorado Mountains. It's supposed to be rich in both silver and gold. In the 1840s, Apache raids drove people away, and after that, the location of the mine was lost. Or so the story goes."

"Is there anything else you need to tell me?" Ramirez asked.

"It's in the links I sent. The old Heintzelman Mine—the Cerro Colorado Mine—was a real working silver mine in the late 1850s. The mine's owners left Arizona to fight as the American Civil War began. The story is that in their absence, the mine workers stole silver from the mine. Believing there was more, they tore the place apart, looking for it. Of course, it was never found. There are other mine stories and also many tales of outlaws burying stolen treasure. Name your place. Tombstone. Bisbee. It's all on the list."

"I received it. Muchas gracias, Will. Your comments are very useful."

"I enjoyed it—but you said something earlier about protecting someone. Can you tell me what this is about?"

"I appreciate your help, but it's very complicated right now," Ramirez said. "I can only say it is possible that not all of the stories of hidden treasure are myths. Please keep this confidential." She ended the call.

Real treasure? Will was puzzled. He decided to archive the links in case they were useful later.

4

RODRIGO TELLS A TALE

R amirez drove Chuy to the house in the police SUV. Chuy told her that after Rodrigo called, he'd arranged for the man to stay at Omar's family *casa*. Omar had been Chuy's best friend until his death by El Jefe's *sicarios*. Chuy blamed himself. Omar had never been involved in drugs. His only crime had been being Chuy's best friend—his *wey*. After Omar's death, Chuy helped support Omar's mother and sister. When Rodrigo returned to town, the two women were pleased to let Rodrigo stay. Omar's sister Alicia remembered Rodrigo from school as a quiet boy who kept mostly to himself.

Alicia and her mother both worked, so Rodrigo was alone at the house when Chuy and Ramirez arrived. They saw him pacing in the yard, smoking a cigarette. His reddish-brown complexion was darker from exposure to the Arizona sun. The yard was little more than sand, and the small cinder-block house needed painting. When the two rolled up in the police SUV, Rodrigo crushed the butt into the loose sand with a rolling motion of his hiking boot. He rubbed his shock of unkempt black hair in a nervous reflex and exhaled smoke. Then he paced the yard like a dog looking for weak spot in the fence in order to escape. His jaw was tense, and he didn't meet their eyes.

Chuy gave him a reassuring smile and called out, "Hola."

Rodrigo nodded and massaged the soreness in his left shoulder through his denim work shirt. "Could we just talk out here?" he asked in a wavering voice.

"Okay," said Ramirez, trying to size up the young man. She thought he might take off running down the street any moment, just to burn off his adrenaline.

"Did Chuy tell you about the *plata*?" he asked.

"He did. Would you like to tell me more about it?" Ramirez planted her boots in the sand and crossed her arms in anticipation.

He continued walking back and forth in the small yard, staring at the ground as though counting individual grains of sand. "Chuy says I can trust you…" It seemed to her more like a plea than a statement.

Ramirez nodded. *"Por favor,"* she said in a soft voice. "Tell me."

"I had a crappy part-time job delivering pizza. On one run, I met some guys who offered me a job if I wanted. They said I had to meet the boss, Choto, so I did."

"Okay. Is he here in Puerto Peñasco?"

"No sé. I don't know. I only met him once for a short time, in his car."

"And…?"

"The men, *sicarios* working for the cartel, told me I was smart. Smarter than others. They said the boss would give me a chance to prove myself, you know. Move up in the organization. Demonstrate my loyalty." He waved his hands about as he rattled off the sales pitch.

*"Sí, típico—*the cartels' usual offer."

"A couple of his *sicarios* explained what I had to do, gave me some equipment and told me how to stay out of trouble.

Then they took me through a tunnel into Arizona." His voice was trembling.

"A tunnel? Where is it?" she asked, maybe pouncing too quickly.

"No, I don't want to say," he nearly whispered.

"Okay," she said, dropping her arms. "What are you willing to say?" Ramirez just wanted to get the boy talking to see what would spill out.

"I need help." The words fought to escape.

"I want to help you, Rodrigo, but I need to understand what is happening. What did you do on the mountain?"

"My job was to spot certain vehicles when they passed my location."

"Where was this?"

"Some mountains in Arizona, close to the border."

"How did it work?" she asked.

"I had high-powered binoculars and a radio. I was told what to look for. When the vehicle passed, I recorded the image on the binoculars and reported it."

"Who did you report to?"

"*No sé.* I never knew. It was a code on the walkie-talkie. I was left alone. You hide from everyone, especially *la migra* —US Immigration. I made camp high up with a good view of the road. I had supplies—food and water. I was by myself. Sometimes I came down to meet someone to pick up stuff and exchange the memory cards." He was spouting details, unconnected and disorganized.

"What mountains?" she asked.

"I don't know the names, but they are not far from this town, Arivaca," he said.

Ramirez nodded. "Tell me about the *plata* you say you found.

"I did find it," he huffed. "I gave some to Chuy. Did he show it to you?"

"*Sí,* he showed me." She looked at Chuy standing next to

her, who was trying to encourage him. "How did you find it?"

Rodrigo quit pacing. "We move around to avoid being found. I got a signal to find another location. I was looking around for a new place. I lost my balance and fell." He rolled up his left sleeve to show her some raw skin on his forearm. "I hurt my back and my shoulder, you know," he said, rubbing his shoulder. Ramirez hoped the look on her face was sympathetic. She wanted the boy to relax.

"I fell a long way. I kept rolling. Some rocks stopped me, or I might be dead." His voice was halting as though his extended isolation had affected his ability to speak. He rubbed the denim shirt on his shoulder again and winced. "When I could stand, I looked up, you know, to find my way back. I saw some lumber stacked against the hillside below the ridge. It looked out of place. And a good size. Wood is scarce in the desert, you know. I thought I could use it for a fire. I climbed up, and I saw the boards covered a mine opening. When I pulled them off, I could see inside past the rocks and cactus in front. The hole was dark, but I saw enough to know it went deeper, like a cave, you know." He paused again. "I crawled inside and used my headlamp to light the cave. I saw some old bags stacked in the middle. I opened one—*ah, chingado,* I was shocked! The bag was full of *plata!*"

"What did you do?" Ramirez asked.

His voice rose excitedly. "When I first found the treasure, you know, I was *loco* with joy. How could such a thing happen to me? Me, such a poor person. Why was I chosen to find it? But then I thought of how much *plata* there was. I became afraid. Who put it there? I didn't see no signs of people. If I told Jefe, he would just take it from me. I thought maybe finding it wasn't good. You know?" Shaking, Rodrigo lit another cigarette.

"You could have walked away and forgotten about it, or

told Choto anyway," Ramirez said offhandedly, as though the choice was like deciding between *enchiladas* and *tacos*.

He looked directly at her for the first time. "I did forget it for a while. I went back and set up a new camp. I was too sore to do much of anything except keep to my routine." He paused, seeming far away as if his attention had drifted back to the mountain. "But at night, alone, with nothing to do, I thought about the treasure waiting in the cave. I dreamt about it while I slept. *El tesoro* haunted me, you know. Always by myself, it took over my thoughts. It was like a presence, a being."

He stopped talking and took a slow drag off his cigarette. "I thought if I could take it with me, I could start over. But I didn't know how I would get it down the mountain. What good was it, if I could not keep it?" He flicked a cigarette ash. "I had to figure out how to move some of it and then how to get it into Mexico." Self-consciously, the young man tried to smooth his hair, which was still sticking up at odd angles.

Skeptical, Ramirez searched his tense face for clues. He wasn't telling the truth—she was sure of that. Maybe he was a *halcón*, but this story was too fantastical to be real. She thought about Will Teagarden's research. Rodrigo's treasure story fit the profile of many of the old scams in the information he'd texted her earlier. Old mining tales of buried treasure. Spanish missionaries hiding silver and gold. She thought it was an act, though she didn't think Rodrigo was capable of pulling off a treasure scam like this.

Wrong personality. He's the opposite of Chuy, reserved and somewhat distant. Chuy had a presence that this kid lacked. Chuy could probably make a stunt like this work, at least for a short time. *Who's Rodrigo trying to fool? Cartel maybe. Does he imagine he can distract Choto and then use the uproar to slip deeper into Mexico? That could backfire, putting a target on himself and also Chuy.*

Possibly, the cartel had put him up to it as a test—Choto

had acquired some plata and sent this boy to convert it into cash. *Why?* She believed the cartel had the resources to convert assets. Maybe it was a loyalty test for one or both of them—tell Rodrigo to enlist his friend Chuy to see if they could succeed. *Or is it a cartel diversion to set up something bigger?* If either of those two situations was the case, Chuy bringing this to her put both the boys at risk.

She pressed Rodrigo for more details to see how far he could go with this story. "How did you get it off the mountain?"

His pacing had resumed. "When I felt stronger, I returned to the cave and dragged one of the sacks to the edge of the hill. I dropped it down to the basin below." He motioned with his arms as though dropping the bag. "She was heavy, so she want to fall, you know. I tried to get it to roll, but the sack would get stuck on the rocks and the cactus, so I had to keep chasing her. I rolled her, you know, again and again. At the bottom, I hid the sack behind some large rocks."

"You did this after you hurt your back?" She pressed him.

"*Sí*, it took time. My back didn't ache so bad after a while. Thinking about the money…"

"Was this when you decided not to tell Choto you found the *plata*?"

"This job, I was always afraid," he said, not answering. "I feared I would be seen by *la migra* or the locals. There was so much pressure. I wanted to escape even before finding the *plata*. They joke that they own you. They tell you that. You cannot leave. But when I found the treasure, I thought it was my chance. I thought I could escape before Choto could come after me and find me."

"So you left."

He was spinning a fantastical yarn. *All that was missing was some missionaries and a sighting of the Virgin de Guadalupe.*

"I would think about it every night before sleep. Then, like a dream, it came to me. If they believed something terrible happened, they wouldn't look for me." His voice got louder as he warmed to his story. "I snared a couple of birds, trapped them with some twine. When I cut them open, I sprinkled the blood around the campsite. I made it look like I had been injured and then went to die in the desert. I left *everything* behind—food, water, radio, and bedding. *Todos*. I am not important. They won't look for me."

Ramirez didn't believe that. Rodrigo's first instinct was correct. He was cartel property, and cartels didn't abandon their property. "So you say. After you brought the *plata* down to the base of the mountain, how did you get it into Mexico?"

"I am saying what happened." He seemed like he really wanted her to believe him. "After I set up the campsite, I hiked to the bottom of the mountain. My plan was to steal a truck from a farm. I had to stay off the major roads to Arivaca. Armed men patrol the roads in the dark."

"Border Patrol," Ramirez said, nodding.

"No, *las milicias civiles*, like in Mexico—men in uniforms driving around the desert with guns and flags in their trucks.

"Vigilantes, then?" She glanced over at Chuy.

"*Sí*. I didn't want to get caught, so I had to go slowly and hide in the fields. I passed several houses before I found one with a pickup truck I could start. I drove it back to the mountain and loaded the *plata* in the flatbed of the truck and then drove it to Sasabe."

"If you hid from the citizen patrols, how did you avoid Border Patrol?" He had details that added to the story, but it was all so unreal. He could have memorized something he'd been told. Rodrigo had stopped moving, and she moved closer to him, leaving Chuy by himself.

He shrugged, holding out the cigarette in his right hand. "There are checkpoints in the area, but we know where they are and how get around them."

"You stole a truck and loaded the bag of *plata*. How did you get the silver across the border?"

"Same as I came across, you know. Through the tunnel under the border in Sasabe.

"So now you're willing to tell me about the tunnel?"

He gave a desperate shrug. "It's how they took me across. It is manned only when there is a shipment coming through. They move the drugs through the passage on large *carros*, like little hand trucks, to be loaded into *vehículos*, usually rental trucks and vans. I used one of the *carros* to bring the *plata* across. But I can't tell you where it is."

"Can't or won't?"

"I am afraid to say."

She let it pass. The tunnel was the only part of the story she did believe. *If authorities know that the tunnel exists, they should be able to find it.* It could be useful information that she could share with the drug task force. "How did you get back to Puerto Peñasco?"

"Before they took me across, I did not know the town of Sasabe. It's small, even on the Mexican side, but the *sicarios* told me there are always lots of strangers in town, waiting to cross. So I was sure I would not attract attention. At *la frontiere*, people waiting to cross camped in small tents made from blankets and cardboard or whatever they could find.

"Smugglers?" she asked.

"Maybe, but some told me they were waiting for asylum in the US. They weren't Mexican. They were from farther down. It seemed like Honduras and Venezuela." There was a disapproving look on his face. "In Sonora, I bought an old truck on the street from a man who had a *Sé Venta* sign in the back window. He took some *plata*. He didn't ask questions. I loaded the *plata* and drove the truck home to Puerto Peñasco. Then I found Chuy." His shoulders sagged. Telling the story seemed to tire him.

She didn't believe this part. She was sure he had stolen a vehicle. "Where is it now?"

"It's parked down the street away from the casa."

"With the *plata* inside?"

"No!" Rodrigo said.

"I know a place on the highway—a storage rental the *gringos* use to keep their toys," Chuy interjected. "I told him to put it there for safekeeping. Then I told him we needed to contact you."

"All I want is to exchange it for some cash so I can go back and get the rest of the silver."

Ramirez had two immediate thoughts. The first was to get Rodrigo out of Omar's home and out of sight, away from the family, so they wouldn't be caught up in the boy's problems. The second was that after Rodrigo was safely hidden, she wanted to set up surveillance of the storage facility where Rodrigo said he'd put his silver.

To solve the first problem, she called her friend, expat Dave "the Sandman" Sanderson, a retired Phoenix homicide detective who lived in Cholla Bay. After a quick explanation, the Sandman agreed it was best to get Rodrigo out of harm's way. He also agreed that the best place on short notice was to put him up at his house in Cholla Bay. At least until things were sorted out.

Arrangements made, she asked Rodrigo "Have you spent any of this *plata* in other places besides Sasabe?"

"I was hungry. I bought some food and gas. It was no problem."

Well, it is a problem. Regardless of where the silver came from or the truth of his story, it was potentially a very big problem.

5

SANDMAN'S RESIDENCE BECOMES A SAFE HOUSE

R odrigo was unsure about the whole thing. He sat silently in the back of the police SUV, chewing on the nail of his left index finger and rubbing his sore ribs with his other hand. He didn't understand why Chuy had called the police. All he'd wanted was help converting the *plata* into money. Instead, he'd been questioned by the police chief, who now knew where the *plata* was. And both of them were explaining to him why the *plata* was a burden. He wanted help, not their opinions.

What if this Ramirez woman is on the take and wants to steal my plata? Chuy worked for the cartel. Ramirez had to know that. Maybe the police were also working for the Mexicalis. If they turned him over to Choto, he'd be in more trouble than if he just left his post.

Rodrigo had always believed Chuy was a little sketchy. That was why he trusted his high school friend in his current situation. He needed a friend who knew the dodgy parts of town. But he never trusted the police.

Chuy said the chief was okay, but what if he's wrong? Why would Chuy work with the cops, especially a woman? And now they were in a police truck, driving out to Cholla Bay, *gabacho* town—full of North Americans—to meet another cop, an old gringo. *Ah, chingado!*

The garage door was up at the old cop's casa, and seeing the open space, the police chief pulled the police vehicle inside. A tall, thin *gringo* greeted them at the door leading into the house. "You are Rodrigo," the man said, looking at the newcomer. "Welcome. They call me the Sandman."

Rodrigo nodded, suspicious of his host.

"C'mon inside." Sandman wore sandals, board shorts, and a faded olive-green Hawaiian shirt. He took them upstairs to one of the guest bedrooms on the second floor of his multistory home.

Looking out the window, Rodrigo could see a third floor with a rooftop terrace that overlooked the Sea of Cortez and was partially covered by a large palm-leaf *palapa*. He was surprised by the opulence of the room. The bed was big and firm when he tested the mattress. He sat on the edge, looking around the unfamiliar room. Several small watercolor paintings of the beach and mountains hung on either side of the bed. A full-length mirror was attached to the wall next to the door. He looked at his reflection—his shabby work clothes and his poor haircut. The bedroom was like nothing he had ever been in. The house reminded him of his parents' stories of large haciendas and pictures he had seen in telenovela magazines. But he himself had never been in such a place. He imagined this was how the cartel bosses lived. This was how he wished to live now that he had the *plata*.

"Gracias for the hospitality," Ramirez said to Sandman.

Sandman stared at the boy's dirty denim shirt and worn blue pants. Rodrigo could feel everyone else looking at him in his ragged clothes. "Let me see if I can find you pair of shorts that aren't too big and a fresh T-shirt," he said smiling. He was half a foot taller than Rodrigo, with smaller feet.

Rodrigo nodded. He didn't understand much English, but he figured out what the old cop was saying. Sandman stepped out of the room and rummaged through a closet in the hallway. Chuy gave Rodrigo a reassuring look. Ramirez appeared nervous. Rodrigo thought she wanted to say something but was holding back.

"Okay," Sandman said, returning to the bedroom with some clothes. He handed Rodrigo a T-shirt and some shorts that were too big. *"I'm sorry—lo siento.* That's the best I can do for now. There are towels in the *baño,* which is at the end of the hallway. *Es todos. Quiere comida?"*

Rodrigo shook his head no. He didn't want food. He wasn't hungry. His stomach was still flipping around.

Ramirez kneeled in front of the boy, her bootheels above the carpet. "Rodrigo, you need to stay here, understand?" She leaned her elbows against her leather holster and utility belt and looked him in the eye. He was jarred by the warmth in her voice. "You must stay out of sight for your own protection." Her face was close to his. "You need to stay here —*quédate aquí!"* she repeated. "We want to check the storage facility to make sure the area is secure. We're not going to take your treasure. Settle in, take a shower, get cleaned up, and we will return soon. Okay?"

"Sí." It was the first word Rodrigo had spoken since they arrived. He remained on the bed and looked around the room when they left to go downstairs.

"I need help, but the treasure is mine," he called after them.

Ramirez thought "I need help" was an understatement. Trailing Chuy down the stairs, she asked, "All you've seen was that small sample?"

He nodded without turning around.

"Did you go with him?"

He stopped on the stairs and turned toward her. "No,"

Chuy said in a low voice. "He was too suspicious to let me help."

"Hmm. Does he have family here?"

"Not anymore. His parents are dead. Brother moved away, and Rodrigo said he doesn't know where he is. I didn't know where else to take him except Omar's family. I'm glad you moved him."

Ramirez agreed. "Who else knows about this?"

"He says only me, and now you and the Sandman." He smiled his most honest-looking smile as the Sandman joined them at the base of the stairs. "He says there is more than he could bring back," Chuy said. "Most of it is still at the mine."

Ramirez rocked on her bootheels, her thumbs pulling on her police belt. "I asked you before, but did he ever say how much?" She was confused about the game Rodrigo was playing.

"He says didn't count them, but at least a dozen sacks."

She was incredulous.

Sí, claro." The young man nodded. "*Hay muy mucho.*"

If you're going to lie, you may as well tell a big one. Go big or go home. Ramirez heard gringos say it all the time, usually after one of them had done something really stupid. *Mucho? What does "mucho" mean? A kilo, a ton? Something in between?*

She was debating whether Rodrigo was slow-witted or naive or both. Whether or not any of his story was true—and she didn't believe it—the young man showed a certain cunning in coming up with the fable's details, like how he brought the *plata* down the mountain and into Mexico. The audacity of it was stunning. But for all his cleverness, Rodrigo failed to grasp just how much trouble he was in. She doubted the cartel would believe his faked disappearance. And if he left a trail of even small amounts of *plata* across northern Mexico to Puerto Peñasco, the treasure would become a curse, not a happy fairy tale.

"Should someone stay with him?" Sandman asked. It was more a recommendation than a question.

"I need him to trust us. And I have no way to hold him legally. We should just go."

Sandman grimaced and rearranged his fishing hat.

The self-storage facility was on the main road between Sonoyta and Rocky Point, just outside of Puerto Peñasco and a convenient site for tourists to drop off and store their toys—ATVs, Jet Skis, and rafts—rather than haul them back and forth between Mexico and Arizona. The rows of low-slung buildings sat behind a nine-foot wall of terra-cotta brick with razor wire and chunks of broken glass cemented into the wall's cap. A long rusty paneled gate was tethered with a steel chain during business hours and was the only entrance into the storage area. It would take some planning and effort to scale the wall.

"Chuy, is this it?" Ramirez asked, looking at him though the rearview mirror.

"*Sí*, but he didn't tell me which unit."

"Good choice," said Sandman surveying the compound. "So, Chief, what do you want to do? Should we bust open the place and steal the treasure?"

Ramirez laughed. "You know I'm not going start my tenure as chief by breaking into people's property." She drove through the gate and slowly rode up and down the rows of lockers fronting each other. Each locker entrance was the width of a one-car garage but taller—high enough to store a decent-sized boat.

"It looks as secure as any place," Sandman said. "Especially since there's probably nothing there."

"I will have patrol keep an eye on it in case this is a

diversion, or the cartel is inviting an attack and booby-trapped the space."

When they returned to the Sandman's house, the front door was open. Ramirez drew her weapon. "Rodrigo, where are you? *Donde esta?*" There was no response.

The door to the house wasn't forced, suggesting the young man might have left on his own. Sandman and Ramirez checked the house room by room, Ramirez moving first with her gun covering the space. When they reached the second-floor guest room, they saw Rodrigo's dirty shirt and pants folded neatly on the bed. It appeared he'd showered and put on the clothes Sandman had given him. Sandman did a visual inventory, checking for missing objects and money. He looked in his closet on the third floor, where—he told Ramirez—he kept an illegal Glock locked in a gun safe. It was untouched. Nothing was out of place, so it appeared that Rodrigo had simply gotten cold feet and walked out.

"*Ah, chingado!*" snapped Ramirez, picking through the clothes Rodrigo had left on bed. "I should have listened to you, Sandman."

"You made a judgment call," he said.

"Now I'll have to inform the mayor." She sighed.

Ramirez called a BOLO for police to pick up Rodrigo on sight. "I assume Rodrigo will go back to the lockers at some point to pick up his treasure. But I don't have the manpower to stake out the storage facility. Patrol can run by it when they can."

"Either Rodrigo walked out on his own, or the cartel picked him up because the trap is set," said Sandman.

"Or he was lured out by someone involved with the cartel. We were careful, but someone could have seen us when we brought him," she replied. "I am very concerned for his safety and ours."

"It's a lot of money," Chuy chimed in.

"Only if it's true," Sandman said, letting the words drop.

"Even if it's not, *someone* will show up at storage shed at some point."

"I agree," said Ramirez.

"I have an idea. Save your patrol until the night shift. Speed is always looking for something to do. We'll stake out the storage locker and cover for the surveillance patrol until the lot closes. Someone will probably show up before then." Speed Duncan, Sandman's Cholla neighbor, was a retired postal employee and Sandman's best gringo friend in Mexico. Sandman called and left a voice message. "Speed, meet me at the house in thirty."

"Gracias, Sandman," Ramirez said. "Chuy, I'll drop you off in town."

6

CHUY REQUESTS PERMISSION

C huy Ruiz had dreams of being a player. The young entrepreneur was thinking big now that his business activities had the unofficial cover of the mayor and local police. Selling party drugs to tourists in Rocky Point nightclubs and discos had only been the first step of his long-term business plan.

He didn't really like being a drug dealer. But it was one of the few professions that offered the chance at real money and was open to a kid from the poorer streets of the resort town, and he had nice clothes, a new Chevy truck, money, and time to spend with friends. But he'd learned the hard way that there was no future in selling drugs. Too many people were dead, including his *wey* Omar, a good man.

His goal to become an independent contractor had been sidetracked. He and his crew had been swallowed up first by the Jalisco Cartel and then the Mexicalis. When he started, he would buy ecstasy, marijuana, and pharmaceuticals wherever he could find them. Then he and his crew of DJs and bartenders in the Rocky Point clubs would resell them to tourists looking for a high. It was small-time but profitable. One of the suppliers he bought from was El Jefe, the local

Jalisco cell leader. But El Jefe wanted to be his only supplier. At first, Chuy was okay with that. Initially, he got along with El Jefe. The drug supply was high quality and assured. They had much in common. Chuy understood the business logic of what El Jefe was doing. Like Chuy, El Jefe had grown up on the streets. But Culiacan was a much rougher town than Chuy's little Puerto Peñasco seaside resort. As time passed, El Jefe became more demanding and ruthless. Chuy felt the pressure. He had to dodge the police and then tread lightly around the increasingly dark threats of El Jefe and the Jalisco Cartel. In Chuy's short business career, he found himself batted back and forth between law enforcement and the cartels like a volleyball on Sandy Beach.

After the Jaliscos killed his friend, Chuy turned on El Jefe. He figured with the cartel gone, he would bleed to pursue a legitimate business on his own. But it only got him in deeper. The mayor and police chief had pressured him to become an informant in exchange for protection from the Mexicalis, the next cartel in line. New cartel, same game. Nothing had really changed. He had some money put aside, but both sides were forcing him to run his drug business. Now he had two bosses instead of one.

And as bad as El Jefe had been, this new boss, Choto, was worse. Chuy could read El Jefe most of the time. But Choto—he was *completamente loco,* a moody *cabrón* who veered from inappropriately giddy to insanely sadistic.

Chuy had a dream, if not an exact blueprint, of how to reach his goal to be on his own. He told himself he wanted to be the Kiki Cruz of Puerto Peñasco. Cruz, the Mexican billionaire and richest man in Latin America, had built an empire in transportation, real estate, media, and telecommunications. Like Cruz, Chuy wanted to expand his business into new areas. He wanted to buy a *farmacia*. It would be legitimate for the most part. He would operate it as a regular drugstore, but it would also give him access to legal drugs. And with some creative accounting, he could cut his expenses for his illicit nightclub sales, raise profits, move toward becoming a legitimate businessperson, and leave the illegal drug trade.

For this, he needed permission. Unofficially, the mayor and Chief Ramirez had to sign off on his acquisition. Relying as he did on his salesmanship, he was sure he could pitch the idea in a way for them to agree. He'd told Chief Ramirez that buying the drugstore would give him another window into the cartel drug trade in Sonora. He could be a source for information on how legal drugs found their way into black market sales. Buying the *farmacia* would make him more valuable as a confidential informant. He ticked these points off in his mind. He'd told them to Ramirez and would recite them to the mayor if necessary. Technically, they couldn't stop him from buying a *farmacia* business, but they could make his life difficult in all kinds of ways if they disapproved.

Ramirez and the mayor weren't going to be the problem. He could handle them. His new supplier, Choto, was the question mark. The man sent from Tijuana to run the Mexicali Cartel cell after the Jaliscos were destroyed was erratic, ignorant about almost everything except surviving cartel life, and in need of constant flattery. Despite his paranoia, Choto was less careful than his former boss, El Jefe, had been. Chuy knew the only way Choto would let him acquire a *farmacia* was to cut him in on the deal and make it seem like it was his own idea.

Chuy had arranged a meet with Choto, who was lunching at his favorite downtown eatery. The small restaurant, a separate one-story building on a side street near the *malecón* —the seafront promenade—catered mostly to locals and resident expats. The limited number of tables were set formally, with white linen tablecloths and stemmed crystal wineglasses, even at lunch. Choto liked the place because the staff was effusively servile in a way that appealed to his ego.

The restaurant's menu featured dishes from Mexico City rather than the typical Sonoran beach food of tacos, rice and beans, guacamole, and shrimp ceviche that most downtown restaurants served. Choto fancied himself a person of discerning taste with a refined appreciation of high cuisine that he'd honed in Tijuana.

After finding a parking space on a side street, Chuy nodded to the two security men who were leaning against a black SUV parked illegally in front of the restaurant. Their dark sunglasses and blank expressions followed him as he walked around the rear of the vehicle and through the restaurant's paneled entry door. He saw Choto sitting alone, tucked into a plate of *huachinango Veracruz*. A white napkin inserted at his collar protected his tailored shirt.

"Can they get you something? The food is very good," said Choto between bites as Chuy stood at the table.

There were eight tables inside the small restaurant, and only two were vacant. Chuy counted sixteen people eating and talking. El Jefe would never have met in the open like this, Chuy thought. Everyone sees everything. But for Choto, that was the point. He liked being the center of attention.

"No, gracias." Chuy calibrated an eighty percent smile.

Choto motioned with his knife for Chuy to take a seat. "It's your meeting," he said, his mouth full of fish.

"You've been teaching me the business," said Chuy after he sat down. Choto bobbed his head and took a sip from his glass of white wine. "And about your idea to expand, I think, if I understand correctly, one way might be to purchase a *farmacia*. With your guidance of course."

Choto put down his glass and stared at Chuy. He was silent for a long time. "You mean as cover for some of our activities?" Choto asked, looking around the mostly full restaurant conspiratorially.

"*Sí*. You have put it just so," said Chuy, hoping he was heaping enough praise into his response.

Choto moved his head from side to side as though weighing the options. "Do you have a particular store in mind?"

"*Sí, con permiso.* You have told me that location is *muy importante,*" said Chuy, although Choto had never told him any such thing. He turned his smile wattage up to the full one hundred percent.

Choto made a face as though he was considering it. "*Sí,* location is the key to everything. The right place at the right time," he replied with great gravity. "Where is it?"

"It is in a small strip mall within walking distance of several Sandy Beach hotels. As you say, it is prime location." Chuy relaxed a bit. Choto must have been enjoying his food.

"Does it make money?" Choto asked between bites. "Not that that is important."

"It will make much more with your help and advice. And as you say, it will cover for things that need to be done."

"You will keep me informed on the progress of the sale," Choto said, wiping his mouth with his white cloth napkin. The fish had disappeared from his plate. He signaled the nearby waiter for coffee, and the young man rushed toward the kitchen.

Chuy could feel the whoosh of air in the waiter's wake as he sped past the table. "*Sí,*" Chuy said, his smile undiminished. "Of course."

"Okay, then" said Choto, ending the conversation. The waiter returned with Choto's coffee as Chuy left the restaurant. Outside in the fresh air, he sighed as he closed the restaurant door. The conversation had gone far easier than he could have imagined. He was about to become a legitimate businessman. Sort of.

7

SANDMAN INVITES SPEED ON A
STAKEOUT

"So are you coming with me?" Speed asked when
Sandman broached the idea of a stakeout. They sat
across from each other in Sandman's den in his old, worn
leather seats. Besides his trademark giant straw hat, Speed
wore a faded T-shirt and long shorts that covered his chubby
knees.

"Yeah, we'll do it together. We'll take turns watching,
switching on and off. We'll find a rhythm, and at some point,
the kid will probably show." The retired homicide cop had
explained as much as he thought Speed needed to know.

Speed was still dubious.

"We're trying to help the kid. He doesn't really
understand how much trouble he could be in."

"See, when you say 'trouble,' I get nervous. The last time
you asked me for help, we wound up kidnapping two
university students in Arizona right from campus." Speed
was referring to the time they'd grabbed suspects involved in
the drowning of Naima Singh in Puerto Peñasco and put
them in Sandman's truck then drove them to the border. He
awkwardly crossed his short, hairy legs, signaling his
resistance.

"That turned out okay, thanks to you," Sandman said. "We're just going to observe. That's what a stakeout means."

"If by 'okay,' you mean we weren't arrested. Promise me there's no danger?" Speed pushed up his large straw hat—the size of a small *palapa*—from his forehead and squinted over his chubby cheeks at his friend.

Seeing those puffed-up red cheeks reminded Sandman of a stubborn child who wanted to be convinced to do something he was about to do anyway. He suppressed a smile. "He's just a confused kid. We're only going to observe the storage unit. See something, say something."

Sandman explained that they would go to the storage lot, rent a space, and pretend to be loading items into it while they watched for any sign of Rodrigo. When the kid showed, they would call it in to Ramirez, and that would be it. Sandman skipped any mention of Rodrigo's connection to the Mexicali Cartel or the boy's talk of a silver stash. The fewer people who knew about Rodrigo's treasure, the better for everyone.

"No kidnapping?" Speed asked warily.

"I promise."

"Okay, could be fun." Speed, visibly relaxing, stood up from the chair. "I'll bring snacks."

"Grab a ball cap. You don't want to stand out," said Sandman, motioning at Speed's head. As they moved to the kitchen, he caught Speed's frown at having to leave behind his signature headgear. "There's café umbrellas smaller than that thing on your cabeza. I'll make coffee."

He retrieved a thermos from a wooden cabinet above the kitchen sink and put a full pot on. Brewing coffee was one skill he'd perfected since his wife, Gloria, died. While it hissed and dripped, he opened the garage door and threw some stuff into the bed of his white king cab F-150, including a couple of webbed blue-and-white-striped loungers, several large red plastic coolers, and some miscellaneous wood pieces that had been stacked in a corner.

Wearing a Mexican-league baseball cap, Speed returned from his house three doors down the sand-packed road, balancing a paper grocery bag full of food. "Carol says hi, and if anything happens to me, she's holding you personally responsible."

"I doubt it. Probably Carol is silently thanking me for getting you out of the house awhile," Sandman said.

Fortified with supplies, they drove to the self-storage facility. The tiny stuccoed office fronted the road. A large chain-link entry gate was attached to one side to the end of the building.

Speed and Sandman entered the office. The only furniture was a rickety ceiling fan, a couple of pigskin chairs, and a drinking-water dispenser topped with an upended murky plastic bottle. A waist-high pea green wooden front counter stood between the renting public and a paneled door signed *Solamente para Empleadas*, Employees Only on a duct-taped piece of corrugated cardboard.

A knock on the door summoned a middle-aged Mexican man with long dark strands of thinning hair and an annoyed smile. "*Sí?* Can I halp you *h*entlemans?" he asked, chewing something and rubbing his hands on his trousers.

At the counter, Sandman looked at a diagram of the locker spaces beneath a piece of heavily scratched plexiglass. A number of locker spaces were not x-ed out in grease pencil. "Sorry to interrupt your *comida*, mi amigo. We want to rent a space. Can you tell me if a young Mexican man rented a locker earlier? And por favor, we would like to buy your lunch for your trouble."

Sandman slid a twenty-dollar bill under his palm across the counter to the man. The man hesitated.

"And we'll buy your dinner as well," Sandman said,

retrieving another twenty from his shorts to lay on the counter.

The man's demeanor improved. His eyes moved from one gringo to the other. "He is not in trouble, no?"

"Not at all," said Sandman, smiling. Speed nodded. "He's helping me on my boat later. I promised I would store some fishing supplies close by."

"He took this one here," the man said, pointing to an x-marked space under the plexiglass counter.

"Muchas gracias," Sandman said, smiling again for the benefit of the clerk.

So at least that part of the story was true. Rodrigo did rent a space here. The locker Sandman had chosen was across the alley from Rodrigo's space and over a couple of spaces. Sandman put down a month's rental in cash.

At the locker, Sandman backed the pickup near the entrance and rolled up the metal door. They took down the loungers from the truck bed and set them up inside the space, angled toward Rodrigo's locker. Speed situated himself in one of the loungers.

"Now comes the fun part," said Sandman, looking over the bed of his pickup toward Rodrigo's rollup door. "We wait."

Speed dipped his hand into the brown grocery bag and retrieved a sealed bag of fried pigskin. *Chicharrón?* I have Cholula." He held up a small bottle of Mexican pepper sauce.

"No, thanks, but I'll pour some coffee. I don't know how long we'll be here," he said, hoping that Speed would take the hint and pace his snacking.

After trading insults for a while, they settled into bored waiting in the darkened rental stall, silent except for Speed's occasional crunching and rustling with the cellophane bag. Between bites, Speed stared across the sandy alley at Rodrigo's storage locker with the stillness of an English pointer. Sandman speculated that his friend would pass out if he maintained that position for any length of time. No one had passed by the driveway between the rows since they arrived.

Sandman leaned against the wall and thought about his brief interaction with Rodrigo. Throughout the borderland's colonial history, the imaginations of pioneers of all shapes and colors had been stimulated by the desert landscapes. The thoughts of many inclined toward larceny. It was easier to make money selling the sure thing of a bogus map or a fake mining claim than laboring in a dark hole in the middle of nowhere in the faint hope of striking it rich. Few of those treasure seekers actually found anything of value. But it seemed like every corner of the Southwest had its legends. In the desert surrounding Phoenix, where Sandman had spent his career as a detective, people still looked for the Lost Dutchman Mine. But he didn't believe in buried treasure any more than in the tooth fairy.

Sandman didn't give much weight to Rodrigo's story of hidden treasure. The kid was just clever enough dig himself a very deep hole. If any silver did exist, it was likely the cartel had sent him to turn it into cash. He and Ramirez agreed on that part. If the Mexicalis were behind this, then Rodrigo's handlers had him and the silver on a very short leash. *Sicarios* would be watching when Chuy and Ramirez took him to the house. And then they could have reeled him back. *It'll be interesting to see who shows up for whatever is in the storage locker.*

If Rodrigo had thought this up on his own, he was naive to think that his employers weren't out looking for him. Cartels groomed people with few family ties and then indoctrinated them or tossed them. Rodrigo had left his assignment. The cartel noticed his absence. The campsite trick wouldn't have persuaded them. Sandman didn't trust this version of Rodrigo's story anyway.

And looking at it from the young man's perspective, he thought there was little reason for Rodrigo to trust any of them either. *Ramirez's gambit of leaving him alone failed. If it's not a cartel scam, she'd better find him before the Mexicalis do.*

His musings were interrupted by her phone call. Ramirez said Rodrigo's truck was spotted in *el centro,* but the vehicle disappeared before police could catch up to it. "I don't know when he'll show up there, but I'm anxious to find him before someone else finds him," she said, echoing Sandman's thoughts.

"Right. We're all set up here."

When dusk came, there was still no activity. A row of clay sconce lamps on the sides of the buildings popped on suddenly, illuminating the locker numbers, and offered just enough light for them to see any comings and goings. They were prepared to stay through the evening, but there was no way to know if they would need to. The kid or someone might show at any moment, or not at all. Sandman rearranged some wood in the back of the truck just to show that they were doing some activity as Speed groaned and stood up to stretch.

"How long are we going to be here?" asked Speed, sounding bored.

"Missing an important meeting?"

"Dinner," said Speed.

"You've been eating since we got here. You couldn't possibly be hungry."

"I need protein."

"Carol must find it exhausting to keep up with your dietary needs. Place closes at eleven. If the kid doesn't show by then, we'll have to leave. It'll be up to police to patrol the outside overnight."

Eleven o'clock came and went with no sign of Rodrigo or anyone else. The pair abandoned their stakeout for the night, and Sandman texted Ramirez as they left.

8

SANDMAN INTERRUPTS RAMIREZ'S
EVENING

R amirez heard her cell phone's vibrating buzz on the hotel nightstand and rolled over in bed. "It's mine," she said, grabbing for it in the dark and clicking on the side-table lamp. A moan from under a pillow was the only response from the other side of the king-sized bed. She glanced at the text message before placing the phone back on the table. "That was your father." She smoothed her hair and rested her head against her pillow. "He texted that he and Señor Speed ended their stakeout, so they were going home."

"Oh, gawd, Toni," said Ericka, popping up and sending her long blond hair flipping around her neck. "Is this going to be a problem?"

"Not for me, it isn't," Ramirez said, reaching with her left hand for Ericka's waist. "For your father, *no sé*. I don't know." She slowly traced the soft skin of Ericka's stomach lightly around her navel with the tips of her fingers and then moved her left hand up to her partner's bare breasts. After a few moments, Ericka let out a sigh, and her body stiffened.

"You know how he gets," Ericka said suddenly. Lately, she'd been talking a lot about her father's potential reaction to her relationship with Toni, whom her father had mentored.

"Uh-hmm, I know him very well. Not as well as I know you."

Ericka was long and lean. Her smooth skin was pale. Toni was especially enamored of Ericka's body. Her own was thicker, her skin darker, and her muscles more defined and harder from years of weight training and police work.

"I'm not sure what he'll think," Ericka said. Her mother knew she was gay, though they didn't talk about it, but her father had no idea yet. "This is all new. I haven't had a chance to talk to him, prepare him."

"The Sandman is a delicate flower. His petals may droop if you do not prepare him for the shock," Toni said, withdrawing her hand.

Ericka snorted a laugh, and the aura of desire was broken. The two had spent the late afternoon and early evening in each other's embrace. Their bodies were spent after hours of pleasure, and they'd drifted off to sleep until the phone interruption with Sandman's status report. She was hoping for another round, but the cell call had changed Ericka's mood.

Toni turned over in bed to face her lover. "I don't talk about it with the people I work with in the department. Not even the mayor. But my sister, niece, and nephew all know I prefer women. It's not so much a big deal anymore. And in Rocky Point, people can find whatever they want."

"That's not it," Ericka said, looking across the bed into her lover's dark eyes. "I'm not sure if he would be that surprised, but we've never spoken about it. Shit, we haven't talked about much of anything important the last few years. We've been going in different directions. It was especially tough after Mom died. She was really the force that held us together." Ericka sat silently for a long moment. "He doesn't know I'm here, does he?"

Giving up on the idea of sex, Toni sat up and rearranged a pillow behind her back. "I understand loss. Gloria's death created a chasm, a space that separates the two of you. You both retreated to your own corners to grieve."

The void left in Ericka's life after her mother's death was familiar to Toni, whose parents' death in a car crash left a similar vacuum between her and Maria, her younger sister. They'd overcome the gulf because they had to. Things had to be settled. Their parents had left the house to both of them. Maria's husband had disappeared years before, leaving her alone with two very young children. There were four people to consider, and they were bound together by family and finance. Maria, a devout Catholic, was more religious than her. Maria was never accusing, but her occasional comments made it clear to Toni that she considered her sister's sexuality *amor prohibido*. Together, they'd worked things out for the children, preserving what their parents had sacrificed for them. But it hadn't been easy.

"You seem closer to him now than I am," said Ericka.

Toni laughed. "Oh, Ericka, that's not true. He is a mentor and professional colleague. It's true that after my parents died, he helped me through the shock and trauma. He assumed a role as a kind of surrogate father. He encouraged me, taught me. Mostly by getting me to concentrate on the job. He called it 'the workaholic cure.'"

"I've heard that phrase before," Ericka said, rolling her eyes.

"When Gloria died, that cure wasn't available to him since he was retired. After that, I consulted him more than I needed to just to keep in touch. But it was Señor Speed and Carol who pulled him out of it, not me. To say I am closer to him than his own daughter… that I cannot believe." She watched as Ericka weighed what she'd told her. She knew that Ericka loved her father, and now there was this growing feeling between Ericka and her.

Ericka's different emotions played over her face. "Are you sure he doesn't know about us?"

"I don't think he does. I didn't say anything."

They'd been lovers only for a few months. Toni hadn't seen much of Sandman since a Thanksgiving fiesta at Speed and Carol's house. When they were kids, she'd been just enough older than Ericka to provide some light babysitting when the Sandersons came down from Phoenix for weekends. Toni helped Ericka with her Spanish and gave the girl her first cigarette. The two spent time together at the beach. She'd been aware that Ericka had a childhood crush on her.

While Toni had always known that she was gay, Ericka told her she's been unsure about her sexuality for a long time. She liked men. She'd had a couple of relationships that were potentially serious, but she had doubts about committing to them because she knew she was also attracted to women.

Ericka came to visit her dad and attend a Thanksgiving gathering at Speed and Carol's house that was, in part, a celebration of Toni's promotion to chief, and the two women reminisced about old times. The attraction was mutual and strong. They began exchanging texts and phone calls. A couple of months back, Toni had attended a two-day Alcohol Tobacco and Firearms law enforcement conference in Phoenix. The panel she was interested in was a hot topic for Mexico—unauthorized straw purchases of guns, a big source of the illegal weapons that crossed the border. The two women met up for a drink and spent every moment outside of the conference program up in Toni's hotel room.

Recently, learning that Ericka had some free time at the public defender's office, Toni had arranged for her to come down to Puerto Peñasco and booked a large room in a Sandy Beach hotel for a couple of days. But after their beautiful evening together, her new love was plagued by guilt—Erica hadn't told her dad she was coming down to Mexico, and the sudden jarring text message from him had her sad and angry.

"I don't know why I feel guilty," Ericka said. "I'm twenty-eight years old and an attorney with a solid job, for Christ's sake. Why do I feel the need to sneak around or have to explain myself to him?"

"Don't be so hard on yourself."

"It must have taken some effort on your part *not* to tell him and to hide the fact from the great detective," Ericka said.

"Do you really think your father and I discuss each other's love lives?" Toni smiled.

Ericka's shoulders relaxed. "Some part of me held out the childish idea that he should have known and brought it up himself. Or that he could just pull it out of me. Did he ever tell you the story about one of his murder interrogations? It's been described to me as legendary. I've heard it from cops about a half dozen times. Once, he got a murder confession from a suspect by walking into the interview room, sitting down, and just staring at the guy for twenty minutes, never saying a word." She laughed softly and wiped away a tear.

Toni shook her head. "Maybe he will figure it out one day. But you have committed no crime. You aren't confessing. You will speak to him about it when you are ready." She turned out the light and drew Ericka to her.

9

THE MYSTERY OF THE LOCKER

S andman and Speed returned to the storage facility early the next morning to find that the lock to the metal front gate had been cut. Inside the office behind a wooden desk, the middle-aged storage manager simply shrugged. "Typical," he said, rubbing his thinning hair. He told them that the padlock had been popped several times in the past, usually by gringos who wanted to get into their storage locker after hours and couldn't reach him by phone. His exasperation suggested he regarded North American tourists as another species with strange behaviors and habits that locals had to indulge and suffer through in order to earn a living.

After the manager noticed that the padlock had been cut, he checked the rest of lot before opening. "*Nada*," he told Sandman and Speed. Nothing else had been damaged that he could determine. Even with the North Americans in front of him, his brown lined face didn't try to hide an eye roll that translated to "Oh, those loco gringos."

Sandman and Speed drove past Rodrigo's locker. The roll-up door appeared undisturbed, lock intact. Sandman called Ramirez to update her. "I know it's probably early in the day to rouse Chuy after his nocturnal business schedule, but you need to bring him down here with the key he probably has from Rodrigo." Sandman still thought that both Chuy and Rodrigo were probably involved in a scam. "Unless you're okay with us breaking in."

"I'm coming." Ramirez told him patrols were supposed to roll by and check on the site at regular intervals, but it had been a busy night, and she wasn't sure how often they'd managed to observe the facility.

Sandman suspected the worst. He waited in his pickup truck with Speed. Since they were going to enter the unit, he would have to fill Speed in on the details.

"Treasure?" asked Speed. He was incredulous. "Where did it come from?"

"We don't even know if it exists. Rodrigo claims he found it in an old mine shaft in Arizona. We assume that something was stored here, and we think there's a chance the local Mexicali Cartel might come looking for it."

"You said there wouldn't be trouble," Speed said.

Sandman laughed. "Speed, you aren't in trouble. Rodrigo was a drug spotter. What we do know for certain is that he left his post and returned to Rocky Point with some tale of recovering a bag of long-lost silver."

"He's in trouble, and he's disappeared?" Speed asked, trying to digest this information. "And there may be buried treasure?"

"We don't know. He's decided not to rely on us for help."

"Is there a treasure map? Isn't that a requirement?" asked Speed, rubbing his chin. "Who were we watching for yesterday? Was it a young man? Maybe we should have been looking for a guy with a black beard and a peg leg and a parrot on his shoulder."

"Something tells me you aren't taking this seriously," Sandman said.

The conversation ended when Ramirez rolled up in a police truck next to them at the storage locker. Chuy hopped out of the passenger's seat, key in hand, his bright-white Nike Air Jordans reflecting the morning sun.

"I knew he had a key. Any update on finding Rodrigo?" Sandman asked as Ramirez slammed the vehicle door.

"*Nada*," Ramirez said, shaking her head, a hand over her cowboy hat.

She pulled out her flashlight and aimed it into the dark interior as Chuy opened the roll-up door. The flashlight confirmed what they suspected—the locker was empty. The only signs of any activity were what appeared to be fresh drag marks in the sand. Ramirez tipped back her white straw cowboy hat and sighed.

Sandman looked inside. At least Rodrigo's bloody body wasn't tied up and lying on the sandy floor. That had been high on his list of potential scenarios before they opened the locker. Ramirez flashed the beam along the ground, but also there were too many old footprints to draw any quick conclusions. Other than that, the storage locker was clean of any clues.

"I have several thoughts, and all of them are bad," she said. "One is that Rodrigo returned early this morning with his truck, popped the lock on the gate, and then loaded whatever he's hiding. I think despite our warnings, he continues to play this treasure scam. Maybe he is trying to sell bogus mine claims by salting the area with *plata*. There are several reports this morning from merchants that someone used *plata* to buy supplies in town. Sound familiar? That will be my next stop."

The mood was as dark as the storage locker, and they all stood quietly contemplating a list of bad outcomes. "The second is that he stole *plata* from the cartel and is converting it as he moves around. If that is true, it is possible the Mexicali Cartel tracked him across Sonora and caught up with him downtown after he picked up their *plata*. No matter which of these cases is true, I don't hold out much hope for Rodrigo's safety."

Speed exhaled in an audible rush of air.

"Agreed," Sandman said. "If he's spending the silver in public, then he's still trying to make his lost-treasure scam work. But I don't think he would steal directly from the cartel. He's naive, but I don't think he is suicidally stupid. That leaves you off the hook, Chuy."

Ramirez glanced at Chuy, who looked relieved. "Any ideas where he might go?"

"I told you I didn't know anything. I was trying to help." Chuy flashed his all-purpose smile, this time meant to convey his seriousness. "*No sé*. Maybe back to Omar's house?"

"We're covering that." Ramirez looked at Sandman for comment.

"Yet you didn't tell us that Rodrigo gave you a key," he said, giving Chuy a hard look. Sandman grimaced and turned to Ramirez. "This doesn't rule out either of your theories. If you're asking my opinion, I would say Rodrigo is still alive. Now he's looking to escape after turning down your help. He's undermining his safety, leaving tinselly little bread crumbs around town in the process. Maybe that's the only choice he thinks he has. But if the cartel is looking for him, he'll be easy to find. It won't take much cash to induce someone he dealt with to talk. I hope they talk to you first."

"We'll follow up on the *plata* reports. Chuy, I need you also to ask around," Ramirez said. "Discreetly. See if Rodrigo has been trying to connect with other small-time *culeros* around town. Maybe he knows more crooks and thieves than we know about right now."

"More than just you and Choto," Sandman interjected, still looking at Chuy.

"Of course," Chuy said, his smile undiminished. He avoided Sandman's eyes. "I want to help him."

Ramirez turned to Sandman. "My other concern is if

people in town start talking about lost treasure and silver mines, it could lead to some kind of mass hysteria." She addressed what they all understood. "Nothing about this story can leave this storage facility. At this point, Hector and Luis don't know the whole story. Rodrigo's health and Peñasco's security may depend on it. If it gets out…" She let the words hang in the air.

10

THE MAYOR DOESN'T LIKE SURPRISES

The office of Puerto Peñasco Mayor Juan Carlos Bustamonte Garcia had been fielding calls all morning from residents about *plata* showing up around town: Where did it come from? Who found it? How much *plata* was found? Did anyone find gold as well? Was there a new mine somewhere in the area? Was it some sort of publicity stunt?

By afternoon, reporters were calling with their own questions: Did the mayor know about the silver? Was there going to be an announcement about some new discovery? Would the mayor agree to an interview about the silver mine? How would this discovery affect the development of Puerto Peñasco and the economy of Sonora?

By the time the young mayor returned from a business lunch touting Puerto Peñasco tourism, Elba, his personal assistant, had a handful of pink phone-message slips, all requesting his personal attention. The mayor, who was using his youth, business smarts, and family ties to cultivate plans for an ambitious political career, did not like surprises. And this was a big one, because he knew nothing about any silver being peddled as currency around his town.

He draped his suit jacket over his leather overstuffed office chair and, sitting behind his massive carved wooden desk, rubbed his hands together and then pressed the intercom button. "Elba, could you please get the police chief on the phone?"

The new police chief, Antonia Ramirez, whom he'd appointed, was his go-to person whenever there was a civic upset, even if it was unrelated to law and order. She'd been born and raised in Puerto Peñasco. Her late father was well known among law enforcement as an honest cop. She came from a good family, and he had bet he could build his administration on the family's reputation.

The mayor remembered her father from his childhood. When Juan Carlos was young, he'd loved trains. The railroad tracks ran through the center of Puerto Peñasco and connected what was then a sleepy little fishing village to all parts of the country, from Mexicali to Ciudad Mexico. He found railroads romantic, moving people and materials to important destinations and doing important things. He liked to play near the tracks, though it was against his father's wishes. Sgt. Raul Ramirez had once caught him tightrope walking alone on a steel rail, the train whistle's ghostly moan signaling closer and closer. He still remembered the whistle's pitch sliding higher and louder as locomotives grew near. The cop scooped him up, set him down inside the police car, and lectured him about safety. But Sgt. Ramirez never told his father, and that created a secret bond between the two of them.

He remembered Raul and his wife's freak car accident and how affected he'd been by their tragic deaths. When he became mayor, he came to trust Raul's daughter Antonia and promoted her from the ranks. His wealthy family had supplied Ramirez and her sister with private security to protect them during the recent skirmish between rival cartels. So he expected that the chief would keep him posted on anything that might be of interest. *Plata* spread around Puerto Peñasco was something the mayor thought qualified.

"Mayor," Ramirez said.

"Chief, what can you tell me about *plata* circulating around our town?" the mayor asked in an even voice.

"*Mierda*," she cursed.

There was a pause, and Mayor Bustamonte Garcia was sure he could hear Ramirez thinking across the connection. Breaking the silence, the chief began to tell the mayor the story of a young drug scout recruited from town by the Mexicali Cartel. The boy tripped and fell from his post in the Arizona mountains. And after his fall, he returned to Puerto Peñasco with a tall tale of how he happened upon a mine that hid sacks full of silver bullion. Then somehow, he managed to convey a bagful of treasure through a drug tunnel and bring it back to his hometown to convert it to cash. At least, that was the story Rodrigo was telling.

The mayor was flabbergasted. He listened patiently as Ramirez described how their drug snitch Chuy Ruiz—the informant he, the mayor had authorized and encouraged— had brought Rodrigo to her to protect him and keep him out of harm's way. And after they stashed him in a safe house, Rodrigo had skipped. The mayor stared at the pile of phone messages with questions and rumors about a new *plata* discovery, all there because of the boy's unsophisticated attempt to go underground. The story was fantastical, but it accounted for the stack of pink slips littering his desk.

"Chief Ramirez, you remember that because of my family, I have resources I can call upon outside the usual government channels," the mayor said. He shouldn't have had to remind Ramirez that his father had been governor of Sonora and his family had considerable wealth and political connections, especially since his father's bodyguards had protected the chief's family for months.

After listening to the pointed lecture, she responded. "I

was keeping this information as tight as possible, not only to protect the boy but also to keep it quiet until I could determine what the facts are."

"Keeping information close does not mean keeping it from me," said the mayor in a clipped voice. Again, there was a pause. "We are on the same team. I need to build trust."

"Agreed," said Ramirez. She didn't try to spin it. "Also, we did not gain Rodrigo's trust, I'm afraid. It's possible his spending around town will bring cartel violence to the streets here."

The mayor hadn't considered that angle. Up to that point, he'd been focused on the public-relations uproar and the potential economic and political damage. It could bring the unwanted kind of tourist, North Americans looking for a quick buck or scheming to rip people off with phony mining promises. Things could get out of control quickly if half the citizens of the town caught prospecting fever and began digging holes all over northern Sonora. He was concerned about the biological reserve north of the town in particular. But the threat of criminals pursuing *plata* inside the town was a much greater and more immediate problem to Puerto Peñasco's security.

"What's your plan?" he asked with new concern.

"We're doing our best to locate Rodrigo and bring him in for his own protection and recover any *plata* he has. I'll keep you informed."

The mayor was quiet. He felt the chief's impatience on the other end of the line and could tell she wanted to get on with the search. He agreed with her in principle—every moment wasted increased the danger to him politically and to the town.

Finally, Mayor Bustamonte spoke. "Whatever resources you need, you will get. Concentrate on finding this boy before the situation becomes extreme. In the meantime, you are to avoid the press at all costs. I will work on a cover story that minimizes the effect of *plata* that's been spent and suggest that it came from outside of Mexico, which is accurate, *sí*? There is no pot of *oro* or *plata* at the end of the rainbow for people to find." Mayor Bustamonte's imagination began to engage with the problem. "Who knows, it might be argued that the whole thing is a Hollywood stunt to promote a remake of the Treasure of the Sierra Madre or some such thing. Find Rodrigo and his so-called treasure before this blows up in all our faces."

Putting her phone back in her pocket, Ramirez didn't see how making up more stories was going to help the situation, but she was happy to sidestep any potential media show and let the mayor handle it.

11

JD GUZMAN PITCHES A STORY

Will Teagarden and his girlfriend, *Tucson Daily Mirror* reporter JD Guzman, were sitting down over dinner in their apartment, he with a local craft beer—Dragoon Wheat—and she with a glass of cabernet. Because of their busy careers, the dinner hours were precious time spent together. Will made jokes about how their drink preferences described them. He was blond and thin like a pale ale, and she was darker and full of life, just like her favorite drink, a full-bodied cab. She had let her hair down from her work-appropriate ponytail. It was a look he much preferred. She sat at the table still in her work jeans, one of her long legs folded underneath her, the other planted like she was ready to leap up from her chair if needed. They'd moved in together to a new downtown one-bedroom apartment over the objections of her Catholic parents, who wanted her to wait until marriage. But there was no holding back JD on most things she wanted, and she wanted this.

The new one-bedroom space was part of an infill project just north of downtown in a well-established upscale neighborhood, close to the newspaper's downtown satellite office and only about ten minutes from Will's space in a small office complex. When they'd decided to live together, she laid down several rules, including that she was in charge of decorating. After staying at Will's apartment and viewing his "lifestyle" and the state of his furniture, she insisted this was nonnegotiable if they were going to occupy the same small space. They also agreed to share cleaning duties, which were described in detail in erasable marker on a white board calendar in the kitchen area. Meal preparation usually meant calling to order takeout, such as the present dinner, a very good Vietnamese pho from a family restaurant in a nearby strip mall. Small talk about work was also strictly forbidden, but that house rule was almost never enforced. Despite their mutual rule breaking, Will and JD had maintained the arrangement without conflict.

"I heard an interesting story in the office today about Rocky Point." JD waited for Will to groan at her violation of the rule against talking about work at dinner.

The two had been vacationing in the Mexican resort town, renting a condo in Cholla Bay, when a Tucson university student was found dead on the beach. The weekend getaway turned into work time for JD, and Will got pulled into it. Since she was already there, JD led the newspaper coverage of what became a suspicious death. Will compiled research for her. It was not the ideal vacation they planned. During that time, they met and eventually worked with Sgt. Ramirez and the retired detective Dave "the Sandman" Sanderson. After posting a number of stories for the *Mirror*, JD and Will had returned to Cholla Bay to attend a Thanksgiving celebration hosted by Sandman's friends Speed and Carol Duncan. Because of the circumstances, Will and JD's memories of Rocky Point were bittersweet.

Instead of complaining about JD breaking the house rule, Will looked at her attentively without protest, so she continued. "Our Spanish-language sister paper, *Espejo de*

Sonora, got an interesting tip from several people down there about some pieces of rough silver that turned up in Puerto Peñasco. Not coin but raw silver or whatever you would call it."

"Bullion? Smelted? Where'd it come from?"

"No one knows," she said, brushing her long black hair away from her face. "The reporter thinks that someone has been exchanging it, using it for currency to pay for things. It's a tip from several sources, but details are sketchy. It reminds me of the old stories of lost treasures in southern Arizona. I was thinking about the old abandoned mines in the mountains around here. Many of them aren't capped, just holes out in the open. Especially on public land. If their story turns into something, I think I'll pitch my editors a sidebar. A cautionary tale about staying away from dangerous old digs and ghost camps. It'll give me a chance to get out of the office and get some fresh air."

Will appeared lost in thought, his spoon idle. She snapped her fingers at him. "You paying attention, babe?" She took a sip of her wine.

After a pause he asked, "Guess who called me earlier today?" Hesitantly, he told her about a phone call from their mutual friend Puerto Peñasco police chief Ramirez, asking for some general research help on silver mines and lost treasure in southern Arizona.

"So maybe there's something to the Rocky Point story," she said. "What did you tell Antonia?"

He exhaled. "I can't share details of what we talked about because of client confidentiality."

"She's a paying client?" JD was skeptical. She focused her gaze on him like a laser.

"No, but I treat her as one, and she asked me to keep the inquiry quiet," he said defensively.

"Kind of late for that, don't you think?" She shrugged at him and put down her glass.

Now that dinner was officially interrupted, Will gave in. He finished his beer then, taking out his cell, texted the search links he'd researched for Ramirez to JD's phone. She thumbed through the links, tagging several for review.

Looking at the screen, she hummed in thought. "I know who I can talk to about this story. I interviewed Dr. Creighton Savage several years ago about a University of Southern Arizona student who won a prestigious history prize. He's a folklorist and a historian. We've interviewed him before about local history. This is great, Wills," she said distractedly, staring at her screen.

"Glad I could be of service," he answered in snark mode. "I thought we weren't going to talk shop or use our phones at dinner."

She looked over at him in mock surprise. "Aw, *pobrecito*," she said, getting up from her chair, phone in her left hand, and crossing the little dining table. She straddled his lap. Facing him, she stared into his eyes and ran her hand through his blond hair.

"If you do call Ramirez, tell her I didn't put you on to whatever it is going on down there," he said, his composure slipping.

"I don't reveal my sources," she said, continuing to look into his eyes only inches away. "Whatever's going on in Rocky Point is not my story. I'm sure the reporter *Espejo* assigned to it has already contacted Ramirez and the mayor. If there's something to it, my idea could be a good companion piece, outlining the present dangers of exploring old mine shafts and a little something about the history of gold and silver mining and searching for lost treasure. Remember that story out of Phoenix recently about the guy who went out in the desert alone, looking for precious metal inside an old mine, and got stuck? It took two days before someone found him."

"Uh, vaguely." He no longer seemed to be paying attention to what she was saying.

"Men are so easy." JD stood up, moved his dishes and beer glass out of the way, and led him to the bedroom. Kitchen cleanup would wait until much later, no matter what was written on the white board.

12

RODRIGO DISAPPEARS

R odrigo felt the blood coursing through his temples, his heart thumping against the sides of his head. His shoulders ached, and his hands gripped the steering wheel hard to keep them from shaking. He tried to slow his breathing to calm himself, but it came involuntarily in short shallow gasps. He felt more alone now than he had been on that Arizona mountain. There was no one to trust but himself. *Since my parents died years ago, isn't that the way it is anyway?* He hadn't heard from his older brother in several years. Flaco might be dead or in prison, who knew. He laughed to himself. Expecting anything different made him seem a fool.

After he'd fled that old cop's house, he figured the police had targeted him. The Mexicali Cartel might be suspicious, but he didn't think so. He was nobody to them. For sure, the cops were looking for him. *Why? I committed no crime in Mexico. They must be after the treasure.* He shouldn't have trusted Chuy.

But that's on me, Rodrigo thought. *I should have planned it better.* It was good that he'd left Cholla Bay. After running away from that house, he hitched a ride with some guys who let him off close to Omar's mother's house. Without saying goodbye, he walked to his truck and split.

He waited hours after the self-storage business closed and then forced the lock to get inside. He was relieved to find his sack of *plata* still on the dirt floor where he'd left it. He feared that the police might have taken it, but it was still there. Now that he had it back, he wanted to just sit with it and rest. But he knew that the woman cop would be looking for him. He didn't dare relax. In the faint light, he put the sack on the floor of the front seat.

As dawn broke, he drove downtown and waited. When the shops opened on Circunvalación, he bought some new shoes, a logo baseball cap with an audio-company label, several cheap blankets, cans of beans, fresh tortillas, and a couple of bottles of tequila. He knew he'd paid too much in silver, but he'd found street merchants who would accept it.

He was rearranging the blankets to cover his purchases and the *bolsa* of *plata* on the floor of the truck's front seat when he saw the police vehicle approach. He jumped into the driver's side and quickly left. The police truck followed him, but he was able to lose it after a couple of illegal one-way turns through the small neighborhood above the *malecón* —seafront. He parked at an active construction site with excavated piles of dirt and sand, hiding his vehicle among several pickup trucks left haphazardly at the future office site until the police truck was gone. The cops circled around the *malecón* several times, but eventually, they left the area.

The close call with the *policía* reinforced his decision to leave town. His thoughts were coming at him rapidly. He saw a road sign and decided he would go to Caborca until things died down. Caborca was only a couple of hours away. It was the closest town of any size where no one knew him and he would not be recognized. If only Chuy could have paid him some more dollars instead of calling the cops, he could have held out until he figured out another way to exchange the precious metal for money. Now that the police knew his truck, he figured he had to dump it.

Checking carefully to make sure the *policía* had left the area, he drove out Fremont Boulevard toward Las Conchas. He passed a public storage building and briefly considered renting another stall to stash his treasure, but he didn't want to be separated from his silver again. He turned on the cell phone that Chuy had given him and saw a stack of missed calls and text messages from Chuy. He used it to call a used car lot and then turned it off again.

Parking on a side street of single houses and small businesses, he left the truck near a family-run *barbacoa* restaurant, next to a real estate office. He looked around to make sure no one saw him then picked up the small bag of *plata* that rested on top of the blanket. He hoped that the rest of his treasure would go unnoticed during the short time he planned to be gone to buy another vehicle. As he left, he checked through the passenger window to make sure the load wouldn't arouse anyone's curiosity. It was a risk, but no one was on the street.

He walked to the nearby car lot and found a smiling older salesman looking to make a quick deal. The rotund negotiator in a rumpled brown suit quickly sized up his customer and showed Rodrigo several older vehicles sitting on the sandy lot in front of the small stuccoed sales office. Rodrigo bought a dark-green Ford sedan with decent tires and a lockable trunk. The salesman called it "well used." Rodrigo thought, *Es una mierda de carro*—a piece of shit—but he bought it anyway. He paid in *plata* retrieved from the top of the sack that he'd shoved quickly into a cloth shopping bag he bought downtown. The salesman nodded and tapped on an old taped-together plastic electronic calculator and made a conversion to pesos. He showed it to Rodrigo. It was a bad exchange rate, but Rodrigo figured the price of both speed and silence was high. Aware of his unguarded treasure nearby, he didn't hesitate, nodding okay. He filled in some phony information on the sales sheet, which the salesman accepted with another nod and a handshake. And with a quick *"Buenos dias,"* he was on his way.

He drove to the vacant side street where the pickup was parked and unloaded the main sack of bullion into his new purchase. He transferred it to the floor of the passenger's side next to the much smaller *bolsa* he carried and covered it all with the blankets. The smell of *barbacoa*—slow-simmered *carne de cabra*—from the restaurant was irresistible, and he used most of the last of his cash from Chuy to buy a hot late lunch and a Coke for the road.

Sitting in his new car, he ate greedily from the Styrofoam clamshell container, dipping a warm flour tortilla into the sauce, and considered what he would do when he got to Caborca, a town he had visited only once years before. *Banks and cambio stands. Spread it around, so I don't attract attention. Convert it a little at a time.* Once he'd changed the *plata* to *pesos* and dollars, he would have the money to visit Arizona legally and claim the rest of the treasure back at the mine.

Then he could start his new life. He could go anywhere he wanted, even travel to Mexico City—do anything. And when he ran out of cash, he'd return to his secret Arizona mine and get more *plata*. The poor Mexican street kid would live whatever life he wanted to live. No more working for the cartel. He would be his own *patrón*.

He tucked Chuy's phone into his jeans, tossed the Styrofoam-clamshell remains of his lunch out the passenger window, and hit the open road.

13

PROFESSOR CREIGHTON SAVAGE

Reporters called him frequently to fact-check some local historical event or get background on interesting area places, so University of Southern Arizona historian Creighton Savage, aka Doc Savage, wasn't surprised when the *Tucson Daily Mirror's* JD Guzman requested an interview. He knew her work—he was a careful reader of the printed morning newspaper.

By a mutual agreement between the unit and him, his campus office was a tiny cubbyhole in a little-noticed corner of the history department. The office location was both political banishment and self-exile. Savage often claimed it kept him away from the pointless hubbub of academic politics. His space was a maze of stacked-paper stalagmites obscuring everything behind them—books piled on the floor next to chairs, his desk, and the overflowing dark-green metal bookshelves. His research collection was a mix of old historical tomes, copied printouts of original-source documents, paperbacks of popular fiction, and folders of articles about local history.

The wall switch next to the door that was supposed to control the overhead fluorescent lights was duct-taped to the off position. Instead, he used a gooseneck desk light and a vintage pole lamp topped by a semicrumpled cloth shade that had been shunted off into an otherwise unoccupied corner. Half-closed slats of Venetian blinds covered the only window that viewed the redbrick wall of the building's other wing. The office resembled the unsorted back room of a less-than-successful used bookstore, but the seventy-two-year-old could pinpoint in a heartbeat where anything was.

His only acquiescence to technology was an old upright computer stashed under his desk, attached by a thick cable to a nineteen-inch cathode-ray monitor he'd retrieved from campus surplus when his previous one died. A basic telephone handset connected him to the outside world. He would have preferred a rotary dial, but the university's digital phone system could no longer accommodate it.

Despite his age, he easily maneuvered about his surroundings in faded blue Levi's and comfortable well-worn cowboy boots. The only decorations on his walls, partially visible above the stacks, were a framed movie poster of an old Tom Mix Western serial, a publisher's rejection letter for his first book on colonial settlement in upper New Spain—the work was published later by different house—and a series of bolo ties mounted on a shiny yellowed wooden plaque.

Guzman arrived promptly, which he appreciated as it was an old-school nod to common courtesy.

"Have a seat anywhere," he said, peering over his reading glasses and holding a book when she appeared at his door. She glanced around the office, and he got up to clear a pile of books from a chair near the door. "Please…" He gestured with his left hand, holding the books under his right arm then, sat back down. "You said something on the phone about old mines, am I right?"

"Yes, Dr. Savage. I'm doing a story about local old mine legends and tales of lost treasure."

Savage snorted a chuckle through his neatly trimmed,

white beard. "Well, I can give you a very brief history of lost treasure in southern Arizona—there ain't none."

Poised to write in her reporter's notebook, JD frowned.

"There's lots of stories. Discoveries of precious metals, lost mines, sudden wealth, outlaws, and bands of Indians. Frankly, they are the real treasure," he said, raising his arms behind his head and leaning back in the chair. "It's the stories that people make up and retell for one reason or another."

She began writing, but clearly, this wasn't what she was looking for. "But there are mine shafts all through the mountains—the Santa Ritas, the Pajarito Mountains. There are lots of tales of buried treasure."

"Sure, Spanish conquistadors were looking for gold and silver when they explored this part of the Southwest. Explorers ignored the native peoples while the missionaries tried to convert them. So, without the stories that attracted them, the soldiers, missionaries, and settlers might have missed the area. Things would be very different than they are now."

He stood up and moved from behind the desk and picked up a folder from a stack of books and paper. "Here's a short article about the history of gold and silver mining in Arizona. Precious metals were found in the area of course. In the seventeenth century, silver was discovered near what's now Alamos, and Spaniards opened a mine. Missionaries moved farther north, and treasure seekers followed. There's lots of theories about the Jesuits mining, but that's all they are. Supposedly, instead of tending the spiritual needs of the newly converted, missionaries sent them to work in gold and silver mines in the nearby mountains and smelted it in secret rooms at the churches. There's no real evidence of that either in found metal or church records. But the stories persist." He handed her the folder and returned to his desk. "Tumacacori Mission, south of Tubac, has a couple of lost treasure stories," he added with a dry chuckle.

"You're obviously skeptical and disapproving of these stories," JD said.

"Disapproving? Not at all. These are wonderful stories because they tell us something about the past, how people viewed where they lived and what made it special to them. A quick example—there is a treasure story about the great church of San Xavier, south of town. There are no historical records that describe the church's actual construction. Travelers who visited it years later and saw all the gold and silver leaf that adorned the great altar sought to explain it. So people speculated that there must have been a local mine to supply it and the remaining gold and silver must be somewhere, probably stashed in secret tunnels under the church." He laughed again. "Boom, instant legend."

He leaned forward in his chair. "Of course, all these many decades later, neither the precious metal nor the tunnels have revealed themselves. Can't disprove a negative, so again, the stories persist," he said, smiling and stroking his chin hair. "You can find similar stories about nearly every old church in Sonora, on either side of the border. You can study the stories, how certain ideas move across the land and how they change. I've had a very successful academic life researching this stuff." He was enjoying the exchange.

"Another quick example if you have time," he said. "In 1736, a Yaqui miner—and supposedly others later—found a slab of pure silver lying on top of the ground in a creek bed. The well-known soldier Juan Bautista de Anza confiscated it until the king of Spain could determine how much of it belonged to the crown. It took years for the answer to return, and surprise—the king decided that half of it was his. By that time, the silver had disappeared. What happened to it? Who knows. No one could ask De Anza about it because by then, Apaches had killed him. There are good historical reasons to believe that the silver existed, but is it missing? Buried somewhere? Most likely, it was pilfered, taken south where it found its way into the pockets of Spaniards along trade routes among the towns and villages. A stream near where people believe the discovery took place became known as Planches de Plata, its Spanish name." He saw she was writing furiously in her notebook.

"So here's my point. More than a hundred years later, pieces of native *plata* begin to turn up at the Tubac trading post. According to a prospector, he bought the pieces from an old Opata Indian who claimed he found them on the surface near Carrizo Creek, not far from Nogales. The story goes that the prospector returned to the creek area and came back to town with bags of silver. And then suddenly, he died without revealing the location. No one else has found the source of the silver field. Boom! A parallel to Planches de Plata! The story comes back in a new form." Another dry chuckle.

JD finished writing in her notebook. "Are there stories about missing mines near Arivaca?"

"Several. What did you have in mind?" he asked, smiling again. "There's the lost silver from the Cerro Colorado Mine, an actual functioning silver mine that fell to ruins. There's the Black Princess Mine, probably a hoax, and then there's the treasure of the lost Sopori Mine." He ticked them off on his fingers. "They're all in the same general area of the Cerro Colorado Mountains, near Arivaca."

"What would you say if someone said they found silver and gold in a mine there?"

"I'd say, bullshit," he said, laughing. "Though I doubt you can print that in a family newspaper. I've hiked the mountains many times. There's hobby prospecting clubs that have been searching that general area for years recreationally, looking for gold and silver. Sometimes they find some flecks of ore—on very rare occasions a small nugget. Amateur groups, people who go out looking for the fun of it, trying to connect with the past. But they don't believe they are going to stumble onto the mother lode. A few hours of wandering the hot, dry hills in the desert sun, and your enthusiasm tends to fade."

"Could you take me out there?" she asked, undeterred. "Maybe I could take some pictures of the area?"

He stared into her determined dark eyes and shrugged. "Sure, why not?"

14

CHUY MAKES AN OFFER

"I think I can help you," said Chuy Ruiz. He was speaking to a middle-aged couple who were behind a dispensary counter of their *farmacia*. Señor Soto was a short, round-faced man with overcombed thinning dark hair and a small gray mustache. His wife, Señora Soto, rested her folded hands on the glass countertop. She had an open face with large dark eyes and graying hair pulled back in a tight bun. Both wore white lab coats with plastic pocket protectors over their clothes to lend a look of professionalism and confidence to the dispensary. They stood silently behind the counter and listened. Behind them was a floor-to-ceiling glass case partition wall displaying boxes of prescription drugs stacked neatly in various categories on shelves.

Chuy wore a new pair of jeans and Nikes nearly as white as his teeth for his best professional look. The Farmacia Soto was in a small mall on a corner near the older section of Sandy Beach hotels. The Sotos' clientele included some of the locals who worked the bars, restaurants, and resorts, but mostly, they were vacationing gringos from nearby Arizona, New Mexico, and California. Tourists would bring their prescriptions from stateside doctors. A lot of it was cash business in dollars. The gringos told the Sotos that Mexican prices were much cheaper than what their US health insurance offered at home. The Sotos had regulars, and they stocked up on those preferred drugs, especially the common ones like diabetes-related medication. It looked like a good business, and their loyal customers were grateful.

To Chuy, the cash business in dollars was particularly attractive from a money-laundering perspective. Leaving that part out of his pitch, he explained his finance idea to the Sotos. "I know you are under pressure from the authorities and the cartels," he said, sympathetically.

The legal prescription drug business was regulated by the government. The paperwork was thick and official oversight slow. The Sotos were subject to inspection of the premises and their bookkeeping records. Money delivered to the right officials was required to move the process along.

Also, the cartels demanded a monthly *mordita*—bite—in cash payments, which the Sotos made for the privilege of being allowed to operate their business. The Mexicali Cartel called it insurance. Sometimes the collectors took some of the Sotos' drugs. Chuy knew the Sotos were being squeezed. With all the demands, they were barely making a living. The small family business required all their attention, and the hours were long. The couple's two teenage daughters clerked for the store sometimes, ringing up customers, but neither was interested in pursuing it as a career. Twice, overly aggressive "insurance" collectors had made suggestive threats to their girls. So when Chuy came to them with an offer to buy the store, he wasn't surprised that they decided to listen. If Chuy became the owner, the cartels could collect from him instead, and the Sotos could retire or do something else with their time.

"It will be just like before, but I will relieve you of all the problems," Chuy said.

Señor Soto said he couldn't understand why Chuy would make him such a good offer.

"Let me deal with the cartel and the local officials. If you agree to sell to me, the two of you will keep running the *farmacia* just as you always have. I will pay you the going price for the business, and I will also give you a decent salary if you stay to work in it.

Señor Soto frowned. "But, Chuy, we told you about the numbers, and you know about the *mordita*. How will you make any money?" He looked at his wife, who also wore a puzzled expression.

After a pause, Chuy said, "Marketing," and gave him a big smile. If they asked that question, he knew they were interested. Now he was sure he could close the deal. "I can increase sales, and together, we will make enough *pesos* and dollars to be profitable."

It didn't matter to Chuy, at least in the short run, if the business made money. He could front the purchase and the operating expenses as well. It was part of his expansion plan, the one in his mind that he called the Kiki Cruz Plan. *Think about how the billionaire operates. One step at a time. Look for opportunity where others don't or can't and be ready to move when it presents itself. Because the opportunity may not come again. Understand what the real underlying business is.*

His business idol, Cruz, knew that the bakery corporation he owned was a really a transportation and distribution business. Drivers delivered fresh bread to small towns and hamlets from regional transportation hubs, doing business with places no one else cared about or wanted to service. The distribution network, not the product, was the innovation. Chuy thought he could do the same thing, linking together mom-and-pop *farmacias*. But he needed to get his foot in the door of a legitimate business, or he would never escape the perpetual and dangerous back-and-forth between law enforcement and the criminal cartels that he knew could eventually destroy him.

To facilitate the Kiki Cruz Plan, he could request help from the mayor and Chief Ramirez for any government issues. In fact, he would insist on it as part of his deal to continue as an informant. He had leverage, he thought. With Choto's approval in hand, the cartel's *mordita* would go away. Instead of a payoff, he could offer the cartel a vehicle to launder cash as a cover to move drugs around town. If he could buy one *farmacia*, then maybe he could buy others and own a chain of drugstores. Then he could transition from an illegal business to a legitimate one.

He also wanted to help the Sotos. They were hardworking, honest people. He liked them instantly when he'd met them several years back. He understood their business predicament. Hell, it was the same as his. And he did notice that the daughters were growing into beautiful young women.

"I promise I won't interfere with the day-to-day operations of the business," Chuy said. "I am not a pharmacist. I don't want to be. I am a businessman, and I want to partner with you. I will accept all the financial risk." He turned up the wattage on his smile. "You will come to the store just as you always have. But at the end of the day, you will go home without worry, leave any problems of the day behind, and enjoy your life. Together with your family." He spread his hands wide for emphasis.

He was pitching a story. The rhythm of his sales talk reminded him of the old days when, as a young teenager, he sold resort time-shares to tourists. It felt like he was back in the salesman groove. He could read their faces. He saw them relax and knew he'd made a sale.

Señor Soto sighed and then, looking at his wife, said, "We would like to think about it, but your offer sounds generous."

She nodded and smiled back at him. "I still don't understand how you will make money, but…" He shrugged.

Chuy knew they would accept. "I have an *abogado* working on the legal papers now. Everything will be spelled out. You'll see. If there is anything you don't like in the sales contract, we can work it out. I promise. Gracias for allowing me to present my offer." He saw one of the Soto's daughters eyeing him with interest from behind the edge of the partition wall.

His phone buzzed with a text. He noticed that it was from Chief Ramirez. Looking up from the screen, he said, "Excuse me, I have to deal with this. Think about my offer carefully, and I will come back," and hustled out the door of the *farmacia*.

15

POLICE SEARCH FOR RODRIGO

"I would like you to be discreet when you ask questions," Ramirez said to Hector and Luis, her two most trusted beat cops. The three of them were standing in the warm afternoon sun by the marina next to the road leading to the *malecón*. Hector had been out on a call, so it took a while for the chief to gather the pair for stall-to-stall questioning. The two police vehicles were parked next to each other off the road.

Ramirez sent them a photo of Rodrigo she'd taken with her phone at Sandman's house. "This is who we are looking for. If they ask or suggest a theory, just say that you are simply trying to locate Rodrigo and can't reveal anything more. We want to find him without raising anyone's suspicions higher than they already are."

"But, Jefe, we don't really know much," said Hector.

"That's why we are investigating," Ramirez said. "We think he could be in jeopardy, but you don't need tell anyone else."

The two had some rough edges, but they'd grown to accept her leadership. She felt their acceptance turning into respect. Sandman had told her it would take time. In turn, she relied more and more on them. Others in the small department were not as pleased to be bossed by a woman. But that had made her more determined. As time passed, memories of the former chief would dim. The town was full of rumors that the chief of police had been murdered or was now running with the Jalisco Cartel. Only the mayor and Ramirez knew the truth—the chief had fled after he was threatened by the cartels. Ramirez had found him and his wife living secretly in a tiny jungle fishing village in southern Mexico. Keeping that secret was an extra burden she carried as she sought to prove herself.

Rusty shrimp boats, with their raised net booms retracted, waited silently at the marina ramp for another day. Some distance away, two boatmen puffed on cigarettes and exchanged small talk as they loitered by the steps of the entrance to a chartered fishing business. A large sandwich board sign by the road touted Half-Day and Full-Day Deep-Sea Fishing Trips and advertised a price in dollars.

A ll three cops walked down toward the *centro mercado* streets and then split up, each taking a side of the street and moving from stall to stall, questioning merchants. Ramirez turned down a side street to interview shopkeepers, and Hector continued on. In the bright afternoon sun small knots of American tourists, lazy from lunch and margaritas, walked slowly along the street, perusing the rugs, pewter serving pieces, and trinkets from deeper in Mexico for sale in vendor stalls. Colorful beachwear, imported mostly from China, hung from metal awnings and flapped slowly in the afternoon breeze coming off the blue water beyond the *malecón*. The fish market's briny smell of flounder, shrimp, and octopus from the morning's catch mingled with the smoke of meat sizzling on open grills. Several vendors sat patiently in front of their stalls on large white plastic paint cans or cheap molded chairs, waiting for potential customers who walked up and down the street.

"Hey, honeymooners, come inside, look around," said one, reciting a well-worn sales pitch.

"We have the best prices in Rocky Point," said a short young woman in a colorful blouse, trying to engage a sunburned couple. "What size you looking for?"

Hector approached a short, thin merchant standing in front of his stall and holding a long pole used to retrieve clothes flying in the breeze from a tall awning above. He introduced himself and showed the man—Manny—Rodrigo's picture.

"Why are you searching for this man?" Manny asked, squinting at the image on Hector's phone.

Hector explained that he was a possible witness, and the police just wanted to find him. Removing his baseball cap and rubbing his dark hair, the merchant was plainly skeptical. "What will happen to him?" After Hector assured the man that Rodrigo was not in legal trouble, the vendor admitted that the young man had purchased blankets and a *bolsa* from him with a nugget of *plata*.

"Could I see it?" asked Hector.

The vendor nodded, and Hector followed him into the stall with team-logo T-shirts hanging just above their heads. The man opened a metal cashbox chained to an iron post by the counter. He removed a chunk of *plata* somewhat smaller than a golf ball and held it in his open hand. Hector examined it and held up his phone to take a photo of the silver.

"Gracias, Manny," he said.

Manny quickly snatched it into the palm of his hand and put it back in the metal box.

"It's yours. I'm not going to take it. Don't worry," Hector said, smiling. When Manny moved the cashbox, Hector spied a short stack of maps with the word "Tesoro" printed in hand lettering across the top. He tugged one of the sheets from under the box and held it up to the merchant's face. "Manny, what is this?" The paper was a map of Sonora with three hand-drawn X's marked on them. Hector noted that one of the X's was in the biological preserve.

"*Mapa de tesoros*," said Manny. "I sold three of them already. After I show them the *plata,* they are interested. "

"Where did you get these?"

"I made them myself."

Hector frowned. "I'm taking these," he said, scooping up the stack of maps. "You're encouraging vandalism. If you try to sell more of these, I will shut you down. *Si*?"

"But it was just a joke," Manny protested. "It's entrepreneurship. C'mon Hector, I have some new XXXL T-shirts in stock. You could test a few for free."

"I don't want your T-shirts. Is that all of the maps? It's illegal," Hector hissed through clenched teeth. He waved a finger in Manny's face. "*Basta!*"

Once he left the stall, he called Ramirez and told her about his encounter with the vendor.

"*Mierda*. This is what Mayor Bustamonte was concerned about," she said.

∾

The mayor had been texting Chief Ramirez all day to get updates on the search for Rodrigo, hoping to prevent a public-relations disaster as well as to find out just how much *plata* was in circulation. The police were still canvasing *el centro* to get a rough idea of how much silver had been passed.

The Puerto Peñasco mayor's office issued a statement by email and Twitter, saying that there had been no silver strike in the area but that *plata* was showing up around the *el centro* area. The statement said there was no evidence of a crime and no cause for concern. In an attempt to shift attention away from the police search for Rodrigo, the mayor's office claimed, without providing any additional information, that it possibly was a promotional stunt by a company.

But the Tweet didn't have the desired effect. The phone calls from local businesses to the office continued, and when the mayor left work in the late afternoon, six television and print reporters were camped outside the entrance to the building when he opened the door. Mayor Bustamonte, jacket hanging from his shoulder, forced a smile as they ran up to him.

The reporters all spoke at once. "Mayor, what can you tell us about the silver that's been showing up in town?" "Señor Bustamonte, who is responsible for the *plata*?" "Señor Mayor!"

The mayor lifted his jacket off his shoulder and held up both hands in front of him. "Por favor, I don't have much to add to the earlier statement," he said calmly. "Our police are investigating to find out the source of the *plata* simply because we don't want this to become a situation that endangers the public."

"Sir, the statement said it could be a promotional stunt. Why do you say that?"

"That's what we're trying to find out. It's spring break time, nearly *Pasqua*, when the town will be full, and it has been suggested that a company might be using the mysterious appearance of the *plata* to get free media and promote a new tequila or something."

"Do you know who that is?"

"No, that's what we're trying to establish. I'm sorry, but I must leave for a meeting," he said, employing his most genuine campaign smile. "Thank you very much. Gracias. Please be careful what you report."

∼

Hector and Luis worked their way down the street from opposite ends, and by the time they reached the middle, all of the vendors knew what they were asking and why they were there. Several other merchants identified Rodrigo from the photo. Some claimed they refused to exchange *plata* for merchandise that Rodrigo wanted.

As they moved from merchant to merchant, the three cops compiled a list of items that the young man had purchased, hoping for a lead on where he was and where he might go. Merchants questioned the officers about the source of the *plata*. The cops explained that they didn't know, adding that there was nothing illegal about it and they were just trying to find Rodrigo. Even after explaining that it was not a criminal investigation, they suspected several vendors were not cooperative, believing the officers might confiscate the silver. The partial list of merchandise allowed them to infer that Rodrigo knew people were looking for him and planned to leave town. Both beat cops were curious about Rodrigo and the silver.

"It's stolen from someone with power and influence," Luis guessed.

"It could be," Ramirez said with a maybe-yes-maybe-no look. "I would like to share more with you, but we don't know. We just need to find this young man."

Ramirez released the officers to resume patrol. They would need to find him quickly, before he could leave Puerto Peñasco. There were only two routes out of the town. One was the Sonoyta road, where he could connect to Federal Highway 2 and go east or west or try to enter the United States through Lukeville. They agreed that it wasn't logical for Rodrigo to try to pass through a normal port of entry.

The only other route was the direct road toward Caborca and points east, where he could travel back to Sasabe. That route would lead him through the town of Caborca, a likely destination. Police had a BOLO out on Rodrigo's truck, hoping to catch him before he got into more trouble. Ramirez's worst fears were being realized. Rodrigo had left a trail of silver bread crumbs all over northern Mexico. The theory that the cartel was planting the *plata* was becoming unlikely. It looked increasingly like Rodrigo had stolen it and was desperately trying to escape. By that point, he'd attracted too much attention for the Mexicali Cartel not to notice, and if the cartel caught up to him first, the boy's future was *nada*.

Ramirez was on her way back to the station when Hector called. "Jefe, we got a tip about a parked vehicle and found the truck. Empty."

"Hector, where are you?"

"Near Las Conchas. The truck is parked on one of the side streets near a restaurant."

"Any signs of violence?"

"Nothing I can see. No broken windows or blood or anything," he said.

"Get it towed to the station, so we can examine it."

"*Claro,* Jefe."

16

DOC AND JD GO HIKING

D oc Savage's property was a classic one-story ranch
house with a peaked roof and covered porch that
surrounded the entire building. In the early-morning hours,
JD arrived at his home on a multiacre desert lot bordering the
Tohono O'odham reservation south of Tucson. After parking
in the dirt driveway, she noticed that the San Xavier Mission
was visible from the front porch of the house. Doc was
already loading a full backpack, extra water, and hiking poles
into his red Dodge pickup under an extended wooden
carport. He wore an Army green all-weather floppy hat with
mesh vents and a chin tie, a long-sleeved all-weather jacket,
tan Gore-Tex pants, and Merrell hiking boots.

"Are you ready?" he shouted as she approached.

"I think so," she said, waving her arms and twirling in a
circle to show him her outfit. "I'm more of a gym rat than a
hiker."

"I guessed that."

He looked her over. She was wearing an Arizona
Diamondbacks Major League Baseball cap, a ponytail sticking
out the back. Her sunglasses sat above the bill. The rest of her

outfit consisted of an unbuttoned men's plaid shirt over a thin knit blouse and baggy sweatpants.

"What's in your backpack?" he asked, looking down at her feet. *At least she's wearing a serviceable pair of hiking boots.*

"A couple of peanut butter sandwiches, water, an LED flashlight, uh, a multifunction bike tool, and a book I forgot was in there."

"Peanut butter and flashlight, good. No sunscreen? I got plenty. Get rid of the book. I'll give you more water to carry. I've got a first aid kit, a compass, an extra space blanket, and some socks for you. I always keep maps in the truck. Your phone isn't going to work where we're going, so there'll be no GPS on the mountain." He grabbed her pack and loaded the additional items into the large pocket, then zipped it closed and placed it in the truck bed.

"I expected that. I'll use the phone mostly for interviews and photographs," Guzman said, smiling.

"Climb aboard," he said, satisfied that they were prepared. Doc's house was not far off the freeway, and they were soon heading south in the pickup. "Guzman. That's a fairly common name." Savage moved through the early-morning traffic. "Has your family lived in this part of the world long?"

"My great-grandparents moved up here from Sonora, Mexico, when they first got married. That was a long time ago. The borderland was a lot more fluid back then. I don't think Arizona was even a state when they came. They eventually settled in Tucson and became citizens. Then some other relatives followed. Now there are lots of Guzmans in Tucson."

"And you're not married?"

"No, but I'm in a relationship."

Doc Savage chuckled dryly. "Is that what it's called?"

"We're together," she said defensively. "We'll see where it goes."

"Seems like a formal way to refer to shacking up—'in a relationship.'" He glanced at her while she made a face.

"Pretty old-guy thing to say. You sound like my father. Wills is a great guy, and we're serious," she said. "We had a friendship before we became involved."

"No offense. I'm interested in cultures and language. The way people refer to things says something more than just the words themselves. In this instance, it indicates a seriousness that another phrase would not. It's saying this is not casual."

"You must drive your wife crazy, dissecting every word like that," she said.

"I used to. She died six years ago."

"I'm so sorry. I noticed your ring. I assumed…" She nodded at the wedding ring visible on Savage's left hand, which was gripping the steering wheel.

"I can't take it off. Don't know that I'd want to anyway. In many ways, Suzanne is still present in my life. See? Words and customs have meaning beyond the obvious." He chuckled again, this time wistfully, and his face became serious. "She died of lung cancer. Never smoked. We learned during her treatment that it's not all that uncommon. She was the best damn editor I ever met. I'm a better writer since I married her. Better man too." His eyes teared up, and he brushed his sleeve across them, focused on the memory.

By that time, Doc had left the interstate and was driving on the state highway toward Arivaca. They sat silently for a while as Doc thought about the day ahead. Finally, he said, "I'm going to warn you, the trailhead marks out an easy hike that many people take. It's not going to be very interesting at the start. But we're going to keep going to the higher ridgeline, which is a trail much less traveled and gives you a better view of the area. You can fill your cell phone with panoramic photos if you like. "

Doc pulled off the highway onto a dirt road and drove about a quarter mile, where it became more rutted. He continued a few hundred yards farther and then found a place to park off the road. "Here we are," he announced.

No other vehicles were present. They got out of the truck and put on their backpacks. The morning was crisp and cool. The vegetation at the base of the mountain included grasses, shrubby mesquite, and prickly pear and other cactuses swollen temporarily by rain. "We're going to follow the trail for a little while, and then we'll do some bushwackin' but nothing worse than a class two," he said, pointing up the trail with one of his poles.

"I have no idea what that means." JD fidgeted with her phone and held it in front of her as they started on the trail.

"We're going to get off the path more traveled and cut across the mountainside then make our own path," he said, looking back at her. "You really are a gym rat, aren't you?"

She gave a pouty frown, put her phone back in her pocket, and followed him up the trail. He used his poles to push plants clear and to steady both of them as they moved up the incline. They traversed across an embedded rock face and kept hiking.

After about an hour hiking at a steady pace, Doc paused and took out his water bottle. He turned and looked down into the valley revealed below. It was a sweeping vista, but it would be even better when they got higher. JD took out her phone and fired off some panorama shots of the area, turning slowly. Then she grabbed Doc by the shoulder, turned the phone, and took a selfie of the two of them together.

"Better save some juice for later," he advised.

They continued upward, and the bushwhacking became more difficult as the mountainside got steeper. They reached the ridgeline about ninety minutes later. The higher sun was warm, but a light chilly breeze kept them cool.

Doc consulted the map and checked their position with a compass. "Where would you like to go next?"

"So, if you were looking for silver, where would you go?"

she asked, holding a hand over her phone and blocking the sun as she took more photos.

"Probably to a jewelry store."

"C'mon, play along," she said, still shooting pictures of the adjacent mountains and the valley. "Think about what might be of interest to readers."

"We talked in the office about some of these places. Here's the general location of the Cerro Colorado Mine…" Doc made a circle on the map with his finger. Then he pointed to a spot below them. "Somewhere over there." He looked back down at the map. "This is the old Sopori Ranch," he said, pointing to an area below the mountains. "The location of the Sopori Mine may have been on the ranch property itself, or it may have been higher up on the mountain, possibly over there somewhere. And the location of the Black Princess Mine resides, most likely, only in the imagination."

JD took a deep breath and gazed out at the landscape below. "I can get a sense of how it felt for the Spanish settlers to have walked this area, looking for fortune or just a way to scratch a living from the earth."

"That's it." Doc gave her a wide smile. "Now you're thinking like a historian. You translate some of that to your readers, and you've got an interesting story. Settlers spent nearly all of their time farming and tending their animals in order to survive. But there are holes all over these mountains, so people did come up here and dig or do some placer mining along the streams—which flowed more often than they do now—looking for gold and silver." He tossed an energy bar at her. "Let's have a snack."

She snatched it out of the air like a first baseman. "So mining was always part of the area."

"Sure, and some miners did find precious metal, but the tales of fabulous wealth just waiting to be plucked from the ground…" He shrugged.

"I'm sure people invented stories, in part, to justify their efforts and not admit they were largely wasting their time," she said. "But some people must have struck pay dirt."

"Yup. A fortunate few. After we refuel for a bit, let's see if we can find the remains of another old mine shaft around here that some poor misbegotten soul put his back into a century or two ago."

17

THE ROAD TO CABORCA

E ven though he'd shaken the local cops and changed vehicles, Rodrigo couldn't lose the sense that he was being followed—nothing he could put his finger on, just a nagging feeling that grabbed his shoulders from behind. He told himself it was his imagination. There was no chance anyone knew where he was. Not even Chuy would guess. He didn't recognize the vehicles in the traffic behind him. He'd been careful. He hadn't stopped anywhere since he bought the car. *How could anyone know about me?*

He figured he still had time before the Mexicali Cartel noticed he was missing. More time would pass while Choto weighed the evidence Rodrigo left behind at the campsite. First, they would look for him on the mountain. Even if Choto didn't believe the bloody scene he had arranged, it would amount to a dead end. He'd taken nothing with him, not even his clothes. They had no way to know where he'd gone. And anyway, he was so low in the organization that no one would care.

He looked in his rearview mirror. The vehicle traffic behind him consisted of trucks carrying cargo across northern Sonora with a few cars interspersed. Nothing stood out among the cars. It was a sunny day, and he was glad to be back in Mexico. He told himself to stay calm. His only worry had been the police in Puerto Peñasco. He thought that maybe the cops were infected by the same cartel scum he worked for. If he'd stayed, they would have stolen his *plata* and turned him over to Choto. He had to admit that the police chief had treated him well, with respect.

But Chuy made an error in judgment. Rodrigo didn't understand why his friend had called the police. By that point, he was sure Chuy had realized his mistake. Rodrigo hadn't liked the gringo they called the Sandman. The old man smiled at him, but it was not a friendly smile. His eyes were blue stainless steel like a *sicario's pistola* and looked right through Rodrigo as if he could read his thoughts. He was hard. Rodrigo could tell that the old cop had seen things, bad things. Maybe done bad things. There was no way he could stay at the Sandman's house. *That's bullshit.* He'd had to leave to protect himself and his treasure.

Rodrigo approached Caborca in the late afternoon. It had been an easy drive despite the road's poor condition. The highway hewed close to the sea until it turned east and inland toward the town. He kept checking the rearview mirror. As he thought about it, there was an SUV a few vehicles behind him that made him nervous. The black SUV hung back, but it had stayed close enough when the road turned toward the town. The vehicle was like a dark shadow that he couldn't shake. He looked over at the blankets covering the passenger's floor and felt weighed down by the *plata* in the car. It was more like a burden than freedom. He sped up and again checked the rearview mirror to see what the SUV would do. It stayed behind. *Maybe it isn't following me.*

He was rethinking what to do with the *plata*. He couldn't just carry it around with him everywhere he went. He couldn't leave it unattended in a motel room. He decided Chuy's idea of a storage facility was sound, and when he got to town, he would look for some kind of rental place to stash most of it so he could exchange it as he needed. It would take time before he could return to Arizona and claim the rest. In the meantime, he would look for a place to stay.

He felt his heart jump into his throat when the SUV began passing traffic on the roadway, getting closer to him. *Tranquilo,* he thought, urging himself to calm down. It was the highway, after all, and the main road between Puerto Peñasco and Caborca.

The sun was behind him, and he lost sight of the vehicle or how far back it was. He felt more like a target than the newly rich man he'd become. Caborca was just ahead, and Rodrigo saw a Pemex station on his right. In a sudden move, he swerved off the road and stopped for *gasolina.* At the pump, he waited until he saw the dark SUV continue on the road before he got out. He sighed in relief and gave the last of his cash to the attendant. The young man in coveralls nodded at the few *pesos* and hooked up the nozzle.

The sun moved lower toward the horizon, and he thought he would find a *cambio* shop to get some *pesos* before it was too late. He didn't want to negotiate the price of a motel room using the *plata.* Looking down the road toward town, Rodrigo turned to see the attendant leaning over the car window with his free hand and looking at the blankets that had slipped slightly at the foot of the front seat. Neither Rodrigo nor the attendant said anything.

After reaching the *peso* amount, Rodrigo waved, got quickly into the car and started off with a jump. He was counting on the town's anonymity as a form of protection— he knew no one, and no one knew him. But it also made him suspicious of everything and anyone.

He drove up and down the main streets of Caborca until he found a *cambio* shop wedged between two small storefronts and parked. It was a stand-alone kiosk with a cement base and a large window. An attractive young woman, little more than a teenager, sat behind a glass partition, stacking coins in a metal holder. She looked up from her task and smiled at him. "*Puedo ayudarte?* Can I help you?"

Rodrigo drew a piece of silver from his pocket. "*Cambié a pesos,*" he said confidently.

She looked at the silver. "It is not common for me to exchange this, but I will check," she said with a shy smile. She pulled her cell phone from her flowered apron and speed-dialed a number. "*Sí,* someone would like to exchange *plata* for pesos. *Sí.*" She turned to look at Rodrigo. "*Cuanto?*"

He pulled several more pieces of silver from his pocket and laid them in the tray so that she could retrieve them.

"*Es todo?* Is that all?"

He nodded, not wanting to reveal how much he had.

She said something softly into the phone that he couldn't hear. Then she retrieved a small digital scale from under the desk and put the pieces on top to weigh them. He felt the hair on his neck rise, but what could he do? He had to start recovering some cash. She smiled at him and removed the pieces of silver from the scale. Running her fingers through her light-brown hair, she spoke into the phone again and then wrote some numbers on a thin slip of paper.

She passed it through the slot below the glass on the tray. "This is the number I can offer," she said.

The terms were much better than what the car salesman or vendors in Peñasco had given him. He nodded. She removed a stack of pesos from a drawer underneath the desk and crisply counted out the bills and coins on the desktop. She counted them a second time and put them in the tray for Rodrigo.

Some real money at last.

"*Buen día, señor.* Have a nice day," she said, and he began to walk away. "Do you have a place to stay?"

He shook his head.

"Try the hotel down the street that way," she said, pointing to her right.

"Gracias, señorita." Rodrigo saw her say something into her cell phone as he walked to his car.

He sat in the driver's seat for a minute and caught his breath. *That went better than expected.* The clerk hadn't asked him where he'd gotten the *plata*. There was no pushback. In fact, she offered him a friendly, almost inviting smile. He again weighed Chuy's idea of finding a self-storage locker for his treasure. He would hold on to his *bolsa* to exchange for money and put the larger sack in storage. No one would notice him coming and going from a self-storage locker. But he remembered the feeling he'd had the last time he was separated from his fortune. He started the car and pulled out into the light street traffic and thought about the hotel that the cute *cambio* clerk had suggested. Maybe he would drive around for a while before settling in for the night.

18

DOC AND JD ENCOUNTER STRANGERS

They'd been hiking for hours, and JD was tiring in the sun and altitude. The azure canopy of the sky was unblemished by even a hint of white. The mountains weren't extremely high, but the air felt thinner. They must have been higher than she'd realized.

She stopped for a moment to catch her breath and take it all in. The old man, Doc Savage, seemed to have more energy than she did, which annoyed her. She'd used up most of her cell phone's battery, shooting photos and some short videos as they made their own way across the side of the mountain and investigated the remains of a mining camp and an old shaft opening that Doc knew about. Just as he'd said, the shaft looked like it had been abandoned long before and appeared to be more than a little dangerous for anyone to enter now. There were no posted warning signs anywhere, and the site wasn't fenced off. She clicked some more pictures of the opening.

They remained outside and talked about the human-caused wound inflicted into the mountainside. Upon seeing the half-covered gash, she'd felt both a little angry and sad. Many years before, someone had spent a lot of time digging the mine, using primitive tools—little more than miner's axe and a shovel—moving rock and earth with only a slim hope and a wild daydream to keep him going. Finding precious ore would have been just the first step in recovering metal of any value, much less generating great wealth. The abandoned mine was a scarred monument to the failure of someone's dreams—and to people chasing fantasies across the years. She was beginning to understand Doc's point of view.

Standing on top of a ridgeline with spectacular views of the area, she wished she had saved a bit more phone juice. It was a stunning landscape. Doc was pointing out various landmarks that were present and others that existed only in memory. The valley turned delicate shades of peach and reddish pink in the afternoon light, contrasting the dark-green patches of shade and vegetation. JD's cell phone was useless for calls—if there was a location that could register something below zero bars, they'd found it. She might as well use her phone for pictures.

She aimed it at a scene below and was taking a panorama series when from behind, she heard a sharp metallic racking sound. Startled, she jumped. JD felt her heel gave way in the dirt and with it, her balance. She raised her arm over her head to steady herself and felt Doc's strong grip on her forearm as her phone flew into the air and tumbled down the mountainside. Despite Doc's attempt to keep her upright, her weight was too much, and she began to slide on her back. To her horror, she saw Doc pitch above her head and over, his poles flying beyond her, and he rolled down the steep slope out of view. As she tumbled, she grabbed at a shrub and managed to stop herself but watched Doc bounce farther down the slope until he slid to a stop near a boulder. He let out a sharp groan and didn't move.

She called down from her position, "Are you all right, Doc?"

He only gave out a moan in response. In her mind, she

ticked off a checklist of her condition—no serous pain, just a few scrapes as far as she could tell without examining further. She felt some loose dirt and gravel roll down and gather behind her head, and she tried to turn to see the cause.

"*Lo siento*," came a male voice from above that didn't sound very apologetic. "Did we scare you?" they asked in Spanish.

JD managed to turn herself enough to see the outline of two men about thirty feet above her, standing where she and Doc had been. "*Pedir ayuda!*" she yelled and added, also in Spanish, "I'm afraid my friend is hurt."

"We are looking for someone," the voice said, ignoring her plea. "A young Mexican. Have you seen him?"

JD was able to focus enough to see that the men's faces were partially covered with rough scarves and their hands were cradling automatic weapons. "No. Por favor. Can't you see we need help?"

"What are you doing up here?" the man asked.

She could hear Doc begin to rouse himself below her. "We're hiking, and I think my friend is hurt. Can you help?" she asked.

"*Tenemos prisa.* We're in a hurry. We can't interrupt our search. This is not a usual spot for tourists," the man said with irritation.

"Por favor," JD said, concerned that she and Doc were in danger from the pair. There was a long pause.

"Stay where you are until we leave," the man said suddenly. It was a warning as well as a command. "*Buena suerte.* Good luck."

And then she couldn't see them. She considered calling out again, but she knew she needed to help Doc. She worked her way down to his location, half sliding on her back, half crawling until she reached him. She saw blood on his pants just above his right knee, and he had already fashioned a tourniquet from a handkerchief around his thigh to control the bleeding.

"Are you okay?" he asked in a raspy voice.

"I'm a little scraped up, but otherwise, I think I'm okay. But you're not. I am so sorry."

He gave a wave of his hand. "Not to worry." He pointed at his leg. "Make sure it's tight." His hat was still tied down, obscuring his eyes, and he groaned loudly when she moved to make the knot tighter around his thigh. "Feels like a broken leg." He exhaled sharply. "God damn, I hate being old," he spat out.

"I don't want to press on it. You've got it clamped down pretty fast. Doesn't seem like there's too much blood, considering."

"Hmm. Old army medic training."

"Any idea who those guys were?" she asked, though she had her own thoughts.

"Cartel *sicarios*, I imagine." Doc tried to sit up. He pulled his hat down farther over his face, so she couldn't see his pained expression and gingerly straightened his injured right leg with his hands, trying to keep from putting any weight on it. "Aw shit, that hurts," he said matter-of-factly. "They're looking for somebody."

"*Sicarios*? I figured cartel, but…" She stopped short and considered how things could have turned out worse.

"There's stories about drug scouts watching the highway and checking on the drugs moving through." He gave a heavy sigh. She hunched over him, confused. "From what little I know, a key part of the scouts' job is to remain out of sight. They want no part of being found. If you don't go lookin', they'll make sure you don't see 'em. But those two weren't scouts. That was a search party. Somethin' musta happened." He took a deep breath and looked down on at his leg. "It doesn't look like I'm getting out of here on my own," he said calmly. "You'll need to go for help."

She stood up, but the thought of leaving him pushed her anxiety front and center. "I don't have my phone," she said, looking around, remembering it was gone.

Doc reached under the flap of his shirt's breast pocket and extracted an old beat-up flip phone. "You'll have to walk back down the mountain yourself and call for help," he said, pitching her the phone.

"I'm not sure I should leave you alone. What if they come back?"

"If they thought we were a threat, they would have killed us right then. We're going to lose daylight in a few hours. When you're within range, don't call 9-1-1. I don't want a fucking parade coming up here. If those two return and see a large group come up the mountain, they might weigh the risk-reward equation a little differently. Could get us all shot after all."

She started to walk away but stopped and looked back at him, confused. "Who should I call if not search and rescue?"

"When you get a signal, open the speed dial. Number two is SP. Tell 'em what happened and where we are. Don't forget the part about the *sicarios*." He was sitting up against the boulder and fishing for his canteen from his backpack.

"SP—what's that?"

He smiled from under his hat. "Friends of mine. A little out of their territory, but they'll still get here faster than goddamn search and rescue." He took a sip from the canteen. "And they're better armed."

"What does it stand for?"

"They're a Tohono O'odham band called the Sand Papago. Ex-Marines, though I don't hold that against them."

He chuckled his reflexive laugh, which reassured her that he was not going to perish anytime soon. And then it clicked with JD. "I know about them."

"'Course you do—you're a reporter," he said with another chuckle. He pushed up his hat and gave her a look that said,

"Why are you still standing there?" which caused her to turn down the hill and start walking.

"You have a pass code on this phone?" she asked over her shoulder, holding the scuffed black instrument near her head.

He scoffed and shooed her away with his left arm. JD picked up her step and began some serious bushwhacking down the mountain slope toward help.

19

RODRIGO DODGES CHOTO'S SICARIOS

R odrigo drove around Caborca after leaving the *cambio* shop to explore the old town, first settled by the Spanish. It was smaller than Puerto Peñasco with many fewer American tourists. The gringos who visited were mostly on day trips to see the tiny historic church built by missionaries two centuries earlier. The late-afternoon sun hung low in the west, casting a yellow-orange glow on the many white buildings. The end of *siesta* added to the bustle and movement on the streets. Moving through the traffic, his old beater felt sluggish and weighed down by treasure and anxiety.

He steered through the streets aimlessly for a couple of hours, weighing his next move, and then turned the street corner of the *cambio* shop again. He thought it was a sign, signaling what he should do next. The girl at the *cambio* shop had suggested a hotel in the area. A good night's rest would help him decide on a plan.

She said it was down the street. With the *cambio* shop as his landmark, he drove past the change booth toward the hotel. He glanced at the building as he slowed to the hotel's corner.

The L-shaped two-story hotel was a white-washed stuccoed building with an ornamental clay-tile roof over the carport leading to the lobby. He was just about to turn into the hotel entrance when he spotted them. Fear gripped him instantly. He felt his heart race in a burst of adrenaline as he recognized two of Choto's *sicarios* standing in the parking lot, idly smoking between cars. He held tight to the wheel and tried not to panic. Reflexively, he put his foot on the accelerator and then backed off. The car lurched forward then gained speed moving past the hotel.

"*Tranquilo,*" he said. He turned his head away to avoid being identified. The two men were among the *sicarios* who had smuggled him into Arizona through the drug tunnel. They would know him by sight.

Thoughts rushed through his mind. Somehow, they were on to him. *How did they find me?* He considered the timeline. By that point, they'd probably discovered he'd left his post, as he expected. *But why would they look for me here?*

He couldn't concentrate. His feelings were jumbled as he tried to understand how Choto knew where to find him. Ideas bombarded another part of his brain with conflicting thoughts of what to do next. He started driving toward the main road. As the minutes went by, he realized he was driving back toward Puerto Peñasco.

Renting a storage unit in Caborca wasn't a good idea, but he had to do something. The *plata* was slowing him down. If they found him, they would take it. Looking at the buildings on the highway, he saw a hardware store on the outskirts of town. The best option was to bury the treasure somewhere. It had to be a place where he, and only he, could get it.

Rodrigo parked on the side of shop not facing the road to avoid anyone seeing his car. His hand shook when he shoved the shifter into park. He sat inside the car and checked to see if anyone had followed him or stopped suspiciously nearby.

He saw nothing to alert him. Taking a deep breath, he stepped out of the car. He locked the car doors and went inside the small store.

He grabbed a shovel with a pointed tip, snatched some cheap leather work gloves from a hook, and picked out a flashlight at the checkout counter. As he left, he stopped briefly and looked through the glass of the hardware store's door, checking the road. Seeing nothing unusual, he went outside and loaded the car then pulled back out on the road, making sure to keep up with the traffic. The purchased shovel listed awkwardly on the head rests and on top of the rugs covering his treasure. It vibrated as he cruised the highway.

He kept driving. He sped up and slowed down, passing trucks and cars and then hiding among the 18-wheelers. He weaved his way between the trucks in the line of traffic, his eyes bouncing from the side-view mirror to the rearview, looking for any sign that he was being followed. He didn't see any vehicles trying to mirror his movements.

Rodrigo breathed a heavy sigh and looked ahead. It was good that he was going back to Puerto Peñasco. Maybe it was fate, or God was directing his actions. He would look for a remote location outside of the town and bury his *plata*. That seemed like the best idea. No lockers, no keys, and no way for anyone to take it from him.

Dusk enveloped the flat seaside terrain like a dark fog as he drove down the highway. The oncoming vehicles switched on their headlights. Cloaked in the impending darkness of a moonless night, he felt safer and a little more relaxed. He turned on the car's radio for the first time, tuned it to a *ranchero* music station playing a song heavy with guitars, and hummed along.

When the song finished, the announcer reported an unusual storm system off the coast of California that could develop into rain for the area. Peñasco received less than four

inches of rain per year. March marked the end of the chance
for any wet weather until July or August. An unusual cutoff
low, said the announcer, was spinning southeast off the main
storm in the Pacific Ocean and could deliver some showers
over the next couple of days.

Rodrigo knew he would have to contact Chuy again for
help. *This time, no cops.* In exchange for hiding him, he would
offer his friend some *plata* from the *bolsa* sitting on the
passenger seat. That was what he should have done the first
time. He had tried to explain his situation—he even gave
Chuy a key to the storage locker to show he trusted him. But
Chuy hadn't understood. What Chuy understood was money,
so Rodrigo resolved to pay him. He would bury the *plata*,
then he wouldn't feel so vulnerable.

Rodrigo approached the coastal area near the lavish new
resort, the Montezuma Palace. The resort occupied a large
parcel of coastal land that included a hotel and conference
center and custom hacienda lots in a gated community about
twenty kilometers from downtown Puerto Peñasco. Traffic
had thinned to a few cars and trucks, their headlights
beaming a path through the darkness. He looked for a place
on the inland side of the road where he could dig. The estuary
was remote and far enough from town. There was little
chance of someone walking through the area.

He pulled to the side of the highway and just off into
grassy bottom land and then stopped and turned off his
lights. He waited. An occasional commercial truck passed by,
but that was about all. When he couldn't see any more
approaching lights, he clicked on his flashlight and looked at
his *bolsa* on the passenger floor. *How much plata do I need for the
immediate future?* He reminded himself that he still had some
cash. He upended the bolsa onto the rug that covered the
passenger seat and examined the pieces.

As he unpacked it, he discovered metal of a different color

at the bottom of the sack. *Gold!* There were numerous smaller irregular chunks of the bright-yellow metal mixed with the silver. He'd left the *mercado* in a hurry earlier and had just dumped some of the sack's contents into his shopping *bolsa*. He was flabbergasted beyond words at his finding. Rodrigo let out an involuntary yelp. His skin tingled, and he felt his lip quivering. *This is like finding a second treasure.* He had no idea how much *oro* there was or what it was worth, but he knew it was even more valuable than the *plata* he'd exchanged. He wondered if there was gold at the bottom of the other sacks he'd left back at the mine. Maybe it was in all of them. The thought made him dizzy. He wanted to bury it as quickly as he could manage. With his new discovery, there was more than enough for his immediate needs. *Hell, way more.*

Rodrigo checked the road again and grabbed the shovel. He would dig a deep hole, line it with the cheap rugs he'd bought in Rocky Point, and bury the larger sack. It wouldn't take too long to dig in the soft soil.

A sea breeze pushed ahead by the approaching storm hit him when he left the car and began to dig. He took his time shoveling the hole in the sand and lined it in the dark. He was sweating from the effort even though the night air had cooled. He didn't risk using the flashlight except in short bursts when the nearby road was empty of traffic. He smiled in the pitch-black night. First there was *plata*, then he discovered *oro*.

Yes, this has to be a sign. Maybe God put it in my bag after I found it. God was looking out for me. This is the best day of my life. Even better than when I found the sacks in the first place. Now the treasure is secure. For the first time since the day that he discovered the mine, he felt the treasure was truly his.

He covered up the hole with sand and dirt. Using the shovel, he pried some nearby reedy grasses from the estuary

and replanted them over the freshly turned earth to disguise
the hole's location. He paced the area and estimated the hole
to be about a hundred meters from the road. Memorizing his
steps, he flashed his light around, when he could, to set the
place in his mind. There was no way he could forget it.

Rodrigo threw the shovel into the now empty trunk,
started the car, and kept the lights off. When he turned onto
the highway, he switched on his headlights and looked for a
unique landmark. He picked a black tire mark on the road to
identify its location. Then he set his trip odometer to zero to
chart the distance to Peñasco.

Maybe it was his imagination, but the car felt so much
lighter without the weight of the precious metal. He felt
lighter as well. He was free, and he was rich. The lights of
Puerto Peñasco ahead of him grew nearer. He was humming
along with the music and thinking about all the things he
could buy with his fortune when flashing red and blue lights
appeared in his rearview mirror some distance behind him.
The shock of the lights in the darkness sent an electric pulse
up his spine. The lights grew bigger, and he could see two
police vehicles in tandem bearing down toward him.

"*Tranquilo, tranquilo,*" he said out loud. "Don't panic.
Maybe there was an accident."

One vehicle, a white SUV with Sonoran State Police
markings, passed him, light bar flashing, and sped ahead. He
sighed and thought it would move on. But the second vehicle
moved within a meter of the rear of his car and, with quick
blasts of the siren, indicated for him to pull over. He could see
two cops inside.

The police SUV that had gone by slowed until it was just
in ahead, less than two meters from his front bumper, forcing
him to slow down as well. Rodrigo braked, followed the
police SUV to the side of the road, and rolled to a stop. He
waited and saw a cop from the rear car in his side-view

mirror approach him on the highway side. The cop made a motion for him to roll down his window. He complied.

"Rodrigo, we've been looking for you," said the cop, leaning in and smiling. "We're glad that you are safe. Choto thought something terrible happened to you."

20

SAND PAPAGO TO THE RESCUE

J D saw the truck's headlights approaching her at the deserted trailhead. She was a solitary figure pacing in the high beams when the vehicle arrived.

"Hey, you JD?" shouted Frankie Antone, getting out of his truck and walking toward the reporter.

Even though the group was backlit by the headlights, she recognized them immediately. Three enormous men carrying gear gathered around her. The night was pitch-black by the time Frankie and two other band members arrived at Doc's Ram pickup at the trailhead of the mountain. They wore military-style boots and light jackets.

"You're here," JD said with relief. "Thank you."

"Where's the old man?" Frankie asked.

The two other band members pulled an aluminum medical stretcher from the bed of the truck and shoved the gate closed with a metallic thud. They nodded but said nothing. Frankie shone the light for them with one hand and held the straps of an army-style medic backpack in his other hand.

"He's pretty far up the trail. I just hope he's okay," JD said, thinking of her role in causing the fall. "I had to leave him alone. I'm so sorry." She could hear the trembling of her own voice.

Frankie's flashlight focused below her face. "He's hard as the mountain. We'll extract him." He watched her eyes widen at the AK-47s and night-vision goggles strapped into the stretcher. "A precaution. You said something about *sicarios*."

She nodded. "He said to tell you. Two of them were above us after we fell. They startled me," she said, apologizing.

Frankie grunted. "Well, if you saw them… I thought maybe it was an excuse and he was really too embarrassed to call search and rescue." He slipped his arms through the backpack straps, checked his sidearm, and secured it back in the holster. "He used to volunteer with them. Loss of face." She saw his grin in the dim glow of the flashlight. He signaled for them to move out. She hesitated, frozen where she stood hands on her hips, and he looked at her again. "You look familiar."

"We didn't actually meet. I was on a ride-along with the DEA agent Robbins, and we stopped at a village wedding where you were playing. I wasn't sure if you would remember."

"I remember. You and some little dude with white teeth were standing next to his car. The ex-Marine cop suspected us of carrying drugs." He snorted. "We let him search the van. Gave him some CDs to take home."

That encounter hadn't made it into any of her reporting about the major drug intercept. It was only an investigative lead that Robbins had followed, and it had gone nowhere. But seeing the weaponry the crew carried, she reviewed the possibility that these guys were more than just a *waila* band.

"Hey, bro, let's move," said Tim. The unspoken urgency was that if Doc were bleeding internally, every second would count. He and Danny, the other Sand Papago band member, held up the stretcher.

"Okay, stay behind me," Frankie said to JD.

They began moving up the well-worn lower trail, Frankie shining the flashlight, illuminating the ground ahead. The night air was cool, but there was only a slight breeze, and it wasn't uncomfortable. The group moved slowly behind the light. The absence of any moonlight made it tough to measure their progress. They walked along silently upward on the narrow tourist path. The nocturnal wildlife shift was active— JD could hear the disturbed rustling of small mammals and reptiles crawling around in the darkness as they climbed upward. The climb was slower going than her day hike, and she felt guilty that she'd dragged Doc out to the mountain.

"If I hadn't begged him to take me out here, none of this would have happened," she said into the back of one of Frankie's enormous shoulders.

Frankie laughed. "Begged him? Doc's been tramping around these mountains forever. He's ground down more hiking partners... if he made you think he was doing you a favor..." He laughed again. "Today, the mountain didn't want you up there. It's protecting its secrets."

They continued with JD searching around Frankie's large shoulders to see the spotlighted trail. She pointed out the junction from the main path she had marked on her way down.

"Okay, stop," Frankie ordered. "That's good you marked the trail." They slung their rifles onto their shoulders and strapped on the night-vision goggles. "I hate these damn things, but we might need them to avoid being seen when we get close to Doc."

Tim and Danny stopped and rolled the empty stretcher up into sticks. They carried it above their shoulder for the trip in the darkness.

"Silent mode," Frankie said.

They worked their way carefully across the face of the steeper hill. JD was concerned about how long it was taking to reach Doc. She hoped he was okay and fretted about leading the group to his location. There was no way to contact him, and even if they could, she had his phone. They kept moving. JD buttoned her plaid flannel shirt against the chill of the night air. It was definitely getting cooler. Silently, the procession worked through the rocky terrain, keeping up a pace in the dark. As the time passed, JD felt the ache of her leg and shoulder muscles from the long day of hiking, her fall, and worry over Doc's condition. After another hour of slow but steady progress, the four climbed over the top of a small ridgeline, and JD could see a tiny light in the distance, higher and to their right.

"That's him," Frankie said, breathing rapidly from the exertion.

He killed the flashlight, and the three ex-Marines drew down their night goggles and pushed themselves harder to climb above the ridgeline. It took more time to reach him. The glow from a small campfire grew brighter as the group closed on his location. Within fifty yards or so, JD could see that Doc had pulled himself behind some large rocks where he fell. The rocks minimized the chance of anyone seeing him from above. The flickering light from the fire reflected off a silver solar blanket that Doc used to keep warm. They approached him carefully. No one spoke. Doc looked comfortable, his eyes bright and his face glowing above the small fire.

"*Cathartes aura*, it's the buzzard himself," Frankie said, leaning close, his voice barely above a whisper. "Whaddya do to yourself?"

Doc smiled and in a hoarse whisper replied, "Thank God, you had JD to guide you. You Marines could never have found me on your own."

"No need to employ Marine Corps training. Used our ancient Indian Country tracking skills. Knowledge of the land. Stuff you never knew about. Are you in pain?"

Doc nodded. "Some. It mostly numbed up."

"Do you know how bad it is?"

"It's my right leg. I felt it crack when I went down. Tried putting weight on it, testing it in case I had to drag myself out of here, but I can't stand." He'd been out in desert alone for more than four hours since the accident but was responsive—his usual cranky self—and showed no sign of shock.

"So you sent the *chica* to fetch us."

"Be nice—she's pretty sharp," Doc said quietly. "Did she tell you we're not alone?"

"She mentioned that," he said, looking over at JD, who was standing off to the side, barely in range of the campfire light. The other two were rigging the stretcher for transport and the climb down.

"Two guys, up there," Doc said, throwing a hand above his head. "They're not doin' anything, just sittin' tight. First time JD and I saw 'em, they were in heavy-duty search mode, looking for somebody. Just after dark, I heard them come back. Can't see 'em. They know I'm here, of course, but they haven't said or done anything."

"You want us to roust 'em?" Frankie looked up the hill into the black night, where nothing was visible.

"They've had their chances to come after me, if that was the idea. I think they're waiting for something. A signal? Maybe dawn? Whatever it is, I don't think it's us. Let's get the hell outta here and see what they do."

"It's a bumpy ride down the hill, so we're going to give you something for the pain." Frankie pushed aside the solar blanket and shoved a needle into Doc's right leg to numb it more. "Quick-acting local anesthetic. That'll help till we get you to the truck."

"Where's the rest of the band?" Doc asked.

"Mixing tracks. Working on the next album. We figured the three of us were enough to handle one old man."

They snuffed Doc's campfire and loaded him carefully into the stretcher. Frankie turned on the flashlight. Since the *sicarios* knew they were there, stealth was no longer necessary.

"The mountain doesn't want you here, so it sent Coyote to trip you up," said Tim earnestly. He looked down at Doc's wincing face from the head end of the stretcher. Doc just groaned. "If you want something stronger..." Tim let the words hang.

The suggestion of weakness got him going. "Hell no," growled Doc hoarsely, looking up at Tim. "We can discuss Coyote's role in this another time. Vamos!"

They began trekking downhill, ignoring the two unseen *sicarios* perched somewhere above them. They moved much faster going down the side of the mountain than coming up, Frankie in front illuminating the desert floor, followed by JD and the men carrying the stretcher with Doc strapped to it. The two worked to keep Doc as level as possible on the steep terrain to minimize his discomfort and still make time. The hardpan crust crunched under their faster pace. Their legs brushed against the dry desert scrub. It would take awhile to reach the parking area.

21

RODRIGO AND CHOTO REUNITE

As soon as the cops took Rodrigo from his car, they jammed a black hood over his head, handcuffed him, and shoved him into the back of one of the patrol cars. It was a short trip. He kept track. A few kilometers toward Rocky Point, they pulled over on the roadside, removed him from the car, and led him into the back of a larger vehicle. Still hooded, he couldn't tell what kind of car he was in, but it felt like an SUV. Whoever had taken him kept silent. All he could hear was the vehicle doors slamming shut and at least two people got in with him. Whoever they were smelled of sweat and cigarettes. He could feel the SUV start off down the road, moving at a moderate clip.

Some time passed—it couldn't have been longer than a half hour—and then the vehicle stopped. No one had spoken. In the blackness, the only sound Rodrigo could hear was his own heaving breath and the blood throbbing in his head.

He heard the car door open and a felt stiff wind from the beach hit him through the hood as someone grabbed his arm and pulled him from the vehicle. His best guess was that he was on the outskirts of the town and obviously near the water. He could hear the soft rush of the tide. Two people roughly grabbed him under each arm. They half dragged him up the walkway and then a couple of steps to the front door and inside. He was pushed from behind and stuffed into a tight chair. His hood was removed to reveal Choto glaring at him a few inches from his face.

"I want to see the *traidor* who left his post without a word. *Verdad*, we were worried."

Choto stepped back from Rodrigo in mock concern and paced back and forth in front of him. Rodrigo looked about the large room with little furniture, most of which was shoved up against the stuccoed white walls. Three men with semiautomatic weapons stood around the edges.

He had met Choto in person only once, and he didn't recognize the men who were casually loitering. The state cops who'd picked him up on the highway weren't present. He sat in a plastic outdoor chair in the center of the living room. Looking up at the high ceiling, Rodrigo felt Choto looming over him, appearing taller than his six feet. The cartel leader was dressed in expensive dark trousers and an ornate *guayabera* shirt. He held a large nickel-plated revolver with a pearl grip in one hand and clapped it against his other one like he was applauding.

"We sent some people up to the mountain to find you." Choto's high-heeled, ostrich-hide cowboy boots clicked on the Italian terrazzo floor as he paced. "Do you know what they reported?"

Rodrigo was frozen. Except for the handcuffs, he wasn't restrained, but he couldn't move his mouth or shake his head. Choto's wide eyes held him motionless.

"They say they found your campsite. It was terrible, they said. Blood was everywhere. Stuff scattered all over. No sign of you. Something very bad must have happened there, they said. Very bad." Choto's face was red with anger, and spittle formed on the corners of his mouth. He turned away, showing Rodrigo his back. "But here you are!" he sneered and whirled suddenly, the revolver pointed at Rodrigo, and fired a round only inches above Rodrigo's head.

The sound exploded in the large nearly empty room and echoed off the high bare walls. The bullet sank into the white plastered concrete wall across the room, sending chips and dust flying. Rodrigo jumped in surprise and began to quiver uncontrollably. He shook in the chair. He could feel his bladder release and the warm urine wet his jeans and run down his leg. The three men didn't move from the gunshot and smiled at his loss of control.

Adjusting the crotch of his pants, Choto struck a pose and observed Rodrigo as if he were a bug specimen under a microscope. He dropped his shoulders and relaxed. Firing the weapon seemed to calm the big man down. "Don't worry, little Rui. I'm not going to shoot you in the head. I might cut it off and use it for football practice on the beach. What do you think? Do you like football? We could have a game, kicking your cabeza around in the sand." He made a face as though seriously pondering that option. "Goaaaaaaaaaaaaaaaaaaaaal!" he howled suddenly, head raised toward the ceiling like a television football announcer, and then laughed. He seemed to enjoy his own jokes. He looked carefully at Rodrigo again. "Aren't you going to thank me for not shooting you?" Choto smiled like he'd just made a clever remark.

"S-S-Sí," Rodrigo stammered hoarsely. "Gracias, Jefe." His throat felt dry and scratchy, and he could barely catch his breath.

"Do you know why you are still alive and your tiny cabeza isn't rolling around the dunes?" He waved the gun toward the sliding glass doors that led to the sea.

"No sé, Jefe," he croaked. "I don't know."

"Because Choto is not stupid. *Me tomas por tonto?*"

"No, Jefe," he said. "You are not stupid."

"No, because you are *tonto*. You are the stupid one," Choto spat out. "How ironic for you that being stupid turns out to be an advantage. Choto heard about the *plata* that you flashed around. Choto followed it all over northern Mexico. We didn't know who was spreading it around until you appeared like magic at our *cambio* booth in Caborca." He laughed at his cleverness. "Were you asking to be caught? Did you want to be captured? You see. Stupid. *Tonto*."

He tapped the barrel of the gun against his temple. "Choto runs all the *cambio* shops. That's right. *Sí, correcto*." Choto looked over at the security men standing against the walls. "*Correcto, sí?*" He waved the gun around inviting them to respond.

Sí, verdad," they mumbled without unison or enthusiasm.

"You, little Rui…" Choto used the shiny, long-barreled weapon like a pointer directed at Rodrigo. "You tried to take from Choto." He rushed at Rodrigo and pressed the Smith & Wesson 27 against the boy's forehead. "You tried to take what is mine!" His eyes widened. "I should shoot you anyway," he said mockingly as though he was reconsidering. "You are a liar and a thief." He spoke through clenched teeth, his dark eyes burning.

Rodrigo could smell the *tequila* on Choto's hot breath.

"But unlike you, Choto is *not* stupid. So you get to live for a little while." He walked away again, scratching the back of his coifed hair with pearl grip of the revolver, and posed again. "You are going to tell us everything you know about the *plata* and the *oro*. Ah *sí*, we know about the *oro*. We have your little shopping bag from your car. So," he said, turning again to wall. "Is that all of it?

"Uh, *sí*, Jefe," said Rodrigo hopefully.

"Motherfucker! Liar!" shouted Choto, firing the gun at Rodrigo's feet. The bullet ricocheted off the terrazzo floor and lodged in a wooden door on the far side of the room. It was close enough to the men standing guard that they flinched. "You want me to get the auto battery and hook it up to your tiny *huevos*?"

"*Perdon, perdon,* Jefe," Rodrigo wailed. "There is more."

"How does Choto know that you lied? Because. As I told you before, Choto is not *tonto*. There is a *pala* in the back of your car. Look at your shoes and pants," he said, pointing the weapon again. "Is that *mierda* on your cuffs, or is it something else? We don't smell anything, so Choto believes it is mud. Will you take that bet? No?"

"*Sí, sí,* I buried it in the marsh near the resort."

"And?"

Rodrigo was puzzled. He was afraid to guess again, so he stared blankly back at Choto.

"And?" Choto cocked his hip again, pinning the side of the revolver against it. "You will show us where it is. Is that not what you were about to say?"

"Oh, *sí,*" said Rodrigo, nodding rapidly. "I will take you there."

"You're getting smarter, sitting there in your own *mierda*. Maybe stewing in it raises your intelligence. *Bueno.* In that case, Choto will let you live a little while longer." He smiled a wide smile as though pleased with his own benevolence.

22

DOC TO THE EMERGENCY ROOM

The Sand Papago loaded Doc into the back of the pickup for the ride to the Southern Arizona Medical Center. Danny drove Doc's truck while Tim and JD rode in the back.

"Doc, I'm so sorry about today," JD said as they prepared to leave.

"I'm not. It was a hell of a day. I was happy you shared it with me," he growled.

Driving the band's truck, Frankie pulled out first, and Danny followed. They drove fast but not too far above the speed limit.

The painkiller Frankie had injected into Doc earlier was wearing off, and the old historian was in some pain. "Don't hit those bumps so hard," Doc shouted toward the truck cab.

Danny ignored him and concentrated on navigating the interstate traffic. The two vehicles took nearly another hour before they rolled up to the university hospital's emergency entrance. They parked in an ambulance bay, and the ER staff moved quickly, jumping into the back of pickup, surrounded his stretcher, shifted Doc over to a hospital gurney, and rushed him inside. They hovered over the old man and barked medical observations while examining him on the

portable bed. A large nurse with Popeye forearms cut away
Doc's hiking trousers with surgical shears above his
suspected broken leg.

"They're Gore-Tex," he protested. Do you know how
much these pants cost?" He glared at the tattooed nurse, who
ignored the question.

JD, Frankie, and the others camped in the ER waiting
room. The doctor arrived with a pod of medical students,
looked at a quick X-ray on a digital screen and declared that
the thigh bone was cleanly broken. Most of the blood on
Doc's pants came from a surface scrape and not from the
compound fracture the group had feared when they brought
him in. After an overall examination, the doctor informed
them that there was no apparent internal bleeding. The
hospital staff recommended that Doc be held overnight for
more tests to make sure.

"You were right not to try to walk on it, Dr. Savage," said
an earnest young resident who was assisting the
orthopedist. "It could have resulted in much more damage
to your leg."

Doc pretended not to be relieved by the news. Otherwise,
he appeared to be no less ornery than usual. Under
supervision, residents set the leg and put it in a cast. The
ortho doctor seconded the decision to admit him. He made a
notation for the orthopedics department to follow up with a
subsequent exam of the leg to check how it responded before
sending him home. Despite Doc's protests, he wasn't going to
leave the hospital that night.

"They love my insurance," Doc complained.

They were waiting for the hospital paperwork and Doc's
room assignment when Will arrived at the door. JD had texted
him from the bottom of the mountain, and he was agitated.
"Are you all right?" he asked, out of breath, at the door.
"What happened?"

JD rushed toward the entry, embraced him, and held on. "I

couldn't call earlier because I lost my phone on the mountain. I'm fine."

"I'm the patient," said Doc from his bed, sitting up against the pillows and peering at the two.

"I'm Will Teagarden. I'm so sorry about your injury."

"This is your in-a-relationship guy?" Doc asked JD.

"We were on the mountain," JD said to Will. "I heard a noise, lost my balance, and began to fall. Doc tried to grab me, and we both went down. He broke his leg." She still felt guilty about that.

"She did fine," Doc barked. "It was those fucking *sicarios* on the mountain. We made it down, and everyone's okay. Even me."

"*Sicarios*?" Will asked, alarmed. "I thought this was supposed to be a nice little feature story. Fresh air, the standard 'Don't be stupid' warning on the dangers of old mines."

"Will, they didn't come after us. They disappeared after the accident. We think they were searching for someone while we were there, and we surprised each other." She noticed Will's stricken look. "I wish I could have called you sooner, but we were in a dead zone. Uh, unfortunate choice of words."

"That makes me feel better," he said sarcastically.

After the admission papers were completed, aides arrived and wheeled Doc into an elevator and up to his hospital room. They parked his bed against the back wall and fiddled with the oxygen hose and a stand for his drip line. The room was private with a typical pull-around curtain and small lamp behind the head of the bed. The five of them gathered around Doc's bed after the hospital nurses left the room.

"Fun's over. You can all go now," Doc said, waving the hand connected to the drip line.

"Too late to leave the big city. We'll stay," said Frankie, plopping his huge body into a chair. The others nodded.

"Can't wait to see you navigate to the bathroom in that cute little gown they put you in."

"You're having too much free entertainment at my expense." Doc grumbled. "I'm thinking of charging a speaking fee."

"Damn, I almost forgot," JD said. "My phone is still on the mountain. It has all my photos and notes from today. I'm lost if I can't get it back."

"We can return to the mountain and retrieve it," said Frankie. "After the old buzzard is settled back in the nest."

23

HECTOR AND LUIS RECOVER A
TREASURE

E arly in their shift, Hector and Luis drove a patrol
vehicle to the Montezuma Palace resort hotel out on the
Caborca highway to drop off photos of the missing boy,
Rodrigo. Maybe hotel guests on a shopping trip in *el centro*
saw him or noticed something from the resort van while on
the road. Jefe was desperate to find the boy before the cartel
did, and the two cops shared her concern about the vanished
kid. The high-end resort was carved out of a large piece of
land that included extensive beachfront property, an
internationally designed golf course that ran parallel to the
sea, and a huge hotel building with private beaches, pools,
and other amenities. The master development included
expensive seaside residential sites for present and future
construction. Some home sites had already been developed.
With its own extensive private security, the exclusive property
was not part of their regular beat.

Driving the nearly deserted highway that separated a
marshy area from the seaside property of the resort complex,
the two cops were about ten minutes away from the entrance
to the property. Luis looked up from examining the stack of
printed flyers in English and Spanish that showed the chief's

photo of Rodrigo and a stock picture of last known vehicle he'd been driving. On the inland side of the highway, some activity in the marshes caught his eye.

"Hector, check it out," he said, reaching across the left side and pointing out the window. "There's an SUV off the road." Getting closer, they saw several men huddled in a cluster surrounding an inland area of sand and brackish water. They were watching another man dig a hole in the estuary with a *pala*.

"I think we should take a look," said Hector, speeding up and then turning onto the sandy salt estuary.

The tires dug in, throwing up the dirt and grass. The huddled men looked up as they watched the vehicle approach. Hector and Luis could see that the circle of hotel security men were armed. No one made a hostile move, so the two cops got out of the car, Luis setting down the flyers and unsnapping his holster, hand on top of the grip. Hector rested his hands at his belt.

"Need some help?" asked Hector, approaching the men. He looked down at the young man shoveling in a hole about a meter deep in the soft marshy land and saw that it was Rodrigo, but he said nothing. He shot a look at Luis, knowing his partner recognized him as well.

"Our guest is looking for something," said one of the men. "He reported it to the hotel." The group stood above the muck, keeping their clothes clean. The speaker wore a sharp pair of slacks and the green company polo shirt with Montezuma Palace stitched over the pocket. His sidearm remained comfortably on his hip. The other men, wearing hotel uniforms, just looked at the cops.

"What are you looking for?" Luis asked the digger. Not answering, Rodrigo kept shoveling, the rhythmic *shuff* of the *pala* sliding into the wet sand. The first man's jaw tightened.

"He lost something valuable," said a second man, also dressed in the company shirt. He stepped closer to the first man. "And we're helping him find it." He smirked openly at the cops.

"He was out here, partying with friends, and he left his watch somewhere in this area," said the first man. "We're with hotel security," he said, pointing at the logo on his shirt.

Rodrigo kept digging, ignoring the two cops.

"He needs a *pala*?" asked Luis.

"Well, you know—the tides," the first man said matter-of-factly.

"Señor, you should come with us and fill out a police report," Luis said to Rodrigo.

He leaned over and yanked the shovel from the boy. The first man put his hand on his gun grip, but Hector had already pulled out his Glock and shoved it into the man's back. The man stiffened but didn't try for his gun. The two other men were frozen by the surprise move, and Hector scowled at them, his look pinning them in place.

Luis grabbed Rodrigo's wrist and yanked him hard from the shallow hole. "*Vamos aquí*, come with us." As he passed Hector, Luis added in a low voice, "*Tengo control.*"

Luis took Rodrigo to the police vehicle and whispered something to him, and Rodrigo got into the SUV on his own. When he returned, Luis came to Hector's side with his gun drawn. They stared at the men.

"We're going to take this boy to the police station and help him file a lost property report. With luck, he might recover his lost watch. Any objections?" asked Luis. None of the men responded. "Gracias for your help, and I'm sure you have other duties and guests you need to attend to. We won't keep you from them. *Buen día.*"

The pair backed away from the group with their guns pointing at the three men until they reached the vehicle. Hector caught a view of Rodrigo in the back seat from his driver's side-view mirror and climbed into the vehicle with his left hand pointing his weapon over the top of the mirror.

Luis waited until Hector had situated himself in the driver's seat and started the SUV. Then, keeping a steady eye on the men, he walked around the back of the vehicle to the passenger's side. The three still didn't move from the hole. The moment Luis got into the vehicle, Hector pulled away. Luis slammed his door. Tires fought for traction in the sand and mud as Hector turned the vehicle around, and then the rear wheels grabbed enough to accelerate back to the highway. Hector looked in the rearview mirror to see if the men were following, but they were still standing around the estuary.

"Rodrigo, we are Puerto Peñasco municipal police," said Luis, turning his head to look at the boy. He looked surprised. "You are very popular. Everyone is looking for you. What was that all about?"

"Choto's men," said Rodrigo from the back seat, still jumpy from the confrontation.

Hector nodded. "Even with the uniforms, they didn't look like hotel security."

"Why were you digging?" asked Luis.

"I buried something in the marsh, and Choto sent them to make sure I found it and gave it to them."

"The *plata*," said Hector.

"*Sí*, how did you know?" Rodrigo's eyes widened.

"Everyone knows," said Hector. "The town is talking about nothing else."

Rodrigo sagged in his seat.

Luis had turned back around to call the chief on his cell. "Hola, Jefe, we found the boy." He put the chief on speakerphone.

"Good work," said Ramirez. "Where was he?"

"Off the Caborca highway, digging a hole, surrounded by some men with guns. They claimed to be hotel security from the resort. But Rodrigo says they were Choto's *sicarios*."

"Anyone injured? Is everyone okay?" The chief sounded concerned. "Was there trouble?"

"We managed to collect him without shots being fired."

"Are you being followed?"

Luis glanced at Hector, who shook his head. "Not that we know, but we'll keep watch.

"Did he have anything else with him."

"You mean like the *plata*? No. He hasn't said anything."

"Bring him to the Sandman's house. A swarm of reporters might be waiting at the station."

"I hope the Sandman has plenty of soap and towels. The boy stinks from the marsh and God knows what else," Luis said.

Rodrigo sat silent in the back seat. He didn't say another word about the gold and silver.

24

A NEW MILITIA IN TOWN

The headlines in *Espejo de Sonora*, the *Tucson Daily Mirror's* Spanish-language sister publication, were all about the rumors that *plata* had been discovered somewhere near the resort community of Rocky Point. The story featured interviews with two vendors on the *malecón*, who speculated about the origins of the *plata*, the identity of the person who'd found it, and some comments from tourists, accompanied by a photo of a rough piece of silver smaller than a golf ball in the hand of a merchant. The treasure map that Puerto Peñasco *policía* had confiscated was prominently featured in the story. The mayor was quoted as saying there was no new silver discovery in the area while casting doubt on the theory that the *plata* was from some cache of buried treasure. He again floated the idea that any silver passed around was some kind of promotional stunt, and it would all be cleared up in time.

After that story posted, JD's editor wanted her to expedite her sidebar story on old treasure tales and abandoned mines as soon as she could manage it. The group had taken Doc home. They left him sitting on his sofa, his broken leg propped up by a metal stand and the couch crowded with an old laptop, water, pills, and a pile of books for him to read.

"Don't forget to give me back my cell," he said to JD.

Now that Doc was at home from his overnight hospital stay, she wanted to retrieve her phone. *Will I be able to find it? What condition will it be in?* Without her pictures and notes from the trip, she would have to start over on the story. The Sand Papago advised against going back without an escort, so Frankie promised they would accompany her and Will.

"Could we go right now?" she asked.

"We're here already. Why not?" Frankie said.

They stopped at a convenience market for gas and supplies, and once again, they made their way back to the border area. JD sat in the cab with Frankie driving. Tim and Danny rode in the back with Will. JD asked Frankie how the Sand Papagos began.

"When I was eight, Pop got a landscaping and general construction job in Ajo, and we moved off the reservation. The mine had closed years before. A lot of vacant company houses needed to be buttoned up and maintained. The longer we stayed in town, the more we lost touch with our people on the reservation, our community. It happens to a lot of families now. After high school, there was nothing much to do, so I joined the Marines, and my brothers followed. Our parents stayed in Ajo. I was in the Marines for six years. I did two tours in Afghanistan, Tim was in Iraq, and Danny also did a tour in Kabul. When I got out, I moved back to the reservation. Tim and Danny came back too. We played instruments in school, so we decided to form a band. We played music we liked, the music we heard growing up— changed it into a souped-up version of traditional *waila* music.

"It was from music, playing for the community, that we found our way again. We talked to elders about the old ways, how the people had farmed, the planting of traditional crops, and using the water that fell on the land. Tim is interested in the old songs and the traditional medicine, using the roots

and herbs our elders knew about. He believes he might be a
medicine man. Elders appreciated our effort to learn about
the past. After playing gigs and meeting people from other
villages, we learned more. When they heard that we were ex-
Marines, people came to us to ask for help. Sometimes it was
a ride for an elder. Other times, it was more complicated.
Drugs, gangs, family interventions. We've broken up fights,
patched people up, taken elders to receive special medical
treatment off the reservation. Paid for it ourselves."

"I can understand. I cover federal courts, immigration
mostly, and it's true—even simple crimes on the reservation
are tried in federal court."

"The elders, some don't trust any government, especially
the nonreservation white government. *Miligá:n,* the white
people, have always built fences, drawn lines on maps to grab
property and destroy the earth. They never stop. A copper
company wants to dig a huge mine on land our ancestors
walked, places used in sacred ceremonies. We don't believe
that the earth is separate from ourselves. We are part of the
land and everything that is there."

"I assume the BIA is no help."

"It's a colonial relic. Even the supposedly enlightened
whites, the ones who say they want to protect the land—like
the Organ Pipe parks people—are ignorant," Frankie said in a
calm, quiet voice. "They trashed our cultural sites, tore down
houses, and destroyed traditional fields that were inside the
monument. The federal border barriers disrupted our way of
life, separated us from our traditional areas in the south. The
patrols by the greenies, the Border Patrol—they act like
occupiers, like they're in Afghanistan. They know nothing of
the land or our people. So, all my brothers are dedicated to
helping our people remember and reclaim who they are."

"What about the tribal government?"

"Some of the people live in places where it's hard to get
services. These are our people. We want to help, and we have

skills and knowledge of how things work in the white world that some of our people don't." He changed lanes to pass a slow-moving semi.

"The first time I saw you guys, it was at a wedding in a remote village," she said. "You remember—I was shadowing Agent Robbins for a story on a potential cocaine bust. He seemed to think you were somehow involved in drug smuggling. He didn't find anything, but it didn't end his suspicions."

"He was an untrusting dude. We gave him space 'cause he's ex-Marine. We share that brotherhood. We've seen stuff, done some things, cut some deals. We aren't *santos*. But it's always been to help our people and keep them safe. We've put the word out that we won't tolerate the cartels moving drugs through our land. The drugs—I watched Marines get hooked on them after returning home injured, with PTSD. It is poison. The federal fence doesn't keep people from dying."

"How did you meet Doc?" JD asked.

"The professor came out to talk with some of the elders. He was doing research. His wife, Suzanne, was with him. We helped with the interviews, so we met him then."

"Really? What for?

"He was researching a book about land fraud in Arizona before it became part of the United States. How it screwed up the economic and social development, especially for us, the O'odham people and the Yaqui. The elders liked talking to him about the old days. He is a good listener. In his own way, he seems to get it. We learned a lot about our people just by being there and hearing the stories. He might tell you about the book if you ask."

"I will."

"Suzanne was part of the research. We found we had some things in common," Frankie said.

"Military?"

"Yeah. Doc won't tell you, but he was in 'Nam during

some nasty fighting. Saw some heavy-duty shit as a medic. Earned medals he won't talk about. Wounded. Purple Heart. Hiking was part of his rehab, and he never stopped."

They continued down the freeway. Will sat in the open pickup bed with the other Antone brothers. The wind noise made talking difficult. They mostly sat in silence, but JD could hear them laughing every once in a while as they traveled down the interstate on the crisp pleasant morning. If only she'd been more careful. She couldn't help thinking about Doc. Despite what Frankie had told her, she still thought the accident was her fault.

On the highway to Arivaca, a few miles before the turnoff to the trailhead, JD saw an encampment on her right—tents, several small fires, and about a dozen camo-dressed armed men milling around. At first glance, they looked like a large hunting party. Then she saw the pickup trucks festooned with American flags and other insignia parked down the road.

"This wasn't here yesterday. Stop up there," she said suddenly.

Frankie parked about ten feet behind a pickup truck with a large Take Back Our Country decal across the back window. An American flag stuck out at an angle toward the road from the driver's side. JD immediately jumped out of the truck and approached a man wearing an initialed baseball cap, combat boots, and a sidearm on each hip. He stood behind the pickup, holding a leather leash with a panting pit bull attached to it. The dog acted like he was waiting for a treat.

"Excuse me, sir. I'm JD Guzman from the *Tucson Daily Mirror*. Is everything all right?"

"Lamestream media, huh? You gotta go talk to our public affairs officer," he said, staring from behind aviator sunglasses and petting the pit bull.

"No, I'm not looking for an interview. What's going on?"

"We jes' moved our camp here and now waitin' before it's

time to patrol." His aviator glasses moved up and down, taking in her appearance. "Are you from around here?"

"Yes, I am. Where you from?"

"Nevada," he said, spitting some dark juice toward the ground on the side opposite the dog.

"What are you patrolling?

"Our group supports the understaffed and overworked Customs and Border Protection agents in this sector. We're patriots. We look for suspicious activity and traveling groups, smugglers, and illegals—your Guats, TONCs, and the like." His attention shifted, the sunglasses looking above her, directed toward the three men standing up in bed of the pickup.

"Where y'all going?" he asked in an official-sounding voice.

"Hiking. What do you do when you find suspicious activity?" JD could feel the hair on her neck stand up.

"We call it in to the BP."

"That's a lot of weaponry just to make phone calls," she said, pointing at his gun belt. "What's a TONC?"

"Temporarily outside native country. That's what we call 'em, you know—the border hoppers." His shoulders sagged as if he knew this wasn't going well, but like a runaway train, the momentum continued, and he couldn't stop talking.

Danny, Tim, and Will came up behind her. Danny and Tim carried their assault rifles, which were difficult to ignore.

"Who's 'we'?" JD pressed.

"Uh, the National Patriot Militia, Nevada Chapter." He pointed to the NPM insignia on his baseball cap. "Thought y'all were goin' hikin'," he said, looking nervously at the men cradling rifles.

"Rabbits," said Danny definitively. The man looked over his sunglasses at the large globe-and-anchor Marine tattoo on Danny's neck.

"Is there some kind of problem here?" asked Frankie, who'd joined the group.

"No, sir. Y'all come up to me. I'm just minding my business." He adjusted the baseball cap. His eyes above his sunglasses darted from one man to another.

"JD, let it go," said Frankie. "Don't waste the daylight." They turned around and walked to their truck. The dog wagged his tail in regret, looking disappointed at the group's lack of attention.

"I thought you were going to start something back there," said Will, putting his arm around her as they walked.

"That kind of shit just aggravates the hell out of me," she growled.

"They're just wannabes playing soldier," said Frankie.

"Don't want to lose that journalist objectivity," Will said, trying to kid her out of her anger.

"TONC. Did you hear that?" she asked. "What kind of racist bullshit is that? And from Nevada? What the hell are they doing running around down here? We should make them to go back where they came from."

"Too bad our ancestors didn't think of that three hundred years ago," said Frankie, opening the truck door for her.

25

CHOTO'S BREAKFAST IS
DISAPPOINTING

C hoto thumped down the stairs from his second-story bedroom in the late morning, wearing an oriental silk dressing gown, satin boxer shorts with a pronounced bulge in front, and his high-heeled ostrich cowboy boots. Two women, also in robes, followed a step behind him on either side. They were young, top-heavy, and voluptuous. The one with auburn streaks in her hair placed her feet delicately on each step like she was trying to avoid exacerbating the soreness between her thighs. The other carried a plastic *mercado bolsa* containing their clothes. At the base of the stairs, Choto smiled and dismissed them with a wave. They retreated to a powder room off the living room to compose themselves for the day.

His beauty sleep had been interrupted by a text from the three men he'd sent with Rodrigo to retrieve the treasure. He was not happy and paced the living room, waiting for his three *sicarios* to return from the trip to the estuary. His two personal guards were trying to calm him down. Not only had the three failed to return with the *plata* and gold as ordered, but they'd lost Rodrigo as well. They'd sent a text because they didn't dare directly speak to him. They knew Choto would fly into a rage on the phone. He distracted himself by balancing a pair of daggers in his palms as he stomped back and forth across the terrazzo floor in the living room of the mansion.

Faces blank, the three men with muddy shoes and pant cuffs entered the room and stood before the ranting cartel leader.

"Do you forget to bring the *plata*? *Oro*? Surely you brought that? Or did you leave it in the *carro*?"

"No, Jefe," said Ricky. He tried to look Choto in the eye because he didn't want to show weakness, and Jefe was capable of anything if they looked away.

"I don't see the little beach boy. Did you leave him in the *coche*?" Choto felt his temples pounding while he tried to keep his anger from boiling over. The silk dressing gown was open to the waist, showing his hairless chest.

"No, Jefe," said Ricky again, finding himself the sole spokesman for the three.

"Do you think Choto is happy with this result?" Gripping the daggers in each hand, he leaned forward like a miler at the starting line.

"No, Jefe." Ricky's shoulders were hunched, and his jaw was set, as though he was prepared to absorb whatever blows were coming for the three of them.

"Where's the boy?" Choto asked.

"He was digging in the estuary for the treasure, and two *policía* from Puerto Peñasco saw us. They asked what we were doing, and I said the boy lost something. They grabbed the boy and said that he had to go with them to fill out a police report."

"When they took him, what did you do?"

"We thought that maybe you sent them."

"So you did nothing?"

"There was nothing we could do. My gun was at my side," Ricky said.

Choto pretended to consider the situation.

"We'll find him, Jefe," said Ricky. It sounded aspirational rather than reassuring.

Choto stared at them. "And the *plata*?" He spit out the *p*. "The *oro*?"

"After the cops took him, we continued digging. But the hole was empty. *No sé*. He lied or couldn't remember."

"*Pinche changas*! Fucking monkeys! I am surrounded by idiots. I can't trust you three to do a simple recovery job." He stomped his boots.

"We will find him," Ricky repeated.

"No, you won't!" Choto screamed. "Choto will find him." He turned away in disgust, the daggers at his sides, and resumed pacing the floor, tapping his boots loudly on the terrazzo. "Get out of those ridiculous hotel costumes! The three of you. Go back to Arizona." He hissed the Z in the word. "Find the two men who are on the mountain, and search for the mine. Contact them, and try to do something useful. Check the camp Rodrigo abandoned. *Vamos*, before I shoot all of you *pinche* fucks. Go find the mine! *Rápido!*

The three backed out of the room, facing Choto, like peasant rats retreating from a royal rattlesnake. Choto glowered as he watched them leave. They slammed the front door behind them when they left.

"Where's my gun?" he asked his two remaining guards, who were still standing at attention.

"It's locked away, Jefe, for safekeeping," said the first guard.

"Safekeeping? How is it safe if I don't have it?"

"We'll get it, Jefe."

"Never mind now," Choto said. "Find out where the cops took our little Rui while I finish my breakfast. Our informants must be good for something. *Vamos*! Ticktock." He wagged his finger like a pendulum. "As soon as you find out where he is, we're going to get him back." He paused and then yelled,

"I want my *plata*! My gold! Can't I find anyone to give me what I want?" His face was hot with anger.

His silk robe fluttering and boots clicking, he walked out to the patio, which was only meters from the Sea of Cortez and had an expansive view of the water and private beach. He sat down to breakfast and waited impatiently for his chef to serve him *desayuno*. He could feel the morning sun behind him, warm on his shoulders. The soft breeze was calming. His head was pounding. He closed his eyes and inhaled deeply, distracted momentarily from the debacle of the missing boy and his—Choto's—stolen precious metal.

Steal from Choto. It's unthinkable. A very public example must be made of this boy's insolencia. *It would be a pleasure to carve him up. But little Rui is a cunning* pendejo *who managed to expose his organization's weakness. It never should have happened.*

Choto needed to fix this before the bosses learned of it. *Better to tell them about it after Choto has solved the problem.*

He took a deep breath, picked up a white linen napkin from the table, and looked out over the blue water. It was all very nice, *muy bonita*, but he was anxious to return to Tijuana. He missed the crush of people, the activity. You could feel the collective need of *la gente*. The striving, the city's energy—it was palpable. The enormous wealth, anxious poverty, and the scent of desire, and noise and polluted air all mixed together in a sweaty cocktail of life. Oddly, it was in the expansive openness of the rural sea and the sand that he felt trapped. And the quiet—Choto hated the quiet.

He was in exile. The bosses had sent him here to establish the Mexicali Cartel's roots in the sand and lava rock, but he wasn't part of the main action. And he needed to be. He felt wasted in this sand pile of a town. He was running only a small cell in this desert wasteland, not the multiple gangs that had reported to him in Tijuana. He told himself he was being punished for being too progressive, too innovative.

The bosses were still doing things like it was the 1970s.

They needed to get with the times. Cultivating Mexican marijuana and running it across the border using peasant labor no longer made sense. The market was tanking. The profit margin had shrunk. The operation in this part of Sonora had been in place years before he arrived. The country mules recruited from the south carried backpacks of weed and breached the border in rural areas in the bioreserve of Organ Pipe and spaces in the rural O'odham reservation. *Halcones* watched the progress from hidden locations and reported any problems. It was so labor-intensive. It required a lot of supervision. The bosses called it *tradicional.* Choto called it *reaccionarias.*

Heroin was controlled by a cartel based in Guerrero, and everyone had to pay them. They ran the poppy farms, the harvest, and the processing into heroin. They skimmed the *crema* from the top. They had grabbed all the other cartels by the *huevos.* Meth was good business—it didn't depend on the *pinche* Guerrero assholes—but the chemicals could be hard to get sometimes. The supply of precursors was watched closely by the US DEA, who were able to cut it off at intervals. That hurt American producers the most and drove up the street price—good for Mexicans—but there were interruptions in the needed supplies. And manufacture was risky. Unless they were handled with care, the chemicals were unstable. Under his watch, more than one lab had exploded in Tijuana, costing money, time, and rare employees with expertise. Fentanyl was the best. You could order the precursor chemicals in bulk from China as easily as you would a carton of kung pao chicken and bring it in through the port of Guaymas. The manufacturing process to produce fentanyl was relatively straightforward. You didn't have to deal with those cokehead Columbians or the *pinche* Guerreros. It was one hundred times more powerful than heroin, and you kept all the profit. That was what he kept telling the bosses. Replace the street heroin with stepped-on fentanyl. Or mix it as TNT. Single product—concentrate on the profit. They were more interested in maintaining an all-you-can-eat buffet.

The bosses said he could play in this sandbox, but he had to show results. He spent some effort converting the large boathouse next to the *hacienda* into a fentanyl lab. The *gringo* neighbors were far enough away from his casa and were seldom present. They wouldn't see what was going on under their noses anyway, the *rico* gringo *pendejos.* The chemists were working hard. There was a steady stream of drugs flowing through the tunnel into Arizona, moving to Phoenix and beyond. Everything had been going smoothly until this insignificant scout ducked his post and returned to Mexico, flashing precious metal. He needed to resolve the issue before little Rui became a black mark against him with the bosses and left him exiled forever in this small-change fishing village.

His morning breakfast routine was to eat alone at a complete place setting of old-patterned *azul* Talavera dishes, Taxco *plata* silverware, crystal goblets from Spain, and cloth napkins. The menu nearly always included *chilaquiles,* a favorite, served this time *verdes,* with fried tortillas in tomatillo salsa and cheese, along with huevos rancheros— eggs and refried beans—*carnitas,* and more tortillas. One of his security guards brought out the tray and served him while he fiddled with his napkin. He ate hungrily, attacking the plates of food, fuming about his situation. *When will they find out where the policía stashed the boy?*

He ended the meal with his usual topper, a shot of special *blanco* tequila from his reserve and two lines of cocaine, what Choto referred to in English as his "heart starter." He used his silverware knife to arrange the white powder into two very straight rows on the glass tabletop. Choto loved order and repetition. In a practiced motion, he unhooked a tiny length of gold pipe on a pendant chain hanging around his neck, tapped the bottom edge of it three times on the glass, and snorted the left line of coke through the pipe up his left nostril. Then he exhaled sharply through his mouth. He repeated the exercise in exactly the same way for the right side of his nose. He winced from the cold shock of the drug hitting his system and then carefully wiped the gold pipe with his napkin and replaced it on the chain around his neck. His security guard waited until Choto's ritual was complete before approaching with news.

"So, when do we attack the police station?" Choto asked, giving him a strained look.

"Jefe, they did not take Rodrigo to the police station," the guard said. "They say he is in Cholla Bay in a safe house."

Choto nodded and ran his fingers through his black coiffed hair. "It's time for my bath, and then we'll saddle up."

26

SANDMAN AND RAMIREZ PREPARE TO DEFEND THE FORTRESS

Ramirez stood nervously in Sandman's den, waiting for Hector and Luis to bring Rodrigo to the house. The den at the rear of Sandman's *casa* served as his office. He spent most of his time there, sometimes sleeping on the leather sofa if he didn't feel like climbing the two flights of stairs to the master bedroom. The room received light through two sets of sliding glass doors that looked out onto the rear patio. Several overstuffed chairs, including Sandman's reading chair, were arranged around the room.

The morning sun cast a warm light on the bricks and potted desert plants outside, but Ramirez wasn't paying attention. Her greatest trepidations were coming to pass. Rodrigo, God bless him—*Dios lo bendiga*—had flashed his scam *plata* samples all over the place, attracted the attention of his boss in the Mexicali Cartel, and led a manhunt straight back to Puerto Peñasco. A hornet's nest had been whacked, and the insects, armed with powerful stingers, were gathering for an attack. She could feel it. It had been rash of her officers to extract Rodrigo from the cartel without so much as a call for backup. She was relieved they'd rescued the boy, but she would need some answers from the pair.

Did they recognize the men? How many were there?

She was sure there would be repercussions from the Mexicali Cartel. When they learned where he was, they would come after him. Taking the boy away from them would be seen as a provocation, a threat and a loss to their macho pride. A confrontation would go down hard. Her first priority was to secure Rodrigo at Sandman's and keep him hidden as long as necessary. She called the mayor to inform him that Rodrigo was safe and off the streets. They agreed that calling in outside law enforcement would only serve to tip their location. No one had discovered that he had been stashed at Sandman's house, so she believed the location wasn't compromised by Rodrigo's prior visit. Just as important, Sandman had again offered to keep the boy. He and Speed were making changes to enhance the perimeter security. Speed fetched a security-camera system he'd bought on a prior run to Tucson and had never taken out of the box. The retired postal carrier was setting up one security camera to cover the front door and another to view the walled-in back patio off the den. It was the kind of project he enjoyed. Speed was a tinkerer.

Sandman climbed the interior stairs to the rooftop master bedroom to retrieve his Glock 22 from the locked gun safe in the bedroom's walk-in closet. After punching in the combination, he opened the metal safe door and picked up the wooden gun case from a shelf inside. He opened the box and carefully removed the police pistol with a Trijicon night sight then popped a magazine into the grip. He wanted to believe there might be a way to deescalate the situation, but he wasn't hopeful. He knew that carrying the gun made it more likely that he would use it. If the cartel found where Rodrigo was, he had no doubt they would come to the house to retrieve him. There was not much chance of avoiding a violent conflict.

Only once had he fired his weapon in the line of duty. That incident became the source of his nickname. He was a rookie patrolman still on probation when he and his training partner answered a late-night burglary-in-progress call in a south-side Phoenix neighborhood. Arriving on scene, they spotted a man dressed in black and carrying a bag. He was walking out the front door. The intruder saw them exit their vehicle and ran around the side of the property. While calling for backup, his partner chased the intruder and sent Sanderson around the other side of the house to cut him off.

As Sanderson turned a corner, a second man appeared with his gun raised. They were only a few feet from each other in deep shadows. Sanderson, seeing the gun aimed at his face, shot and killed the man. An internal-affairs investigation cleared him of wrongdoing—the pair had criminal records for theft and assault. But the initial investigators' report mangled the rookie's last name, calling him Sandman. His training partner made sure everyone knew about the Sandman who put the bad guys to sleep. As unfunny as the joke was, from that point on, he was the Sandman. Everyone from street cops to police captains called him by that nickname. He was branded.

Sandman grabbed two other loaded magazines and his concealment holster. He clicked the web belt over his board shorts and holstered the pistol. The weapon was illegal in Mexico—he had no permission to carry it. He'd brought it into the country through the Lukeville port of entry hidden in his truck. Ramirez was well aware he had it. Occasionally, they had gone target shooting together in the remote desert.

He reentered the den. Still talking on her cell phone to the mayor, Ramirez smiled as she glanced at the holster strapped to Sandman's waist. Speed was hunched over a laptop perched on Sandman's seldom-used desk. He brought up the remote cameras on the screen just in time to catch the image of a police van rolling up Sandman's driveway.

Sandman went to open the door for the van to enter his expansive two-plus-car garage. "Did anyone see you? Were you followed?" he asked as they got out of the van.

"No, we checked," said Hector. "The Caborca highway was clear. The men didn't leave after us, and we made a little detour around the *malecón* to make sure. We were careful, coming the long way into Cholla."

Rodrigo entered the den with Hector and Luis on either side. He reeked of dank salt swamp, sweat, and urine.

"You're going to have to fumigate the police van," Sandman said to Ramirez.

Rodrigo ignored him and looked over to Chief Ramirez, who appeared more sympathetic. "I'd like to talk to him," she said looking at Sandman.

"Not on my furniture," he said, making a face. "Let me get an old blanket." Sandman left the room for the garage again.

R odrigo stood motionless on the den's tile floor, his clothes still caked in mud. His eyes followed the retired detective as he left, staring at the sidearm belted over Sandman's shorts on his right hip.

Chief Ramirez looked at the two cops flanking the boy. "*Qué pasa?* I need a report."

Luis stretched his thin frame to his full height. "*Pues*, we found the boy."

"*Sí*, I deduced that." Her eyes narrowed. The two cops looked disappointed. They probably thought they had been heroic. "How did you get the boy away from the Mexicalis?"

Speed left through the den's glass door to adjust a camera he'd mounted on the patio roof, which was trained on the wall surrounding the property. From inside, Ramirez idly watched him work. The blue sky began bunching round fluffy cumulus clouds into small piles that looked like they could become bigger ones. He kept his straw hat on.

In the den, Luis pointed at Rodrigo. "We were driving out to the resort to deliver the photos of our subject here. I looked over to the estuary on the inland side on the Caborca road and saw a black SUV off in the sand. Some men stood around near the SUV looking at something. I tapped Hector, who said we should check it out."

"And you didn't call it in?" she asked.

"They looked out of place, not dangerous, so I drove up to them," said Hector, nodding.

"How many were there?"

"I saw the three men right away. They were wearing the green security polo shirts from the resort. Until I approached, they were looking down into a low *arroyo* in the estuary."

"We were careful to follow procedure," said Hector, lobbying in favor of their behavior. "We didn't know them, but they didn't look like hotel security.

"Were they armed?" she asked.

"Oh, *sí*," said Hector. "But we had our *pistolas* at the ready." Ramirez's eyes widened at his admission. Belatedly, he realized how inane it sounded.

"They were watching Rodrigo dig a hole," Luis butted in. "I recognized him right away."

"They claimed that Rodrigo lost something," Hector said, recovering his reporting voice.

"I grabbed his arm and jerked him up from the hole," Luis said. "We told them we were going to take him to file a police report."

Rodrigo stayed busy, staring at his muddy feet.

"I think we surprised them. When Luis grabbed the kid, I pulled and kept them covered while he took the kid back to the van," said Hector.

"And they let you leave?"

"You could tell they were confused. They weren't expecting us. Maybe they thought someone sent us," said Hector.

"Like we were all working for the same people or something," Luis said.

Her anger flared. "Puerto Peñasco *policía* will never become pawns for the cartels," she said defiantly. The memory of Chief Francisco Vargas informing for the Jalisco Cartel then disappearing was still fresh in her mind.

Rodrigo continued intently staring at his feet during the back-and-forth. Sandman returned from the garage with a thick gray Mexican blanket. He unfolded it on an overstuffed leather chair.

"Sit," he said to Rodrigo. "Then you are hitting the shower."

Rodrigo sat. Ramirez pulled another chair in front of the young man, sat down, and looked directly at him. "Rodrigo, tell me where you went after you left this casa," she said in a soft voice.

The young man told her about hitching a ride back to Omar's house, retrieving his bag of *plata* at the self-storage, and then picking up supplies. "When *policía* saw me in *el centro*, I knew I needed to get rid of the truck. I bought a junker with *plata* and drove to Caborca. I exchanged some at a *cambio* there, but then I saw Choto's men, and I turned around to come back to Puerto Peñasco. State police stopped me, and I was taken to Choto."

She reflected for a moment on his claim that state police were doing the bidding of the cartel. "Then they took the *plata*?" She'd hoped he would slip and have to admit that his treasure story was a lie.

"No, I buried it before they found me," he said, his voice barely above a whisper.

She sighed. "Is that why you were digging out in the estuary?"

"I told Choto that I buried the *plata y oro* there."

She noted he didn't directly answer the question. "*Oro*? You saying you found gold too?"

"*Sí*. I didn't see it until I was about to bury it."

Ramirez was losing patience with his lies. "You were digging it up for them?"

"*Sí*, I was digging. Choto said he would cut my head off if I didn't."

"Did you give it to them?"

"No, these cops interrupted things. I am grateful they rescued me. I could be dead now."

"Now Choto has the bag of *plata y oro*?"

"I don't think so," he said vaguely.

"Qué?" She was fighting to remain calm.

"I'm not sure it was the right place to dig. It was dark when I buried it." Then came a rush of words. "I was scared and confused when they took me back out on the highway. It's flat, there are not many landmarks, we were coming from the opposite direction, and I wasn't in the same car when I marked the odometer."

Sandman looked at Ramirez and nodded. She knew he understood more Spanish than he spoke, but you didn't have to be a native speaker to conclude the boy was talking total bullshit. Rodrigo was clinging to some fantasy that he could work his way out of the situation on his own. While she questioned the boy, Sandman stood by his desk and stared at the side of Rodrigo's head. The boy's ear was flushed, surely a sign of stress. In her experience—and probably in Sandman's too—that frequently indicated deception. Ramirez met Sandman's gaze and shook her head. She had nothing yet. Maybe they would try to interview him again after Rodrigo showered and had a chance to think about the events that had led him here.

"Okay, Rodrigo," she said. "You can get cleaned up now. We'll talk again a little later." She took out her cell phone again, quickly tapped a number, and sent a quick text: *Sandman's*. Then she pocketed the phone. Sandman made a face.

Luis and Hector took Rodrigo lightly by the arms and moved him up the stairs to the second floor and the bathroom at the end of the hall.

"*Qué cree usted?* What do you think, Sandman?"

"I assume you just called Chuy. Not sure I'm pleased about that."

She shrugged. "*Chuy es* Rodrigo's *wey*. Really his only friend and any real connection we have to try to get him to cooperate. Despite the fact we got him out of a jam, Rodrigo's told us very little."

"I agree. His story about burying the silver—and now gold—doesn't tell us anything. It's a lame explanation of why he doesn't have it. I'm not sure Chuy will get more out of him. Luis and Hector may have saved the boy only to put us all in danger. I'd lay odds that someone will leak this location to Rodrigo's employers. We should expect visitors."

"I know you're right," she said.

"Let's make sure we're prepared. You have additional officers that you absolutely trust?" Sandman asked. "A few extra hands wouldn't hurt."

"*Todos.*" She shook her head. "This is everyone.*"

27

WAITING FOR GOMEROS

After a fitful night, Vicente Diaz Gámez and his partner Carlos Villar sat waiting around their campfire in the early-morning light. It seemed like all they did was wait. Choto had sent them to look for this kid Rodrigo. For hours, they climbed a trail in the Arizona mountains to find the last known base camp where that little *pinche cabrón* had disappeared. When they found it, Vicente thought it looked like something had happened at the camp, maybe something bad. There was blood all over the place, and the campsite was tossed. Carlos said he didn't see any animal tracks, and there was only one set of human footprints. They weren't convinced by the evidence, but neither of them claimed to be outdoorsmen.

They shrugged and called it in to Choto on a radio, using an encrypted code. Vicente didn't trust the secure radio—they weren't in Mexico—and no one really knew how good the encryption was. For all he knew, the radio messages could be waving a big flag for US law enforcement to come and grab them. He wasn't an expert in this stuff. The gringo cops could have eavesdropping tools no one knew about. They were told to keep looking for the little *culero*, until last night, when the word came down to sit tight and wait. That morning, they were told others would be coming.

A couple of hikers had disturbed their search the day before, but the old man and young woman fell when he and Carlos suddenly came across them on the trail. Choto told them to keep a low profile, not attract attention, so they didn't approach the pair, just left the man and woman where they slid down the mountainside. He doubted the two hikers got a clear look at them, and they weren't the priority. Carlos was all for wasting them anyway, but Vicente argued he didn't want to deal with having to dispose of them. And then there was the noise. If Customs and Border Protection did intercept the radio traffic, then any gunfire might bring them right to their location. Carlos was persuaded for the moment but wanted to revisit the conversation. Vicente told him to be patient.

When night fell, they came back to see a flickering light outlining a large rock a distance below their position. They watched for a while and later detected a small party working its way in the dark toward the lighted rock. When the group got there, they loaded a stretcher and then turned on headlamps for the return trip. Carlos renewed his desire to waste the lot of them, but Vicente rejected the idea, knowing he wasn't serious. Carlos didn't have much of a sense of humor. About the only thing he made jokes about was killing people.

"The problem is solving itself," he'd said to Carlos. Then standing up from his crouch, he turned and walked the path back to their campsite. Carlos shrugged and followed but kept his finger near the trigger of his semiautomatic rifle until they reached camp.

Tired and sleepless, they roused themselves to a chilly morning. The fire they built from scraggly bits of dead mesquite branches, creosote sticks, and dried cholla cactus stems they had scrounged didn't provide much warmth. The

crackling flames burned hot and quickly consumed the dry
fuel, leaving a few coals in a gray pile and sending lazy flakes
of white ash floating above them in the wispy smoke. Their
fire-making skills sucked.

The aluminum pan they'd used to make coffee still sat on
top of the dying coals. It was beginning to have that burned-
shellac smell of old grounds. Vicente refused to drink instant,
so he had put some ground coffee in the bottom and filled the
saucepan partway from his canteen. When the water boiled,
he removed it by grabbing the handle with a rolled-up T-shirt
from his pack. He poured the brown liquid into two tin cups,
trying not to spill it, then put the pot back on the fire. It tasted
only slightly better than instant. He would pray to a dozen
saints that a decent cup of Oaxacan *cafe* would somehow
appear in front of him. They drank the bitter liquid in silence,
occasionally spitting out coffee grounds. Vicente mused to
himself about how much he hated heights and being out in
the desert. He was a city guy. Both of them were. He was a
few years older than Carlos. They'd been recruited from the
same Tijuana streets. That was really their bond.

His chin propped up under his left hand, he looked over
at Carlos, who had decided he should clean his AR-15
outfitted with a custom stock. Unlike Vicente, who was
bundled up in his jacket and still freezing in the mountain air,
Carlos wore a sleeveless military green undershirt. He
balanced his Glock 19 pistol on the large rock next to him,
only a quick motion from his hand. After laying a clean cloth
from his knapsack on the dusty ground near the dying fire, he
dropped the rifle's magazine, checked the chamber, and
pulled the pins to separate the weapon into two pieces. He
removed the bolt and charging pin and lay the pieces on the
cloth. His biceps bulged as he easily worked the carrier bolt
assembly, an oiled cloth in his strong hands. Carlos had his
own custom barrel cleaner, a small-caliber bullet attached to a
thin leather cord that pierced a length of cloth. He dropped

the bullet down the barrel, grabbed it, and pulled the cloth through the interior rifling. Vicente was sure that Carlos had the cleanest weapons in all of Mexico. Carbon and gunpowder residue were probably too afraid to stick anywhere on any gun Carlos possessed. In his practiced hands, the procedure only took only few minutes before he reassembled the rifle and snapped the magazine back into place. He lay the weapon across his thighs, reached for the Glock, and holstered the pistol.

"Thank God I don't have to watch you clean the Glock too," said Vicente.

"A clean gun is a happy gun," said Carlos, looking up from his rifle, looking pleased. "You should work on yours. It's filthy."

Vicente just screwed up his face and held his jacket tighter.

By noon, a coded signal from the expected crew told them that the new guys were on their way up the mountain. Vicente didn't know them well. They were recent additions to Choto's crew, recruited locally, from Sonora. He and Carlos had been with Choto much longer. When Choto was sent to temporary exile in Puerto Peñasco, the two had been part of the team that went with him. Choto had been on a fast track to the upper levels of the cartel. But there were problems arising primarily from his hyper and inappropriate bursts of temper, and it seemed that the *patrons* who ran the plaza in northern Mexico didn't fully trust him.

They all were sent to Puerto Peñasco to set up the local cell after the Jaliscos collapsed. Choto, in the doghouse, would be on a shorter leash than he'd been on in Tijuana to demonstrate his value to the bosses. Except *they* weren't in Mexico. *They*—Vicente and Carlos—were sitting on top of a *pinche montaña* in Arizona. Waiting.

Waiting for what? Waiting for Choto to get his pinche mierda together? Waiting for more men to show. One big happy team. Feliz caballeros. Maybe we could all hold hands on the way back down.

Still shivering in the cold, Vicente declared his intention to rebuild the fire. "I'm going to find more shit to burn," Vicente said, gathering himself to stand. "These guys should get here in a little while."

Carlos, double-checking all his firepower options, grunted in response.

Maybe if he moved around, Vicente could get warm. He looked below to an area of scrub trees and creosote as a potential fuel source. He began sidestepping slowly down the steep pitch of the hillside. Careful to avoid rocks and holes, he worked his way about thirty meters below the campsite and began to gather material. He found a couple of small dried mesquite branches on the ground and pulled some dead creosote sticks from the base of several plants. As he built a pile, he became aware of the sounds of birds chugging in the trees and sweetly trilling in the brush. He could hear scratchy rustling along the desert floor. Creatures—mostly quail, probably—flushed from their morning routine, scurried and chirped in aggrieved protest at his presence. Above his position and off in the distance, a single coyote yipped and howled. *As least someone got breakfast this morning.*

He made his way back to the pile he'd assembled. Mostly it was just kindling, and he thought he'd gathered more than he could carry in a single trip. He picked up as many pieces he could hold comfortably under his arm for the climb back to camp. As he picked up a last branch, he stepped back awkwardly, and the back of his hand brushed against a cholla cactus. A chunk of the plant bristling with needles stuck to his hand.

"*Chingada madre!*" he shouted, causing more quail to scatter. His arms full, he ignored the botanical passenger and climbed up the hillside. Holding his kindling tight against his body, he found the path up to camp more taxing than the way down had been.

The firewood gathering had taken nearly an hour. After

muttering under his labored breath and climbing, he reached the top and threw down the pile. He looked over to see the three heavily armed crew members sitting on rocks surrounding the near-extinguished remains of the fire. They were the newcomers to the crew. Ricky was the *ad hoc* leader of the three, a bit older and taller. The other two were fresh off the farms, *naco*.

"Who's your friend?" Ricky asked, pointing at the cactus stuck on his hand.

"You guys make really shitty coffee," said Paco, the youngest and smallest of the three.

"Continue, and someone could get shot, *muerto*," said Vicente calmly.

"Don't worry," said Carlos, who was oiling the custom stock of his rifle. "His gun is dirty. *Muy sucio.* It will probably jam."

"I swear on my mother's grave, I could kill all of you with only my ball point pen," said Vicente, whose focus had shifted to delicately removing several barbed cholla needles from his skin, using the fingers on his other hand. "If you are finished with your jokes, maybe someone will explain why we waited for you. The code said you would get here before nightfall."

"It is a long story," said Ricky. "It starts with Patrón. That Choto is completely loco!"

"If it's a such long story, then perhaps you should skip to the new part," said Vicente flatly, staring at the red-dot punctures at the back of his hand. Even Carlos, the guy with no sense of humor, grinned at Vicente's joke, chuckling into his super-clean rifle.

28

SHOTS FIRED

J D's mood had not improved by the early afternoon when they reached the trailhead. She told Will that the thought of armed mobs running around the borderland seemed like the stupidest idea imaginable. She knew militias existed, but this was the first time she'd seen that kind of group close-up. At some point, she said, someone was going to get seriously hurt or killed by those undisciplined rednecks.

Frankie parked the truck, and everyone assembled. "Remember, there were people on the mountain when we came out last night," he said, strapping on his sidearm. "Likely, they're still up there though maybe in a different location. Eyes up. Be safe."

Minus the stretcher for Doc, they were able to move up the lower trail at a good pace. Frankie took point with Danny and Tim, eyes left and right, following him, carrying their rifles in low-ready position as they hiked. JD and Will trailed behind. Will was surprised by her flare-up outside the militia encampment. Yokel out-of-state quasi-military groups weren't a new phenomenon near the border. Similar groups had come to the Arivaca-Sasabe area in the past, strutting around the desert with their weapons, claiming they were "helping" the federal government round up criminals and smugglers who were pouring over the border.

There'd been a handful of militia run-ins with the locals over the years. Many of Arivaca's few hundred residents didn't appreciate the "special protection." Officially, Customs and Border Protection regarded them as a potentially dangerous nuisance, though unofficially, many agents quietly encouraged them. But the groups usually didn't stay long. After receiving something less than the grateful reception they'd expected from local townspeople, some members would drop out after a few days and return home. Eventually the leadership would figure out that camping in the open, even on the land of a sympathetic rancher, was not the romantic defense of the homeland that they had fantasized about, and the group would pack up and leave. There was no reason to think this ragtag bunch would be any different. Still, he saw that coming upon them so suddenly must have been a shock to JD.

Will knew she had strong feelings about issues, though he'd never seen her that upset about anything political. She covered immigrant issues in federal court as a part of her beat. However, she held herself away from advocating for issues. One of the things he admired about her was her strong sense of justice, rooted in helping the most vulnerable in society. But only to him did she express her disgust at the mess immigration law had become.

Walking behind the O'odham men, she was in her own head and quiet, eyes focused on the boots ahead of her. He wondered what she was thinking. Maybe it was yesterday's experience with the two sicarios on the mountain. Clearly, she was still traumatized by the episode. He knew she felt bad about Doc's accident, despite Doc shrugging off the whole thing. The image of the old man in a hospital bed with his leg in a cast stuck in Will's mind. Maybe she was embarrassed to have lost her phone, the item central to her work as a reporter.

"You all right?" he asked softly in her ear.

She nodded without speaking. Will knew to leave it alone. They turned off the hiking trail and followed the rougher bushwhacking path the group had walked the previous night.

Will engaged Tim ahead of him, who surveilled his flank. "You were saying on the truck that you believed you were a medicine man. Forgive my ignorance, but is that something you study or get appointed to?"

Tim smiled and continued his watch of the desert as they walked. "You discover you have a gift," he said in that calm even voice all the brothers possessed. "I was a medic in the army, so I was already interested in healing. When I came back from deployment, I walked in the desert without food or water. I traveled our land for days until I could go no farther. I sat under a mesquite tree and received a vision to use my healing powers. After that experience, I learned the herbs and plants from the elders who still know. But some of our knowledge has been lost. My quest is to recapture it, keep it, and teach others. I read the history texts of the Spaniards, the *miligá:n* who visited our land many years ago. So, when the time comes, our people will be able to return to being part of the land like those who came before."

Will could tell he was serious, but he was puzzled. "When what time comes?"

"When all the white people leave," he said matter-of-factly.

"Really? You mean us whites? When will that happen?" Will was paranoid about rattlesnakes, but he listened intently while stepping carefully along the shrubby and rock-strewn path. The path up the mountain from the previous night was recognizable from the displaced brush, but it was still tougher and slower going than the well-worn tourist trail.

Tim walked easily ahead and didn't turn his head when

he spoke. "When they have extracted all the minerals they can find and sucked out all the water under the earth, they will leave. I saw it in a vision."

"I think you're serious," Will said.

"When all the underground water is gone, the *miligá:n* cannot live here. They will have no choice—they will go somewhere else. Only our people, Tohono O'odham, can survive in the desert without the water pulled up from under the earth. We lived on our land for many generations and never drilled wells. It was the white Indian Affairs that forced wells on the people a hundred years ago. Elder Brother prophesized that the *miligá:n* would come and ruin the earth. Elder Brother also said that we would survive it. One reason why our people welcomed the Jesuit missionary Kino was that they were expecting him."

"But you get Central Arizona Project water," said JD, joining the conversation.

"Our ancestors built canals a thousand years ago. CAP water is like a tribute, paying us for taking away part of the land," said Tim. "They built it because they were going to run out of water without it. We demanded a share. If we don't use the CAP water, someone else will. We will help them use it up. You know, the lakes and the rivers where they take the water are drying up. When the water is gone, it won't come back. And there will be no water underground." He said this without rancor as though stating the obvious.

"*Miligá:n* act like it is an unlimited supply, even though they know it isn't," said Frankie from the point position at the front of the group.

"So, you agree with Tim?" JD asked Frankie.

"I believe he had the vision. We argue about the timeline, but what's going on is unsustainable. I told you we left the reservation and moved to Ajo after the mine closed for Pop's job. He worked construction to secure the abandoned properties owned by the mining company. After the mine closure, Ajo was practically a ghost town. We've seen how white people abandon land."

"Talk to us about the story you're writing," said Danny to JD. This was the first time he'd spoken since they left the vehicle. "You said it was about abandoned mines and forgotten treasure. Parallels, dude."

The sun was bright. JD rubbed her temples.

"Punching holes in the land to remove the water and the metals injures the earth," said Tim.

"Ak-Chin ain't just an airport near Phoenix," said Frankie. "In the O'odham language, it means flooded-field farming. For many generations, our people depended on the summer rain to come. They steered the runoff from the rushing gullies and arroyos to flat land for irrigation. In the old days, it was how we farmed. Not so common anymore. Now many of our people drive pickups and eat potato chips out of plastic bags."

"So we're reviving it," said Tim. "We listen to the elders and their stories. We learn about what plants grow when—the tepary beans, the corn, the melons. We have land set aside for farming plots to keep the traditions alive."

Frankie said, "We're curating our history. We gather the knowledge, so it can be passed on, and when it is needed, our people will have it. Also, Doc has been helpful, supplying us with books, and we've helped him connect to some of our people."

Will was leaning in to hear Frankie when he felt the rush of air past his head and a stinging pain erupted on the top of his left earlobe. His brain registered the sound of a gunshot after the pain. Reflexively he put his hand up to his ear and felt sticky blood.

"Down!" Frankie hand signaled Danny and Tim, spreading them out into the brush. They crouched behind the rocks and creosote as more shots followed. "Are you okay?" he asked Will.

"Hurts like a mother," said Will, his hand pressed against his head. It felt like a red-hot branding iron touched the top of his ear.

JD dropped to the ground and looked at Will, shocked. She reached out to him with an anguished look on her face that accelerated his pumping adrenaline.

"You two, stay down, and don't move," Frankie said under his breath.

The three brothers began returning fire to the top of the slope in the direction of the incoming rounds. Frankie signaled that he saw one shooter.

Vicente heard the shots and followed the sound. When he got close, he hit the ground and crawled toward Carlos on his hands and knees, pushing his own rifle out ahead of him as fast as he could manage, approaching his partner. Carlos lay prone on the ridgeline, shooting toward the group below as they moved up the mountain.

Vicente had been checking the little *pendejo's* campsite when he heard the gunfire. The new guys were country types more familiar with the terrain, so he'd taken them with him and designated Carlos as lookout while they searched. *Big mistake.* The object of the search was no longer Rodrigo, the little shit who'd disappeared. According to the new guys, with instructions directly from Choto, they were looking for gold and silver and the place where Rodrigo had found it. Then the search had been interrupted by trigger-happy Carlos.

Vicente thought about grabbing a rock and pounding Carlos's skull into guacamole, but that would have required him to stand and expose himself to gunfire from below. He also thought of strangling Carlos with his hands, but unfortunately, that, too, would be dangerous, requiring him to jump on the *pinche cabrón*, position himself on the small of Carlos's back, and then choke the life out of him breaking his windpipe. Judging by the accuracy of the return fire, he himself would be dead sitting up before he could even find the dumb shit's hyoid bone.

Instead, he shouted into Carlos's ear, "*Qué poca madre!* What are you doing?"

Carlos didn't flinch and squeezed another round. "I saw them coming back up the mountain, and I fired a few warning shots to scare them."

"And how is that working out?" Vicente asked as a volley of bullets ricocheted off the rock formation above them.

"Not so great, I guess. I deliberately nicked one of them as a warning, but the others appear to be trained fighters," said Carlos, betraying his surprise. "I guess I'll have to kill them all."

It was like handing a live hand grenade to a toddler just to see what the *chico* would do with it. "No, you will not. Choto said keep a low profile, and we're going to follow the order. Even now. We have a job, and we need to go and do it." Vicente smacked the back of Carlos's neck hard, snapping the shooter's head against the rifle's optical sight, and cutting Carlos's cheek and forehead above his brow in small semicircles.

Another bullet whizzed by, nearly taking off Vicente's fingers as he raised them. *Mother of God, this is turning into a shit show.*

"Now look what you've done," said Carlos. "I'm bleeding on my just-cleaned weapon." He seemed genuinely sad about the bloody rifle scope.

Vicente thought he might have to kill Carlos before the idiot blundered into getting them both shot. He began backing away, crawling along the hardpan of the ridge. He grabbed Carlos's shirt collar, forcing him away from the targets below. If the two of them stayed low, the group below was disciplined enough to hold fire unless they could identify a target.

It took some minutes of crawling as flat to the ground as they could manage, holding their rifles by the forward sling, before he felt they were clear and out of visual range. Ignoring Carlos behind him, Vicente stood up and slapped a dusty cloud from his pants. He wiped the grit off his weapon with his sleeve. He stormed off among the rocky formations and boulders, leaving Carlos trailing in silence. Vicente kept on ahead while Carlos muttered that they should have just finished the job and returned to Mexico. When they reached Rodrigo's former base camp, only one of the three men was present. The other two had gone off somewhere.

"What were all those shots?" asked Paco, the remaining man.

"My associate decided to engage in target practice," said Vicente. "Unfortunately, the targets shot back. We will need to leave here if we want to avoid another confrontation."

"Just as well. We found something," Paco said, his curiosity apparently satisfied. "Alfonso and Ricky discovered multiple footprints where they didn't expect. They're checking them out. You did examine the camp before we got here?"

"We did, but it was late." Vicente didn't want to go through the whole we-are-not-country-*gomeros* thing with Paco.

"Ricky found a lot of tracks leading down. He thinks they are Rodrigo's shoe prints. The kid was sloppy."

"Couldn't be that sloppy, or you would still have him," said Carlos. He had made it obvious he wanted off that *pinche* mountain.

Paco made a move toward Carlos, but Vicente, much bigger, shoved him aside, staring right through the younger man. "If and when my associate needs a beating, I will be the one kicking his ass. Sit down and wait."

There was a noise on the trail. Everyone became alert, and Carlos, gun raised, found Alfonso in his sights.

"*Tranquilo*," said Alfonso, arms raised. "Jumpy, aren't we?"

"We were discussing the international financial markets." Vicente grabbed the end of Carlos's rifle barrel, which was aimed at Alfonso and pushed it away. "Derivatives can be intense."

"Ricky found some interesting tracks," said Alfonso, ignoring Vicente's comment. "It looks like Rodrigo made a number of trips to and from this camp. Everyone, come." He turned back to where he'd come from and walked away.

Vicente looked at Carlos, shrugged, and followed. Sidestepping deliberately, the four men moved in an awkward single file down a narrow path. Paco took the lead, and Vicente walked between him and Carlos to prevent any more extracurricular schoolboy taunting that might escalate. The trail was unremarkable to Vicente, and he was sure he would not have noticed the carpet-shoe footprints in the dirt among the rocks, cactuses, and lime-hued shrubs, no matter how carefully he searched. He didn't even know what they were looking for. He was grateful to be walking in the opposite direction from the hikers Carlos had engaged a few minutes earlier. He glanced back at his young partner, who had a smirk on his face. Perhaps after they finished with this, Choto would bring them back to Puerto Peñasco, and they could move on to something closer to Carlos's skill set.

They hiked across the face of the mountain and down a couple hundred meters where Alfonso, his hand shielding his eyes from the sun, whistled at the group when he saw Ricky ahead on the trail.

"The trail goes down from here," said Ricky when the group reached him. "You see these small rock and dirt slides below? It looks like he made his way up and down and dragged something." The scraggly branches were broken in the same direction. Even Vicente thought he saw it, now that someone had pointed it out. "The rock face is steep, so I held up before going farther. Wait here. Alfonso and I will go down first."

"Take Paco instead," said Vicente, trying to keep the two near combatants separated. Vicente glared at Carlos. Paco kept silent.

Ricky shrugged. "Okay, Paco and I will go down first." He stepped down backward to keep his balance and prevent himself from sliding on the loose rock and soil. When he stopped wobbling on the incline, he gave a hand to Paco and they half slid, half stepped down the hillside and disappeared below into the brush.

"That must have been some discussion about those derivatives," said Alfonso, noticing the red marks above and below Carlos' eye.

"You never know what's in those things," said Vicente, butting in before Carlos could make some asshole remark. "I like real things, you know—currency, stock, real estate."

Carlos was occupied, taking a cleaning pad to his scope and wiping the dried blood from from the optical shade.

29

ALL THAT GLITTERS...

B y noon, word had spread throughout Puerto Peñasco about the celebrities' public appearance, and hundreds had gathered along the *malecón*. The crowd filled the road, spilling over the sidewalks, forcing the closure of the main street. Pedestrians all through the *mercado* district clogged traffic for blocks.

The darkening sky from the approaching storm didn't dampen the fans' enthusiasm. The port was full of people, many returning for *Semana Santa*, holy week, and American spring breakers were still in town. Sandra compared the crowd favorably to the annual *fiesta* logjam through *el centro* during the Pasqua pageant procession. Commerce had stopped, and stores had closed except a few enterprising merchants who waded into the crowd, selling snacks and drinks mostly to locals who recognized the telenovela stars— Barbara Miranda, Gilberto Javier Romero, and Sandra Perez —gracing their town.

The famous stars themselves waited in the back seat of a black limo for the mayor to introduce them. The stretch Cadillac was parked in a VIP space created by orange traffic cones, set aside on the *malecón*. Staging, reflectors, and a dais had been erected hastily in front of the deep-blue Sea of Cortez backdrop. Clouds hovered over the shimmering horizon. Up on the dais at a lectern festooned with microphones, Mayor Juan Carlos Bustamonte had been orating over a loudspeaker system for ten or fifteen minutes.

Which is what politicians do, Sandra thought. *Still, there is something about him.* She sat at the limo door closest to the stage, part of a glittering sandwich with Barbara on the other side and Latin heartthrob Gilberto in the middle, waiting to be introduced. Despite the mild weather, the vehicle's air conditioning ran full blast to preserve the actors' makeup. In their working clothes, overdressed for a casual seaside resort, they fidgeted.

Barbara kept trying to push her short sequined dress down toward her knees. The back of her legs had been stuck to the heavy leather seats during the entire limo ride from Hermosillo. She'd had to leave her two young children at home with their *au pair* and her philandering *pendejo* of a husband. Barbara had complained that he was probably banging the ripe schoolgirl at every opportunity.

Sandra watched Gilberto repeatedly adjust the collar of his shirt and smooth his long black hair. She held a cigarette aloft in her left hand next to the door, tapped the ashes through a small crack of the slightly lowered tinted window, and with her right hand, flicked wayward bits of gray from her dark-blue skirt.

The actors had been on a promotional tour in Guadalajara, greeting fans of their latest telenovela, *El Dios o Amor,* which had just begun airing to big ratings, when their tour PR manager received a call from the mayor's father, the former governor of Sonora. He'd appealed to the tour manager personally, by phone, to change the schedule and add an appearance in the small resort town of Puerto Peñasco, where his son coincidentally was mayor. It was always good to do a favor for people as rich and politically powerful as the Bustamonte family, so the tour calendar was quickly adjusted.

They flew from Guadalajara to Hermosillo, where the limo, paid for by the governor, picked them up for the drive to Puerto Peñasco. The three stars were told to plug their latest project, of course. The production cast Gilberto Javier, acclaimed by Hispanic media as one of the handsomest actors in Latin America, in the unlikely role of a devout priest torn by desire for not one but both of his very attractive costars, who played bickering partners in an upscale fashion business. The telenovela's plotline created numerous opportunities for impassioned shouting, bouts of extended crying, and knowing looks, all shot in closeup, thrilling Latino audiences and pleasing the three costars.

The mayor's office had informed them that they should respond positively but vaguely to questions about a potential future production, a family saga centered on a tequila distillery and distribution company, with the working title of *Plata*. It was—as they often said in the business—in development. According to the cover story, the project was serious enough for the producers to spend time in town to scout locations and test the marketing waters.

The three knew nothing of the mayor's chicanery before their arrival, and Sandra and her costars didn't care. They were being well compensated by the Bustamonte family for the short detour to the beach town. All had their own stories.

Gilberto, who spoke unaccented English, was seriously interested in expanding his acting career beyond Hispanic heartthrob roles. He was especially eager to meet any gringo fans, particularly young male ones, who might be vacationing in the resort town.

Sandra, also a well-known Latina pop singer, was cross-promoting her new album on the tour and had eagerly agreed to perform her new single, "Orgullosa Chica," backed by a prerecorded music track.

The mayor was still talking. "*Muy guapo,*" said Sandra under her breath but loud enough for Gilberto to hear. He nodded in agreement—the mayor was very attractive. She cracked the window lower for a better view of the young politician and dropped the butt of her cigarette to the asphalt parking lot. The mayor seemed to be winding up his speech, saying how honored they all were to have such famous and talented guests in their town.

"And *chica bella.*" The mayor waved his hand under his chin as if the celebrity hotness threatened to overcome him. "Wait until you meet them in person. Movies and television cannot realistically capture such beauty. And you *will* have the opportunity to see for yourself because they have agreed to stay and sign autographs for all their fans," he said, pumping up the crowd.

Cheers and clapping erupted.

"*Señoras y caballeros,*" he said, his voice rising like a football club announcer. "Ladies and gentlemen, please welcome the stars of a new venture, *Plata,* and the current television hit series *El Dios o Amor*—Barbara Miranda, Sandra Perez, and everyone's favorite leading man, Gilberto Javier!" The program's recognizable theme song, a syrupy mix of mariachi-style strings beneath a soaring, angst-ridden female vocal, drew more enthusiastic cheers and applause from the growing number of people in the street.

"We're up," announced Sandra to her costars, flipping the door handle to the limo and pushing the door wide. In a practiced move, she rotated her hips in the seat to exit the vehicle, careful not to force her skirt to ride up.

Thank God they didn't make me sing that song for the show's soundtrack. Sandra was more of an urban pop diva than a tear-streaked sentimental torch singer.

Gilberto gallantly reached over and opened the opposite

door for Barbara, with whom he shared a deep but platonic friendship. Putting on their public faces, they all assembled in a line at the base of the stage. The three clicked up the stairs in their high heels. Barbara and Sandra went first and then, after a wave of his arm toward his costars, Gilberto, in hand-tooled boots, bounded up to the top of the platform. They radiated broad smiles full of dazzling white teeth and waved to the people in the street, who became even more excited in their presence.

Each star spoke for several minutes, proclaiming his or her personal excitement for being in that *bella y linda* resort town and grateful for the well wishes of all their fans. After everyone had a turn at the mic, it was time for music. With a single move of her hand at her waist, Sandra removed her skirt to reveal long spray-tanned legs and pranced around the stage, singing her chart-climbing song to whistles and cheers. Timed to the percussive final note, she finished the dance move and, hands in the air, struck a pose.

The mayor grabbed her upraised palm and held a hand aloft to great applause. She smiled at him and twirled as though they'd practiced the move, and then the two embraced, laughing. The applause and cheering grew even louder.

Returning to the stage microphone, the mayor thanked the guests again and lauded the respectful behavior of Puerto Peñasco citizens. In front of the stage, the actors sat down behind a long table stacked with color telenovela-series posters of themselves. Sharpies in hand, they graciously signed autographs for hours as hundreds waited patiently in line for a chance to see and converse briefly with the stars. There were only a few questions from the fans about *Plata,* which pleased the mayor.

≈

After the long afternoon of smiling and small talk, Mayor Juan Carlos whisked them off to a scheduled reception and dinner at the Montezuma Palace, the deluxe resort south of the town, where the Bustamonte family arranged for the stars to stay overnight. The hotel had scheduled personal spa treatments and arranged whatever else the celebrities could possibly desire. The stars were feted by local business dignitaries and treated to a four-course gourmet dinner that they dared not consume at the risk of their diets.

The hotel's vice president for operations and the evening's host drew the mayor aside and buttonholed him during the dinner to ask about the treasure maps and the *plata* that he said were "flooding" the town.

"You must do something, Juan Carlos," said Montezuma's vice president, Andres Guerrero. "I can't have people from everywhere running around the resort properties with picks and shovels, digging up the area. It will be chaos. I'm speaking not just for the resort but on behalf of the merchants' association in town."

"Andres, my friend," the mayor responded. "I know for certain that only a few pieces of *plata* have been circulating in Puerto Peñasco. We are confident that the source has been found and contained. As for the treasure maps, an enterprising T-shirt merchant on the *malecón* confessed it was his idea to earn some extra money by creating the maps and selling them to tourists along with his *bolsas* and painted geckos. The maps have been confiscated, and he has been warned that spreading rumors will not be tolerated. If you hear anything else, Andres, please call me." Vice president Guerrero appeared mollified, if not convinced, by the mayor's words.

The mayor removed himself from the conversation and returned to the white-linen dining table where the three stars sat. He noticed Gilberto's eye fixated on a tall *guapo* busboy who patiently waited nearby. Barbara Miranda stared into her phone, texting. Sandra smiled at him and made sure that he sat next to her. She wanted to know if Juan Carlos was on the menu. The sacrifices a mayor had to make on behalf of his constituents and the town.

30

CHOTO'S SICARIOS SEEK SHELTER

The crew moved down the nearly nonexistent path, led by Ricky. "You can see he made several trips here," Ricky said, pointing at the desert trail.

Vicente had to take his word for it. He couldn't see it at all. The disturbed ground looked like everything else—just a rocky mountainside.

"We didn't get below this point, so I can't tell what he was doing in this area," Ricky said. "We should stay together from here. I thought I heard gunfire earlier."

"Probably hunting season," said Vicente, not wanting to talk about it.

"We saw some militia, civil vigilantes on the road before we hiked up the mountain. I think we need to stay together," Ricky repeated.

They stepped carefully down the steep slope trying to follow Ricky's gestures, which pointed to vague impressions in the ground. Vicente pretended to look, nodding appreciatively at Ricky's tracking skills. After climbing over rocks, losing the track, and finding it again, they reached an opening of bare ground. It appeared that something had been dragged across the area.

Okay, even I can see the drag marks now. But with large boulders surrounding the space, it was difficult to tell what happened to the tracks from there. They'd reached an impasse.

Ricky squatted to study the ground while the others stood watching him. Vicente decided that the five of them had trampled any remaining traces of wherever Rodrigo had been going. He tried to pay attention, but his mind wandered, and he gazed absentmindedly at the landscape. He wasn't sure, but he thought he saw some movement in the desert vegetation in the distance far below. While Ricky explained the tracks that seemed to confirm that Rodrigo had hauled something heavy across the ground there, Vicente unslung his rifle and used the sight to identify what it was he'd seen. He found it.

"*Gente,*" he said, still peering through the scope. "They're not the ones from before. Coming up the *montaña* from a different direction. More of them than the first group. Maybe Ricky's militia."

He hadn't actually seen the people that Carlos had fired on—he'd been too busy ducking for cover. But he knew this group was much larger. He focused on a point ahead of the people hiking in single file. He counted seven passing across the scope's sight. Others could be ahead of them. All were dressed in green military-style garb and armed, some with multiple weapons. They walked lazily along the trail, without awareness of their environment, and Vicente decided they weren't government. Ricky stopped talking, and everyone looked at Vicente.

"Did you say something earlier about a vigilante group?" Vicente asked.

"We saw them on the road at an encampment when we came up from the border," Alfonso said.

"They're moving this way." Vicente lowered the rifle scope and cast around, looking for a way out.

"Attracted by the earlier shots," said Alfonso.

Vicente allowed that there could be two groups looking for the source of the shooting. He turned to Ricky. "Any ideas? If we climb back up to the ridgeline, they'll see us." He figured there could be ten or twelve armed men, or more, coming toward them from two directions, like a coincidental pincer move. He didn't like the odds. They could handle the sloppy vigilantes, but the group Carlos shot at would be a much tougher task. And except for Carlos, Vicente's men weren't looking for a fight.

Ricky anxiously scanned the peak above them. It was early afternoon, but the March sun was low enough to cast some shadows and highlight the slope's terrain. He shaded his forehead with his right hand and looked around. Vicente noted that there were no boulders, scrub trees, or anywhere else they might hide to avoid a confrontation.

"There," he said, pointing to something roughly a hundred meters or so above them.

Vicente didn't see anything.

"It looks like it could be an opening in the cliff," said Ricky.

Vicente pointed his rifle toward the spot Ricky indicated and looked through the scope. He still couldn't find it with the scope's narrow field of view.

"It's a dark spot on the hillside," said Ricky. "It may be nothing, but it could be a place to hide. What choice do we have unless we ignore orders and get into a firefight?"

"Fuck the orders," Vicente said. "I prefer not to die on this hill." He didn't want to shoot their way out unless there was no choice. He gave Carlos a hard look and shook his head. *Don't say anything.*

"If we crawl up the slope one at a time, they may not see us," said Ricky. "I'll go first. Everyone, stay down."

Carlos didn't look pleased with the idea. Vicente knew he was all in for a shootout.

"Don't forget your gear. If you leave something behind, it could give away our position." Ricky began climbing through the brush toward the spot he'd pointed to, staying low and using whatever rocks and vegetation he could to hide himself. The others ducked low and watched his progress up the slope. Vicente kept watch on the vigilantes. Ricky was about thirty meters up the slope when he turned toward the group below and motioned for the next man.

"Paco, you go next," said Vicente.

Paco nodded, and the thin young man began climbing the hillside, following the same path as Ricky, who had ducked behind some boulders and was no longer visible from their position. Vicente saw the vigilantes coming, but he hoped they were heading in the direction of the previous gunfire and away from their current position. *Maybe no one will find us.*

"Alfonso, then Carlos. I'll go up last," Vicente said.

One by one, they moved up the slope, leaving large spaces between the climbers. Vicente stood watch until his turn. The vigilantes below had disappeared into the vegetation and out of his view. He hoped the sharpshooters that Carlos had engaged earlier would have better things to do than search for Vicente's men. He wasn't holding out hope that they could dodge both groups. *Maybe the two groups will shoot at each other.*

He shouldered his rifle in its sling and began his climb. Carlos was halfway up, about fifty meters ahead of him. Hewing tightly to the path's slope upward, Vicente could not see the others above him. Trickles of dirt and gravel from the previous climbers would slide down the path, and the rising dust stung his nose. He wished for a bandana to cover his face. The only other sounds he could hear were occasional rocks clicking high above him from the foot traffic and wind whipping past the creosote, shrubby oaks, and mesquites on the hillside.

It took him ten or fifteen minutes to make it to the narrow

flat ridgeline. Ricky, kneeling at the top, offered his hand. Vicente gladly grabbed it, and Ricky pulled him up. He was tired from all the activity that day. First, finding firewood, then crawling around, retrieving Carlos from the disastrous gunfire exchange. Then moving quickly halfway across the mountain and climbing this last part nearly straight up.

Vicente looked around and didn't see anyone else with Ricky, who motioned for silence and pointed behind him to an opening in the hillside. Ricky laid his hand on his shoulder and whispered, "The others are inside. It's an abandoned mine adit."

Vicente nodded. The mountain was probably full of them. He followed the trailblazer into the small opening. *Thank the Virgin for sending someone who's familiar with the desert terrain.* He apologized to whatever saint might be listening for his earlier negative thoughts about country bumpkins.

Vicente crawled through the opening. The small adit, little more than a meter wide and a meter and a half high, ran about five or six meters into the mountain before opening to a larger anteroom with a ceiling just high enough to prevent a person from standing up straight. It was dark, and he waited for his eyes to adjust.

The other four of Choto's men were inside the cave and talking excitedly at the same time. Vicente already felt claustrophobic. He could smell the sweat from their exertion. Someone aimed a cell phone light toward the middle, where Vicente saw a pile of canvas bags lying against each other. Two men were pulling on the sacks under the tiny phone floodlight.

"Choto sent us to look for Rodrigo's treasure," said Ricky to Vicente. "This might be it."

The men's voices grew increasingly loud, echoing off the rock cavern.

"Quiet!" Vicente said much louder than he wanted. He lowered his voice. "Do you want to lead them right to us?"

All the activity stopped. He motioned for Ricky to check one of the bags. Ricky hurriedly untied the horsehair braid wrapped around the sack. He lifted the bag and dumped some of the contents onto the rock ground. It contained chunks that clattered metallically as they struck the floor, and dust rose from the pile. The pieces, roughly the size of golf balls, were a mix. Some looked like silver, and others—much smaller pieces—shone gold.

Vicente coughed after inhaling the dust. "Paco. Go to the entrance, and stand watch." Paco made a face—he was interested in the discovery. But he dropped down to his knees and crawled back to the opening of the shaft.

"Carlos, back him up."

Carlos said nothing and took up a position near the entrance, where the room narrowed. Maybe staring at Paco's *culero* awhile would instill a little humility and give Carlos something else to think about.

Vicente took out a plastic lighter, flicked on a flame, and used the added light to look around. It illuminated more of the mine than the cell phone light. The excavated room was tight for the size of their group. Viewing the closed-in space, he felt his claustrophobia rise. Ricky sat in the middle of the room, next to the sacks, legs splayed, examining the pieces of precious metal. Alfonso sat back against a wall, next to a faded, rough-hewn support beam.

Vicente identified two other dark openings, drifts that were at odd angles to the room. He assumed they probably led to other shafts or even other levels. Those were bigger than the entrance adit, haphazardly made, as though the ancient miners had followed a vein no matter where it led and thrown up the tunnel supports without much thought to the engineering. *The rock appears solid, but who knows?* It was another thing Vicente knew very little about.

The unsettled dust whirled around in the air like smoke, kicked up by all their movements. He could see few signs of animal activity. It was early in the year for rattlesnakes, but that was no guarantee, and a few might have ended their hibernation without checking the date. He held the sleeve of his shirt over his nose and mouth. The cave was an okay hiding place for the immediate present. But with all that precious metal stacked among the five of them, decisions would have to be made.

31

JD LOOKS FOR HER PHONE

B ullets continued whizzing over them as Tim bandaged Will's ear and wrapped gauze tape around his head from the first aid kit they carried. It bled a lot, but it was just a nick. "You'll have a small notch on your earlobe to remember it," said Tim.

"Remembering won't be a problem," Will said, holding the bandage firmly on his ear.

Frankie and Danny returned fire toward the hillside source of the ambush and then waited on the desert's deck behind rocks and other cover. After a few minutes, they stopped firing, when there was no longer a response from the top of the slope. Frankie checked his scope and suggested they press on since he couldn't detect any movement.

They set out on a diagonal, away from ridge where the shots had come from. Hanging back at the end of the group, Frankie kept his sights on the source of the gunfire as they worked their way slowly along the mountain path. The top of the ridge was silent. He kept a wary eye as they pressed on, but the hike became uneventful. After about forty-five minutes, they'd reached the area where they rescued Doc the night before.

JD climbed the side of the boulder where Doc had first landed. She found the remains of his campfire. "We fell from up there," she said, pointing to the ridgeline above.

The slope was steep, and she grabbed some creosote bushes clinging to the hillside to pull herself up the loose rock and soil. Her steps were tentative, searching for a secure foothold, as she climbed. The others looked around for signs of the shooter as she hiked up the hillside. When she reached the ridge, she stood and turned around to face them. She moved slightly to her left and right to pantomime the incident when she'd dropped her cell phone.

"I was standing here. I heard a noise, and the phone slipped out of my hand," she said, pointing to an area below. Her iPhone had a bright-turquoise plastic case. She thought the color would make it stand out among brown and gray-green vegetation and rocks. Keeping an eye on the ground, she lowered herself slowly from the ridge toward the spot. She scanned the landscape carefully as she walked.

"Watch for snakes," said Will.

He and Tim began searching while Frankie and Danny kept watch. It was the proverbial blue-colored, brick-sized needle in a cactus stack. They worked toward each other, JD from the top and the other two from Doc's landing area. Frankie kept watch. JD found a stick and used it to stir the ground and push aside the rare vegetation near her feet as she looked. Another twenty minutes passed, and then she saw it lying flat on the ground near the roots of a scrubby half-dead mesquite.

"I found it!" she shouted, bending over and picking it up. She attached the battery pack she'd bought at the convenience store. It worked. Her pictures from the previous day and all her story notes were there. The phone and all her data were intact.

"Okay, let's go before anything else happens!" Frankie said, still scanning the slope.

With Frankie in the lead, they reversed their course and hiked back on what had become a well-traveled path that they'd trampled three times before. They didn't get far before Frankie spotted a column of figures approaching in the distance. "People ahead." He signaled for them to keep moving. When he got close enough to use his scope, he directed it at the line of people. "It's those pretend militia," he said, still looking through the scope. "I recognize the guy we ran into before—sunglasses and the ball cap. That dog is with him, too. This can't be who fired on us—these guys are coming from the wrong direction and below our position. But I don't trust them. They are completely undisciplined. Who knows why they're coming this way."

"Great," said JD. Her shoulders sagged.

"Let's see what they want and try to avoid anyone getting hurt." He continued, and JD and the rest followed. The two groups moved toward each other on the path. When they got within shouting range, Frankie yelled, "How can we help you, gentlemen?"

"I am Commander Stuart Taylor of the National Patriot Militia, Nevada Chapter!" came a loud, raspy voice over an electronic megaphone. "We heard shooting and rushed to help. Do you need assistance?"

"We're good," Frankie shouted. "We heard the gunfire as well. We're heading down to the trailhead and going home. We will approach."

"Copy, understood," said Commander Taylor, releasing the talk button with an amplified click.

The groups were on the same path and closed on each other. Frankie counted fifteen paramilitaries in the group, in loose single file, all brandishing weapons. The Sand Papago kept their rifles pointed down and away. A fat older man in a billowing long-sleeved camo shirt was leading, with Sunglasses, the guy they'd met on the road, right behind.

When they came together, Sunglasses said to JD, "Hey, I recognize you. You're the reporter from camp."

"Reporter? What's this all about?" asked the heavyset man wearing camo fatigues with the bullhorn, his lined face frowning. His name patch identified him as Taylor.

"Not about you. I was researching a story on old mines on the mountain yesterday with a news source, and I lost my phone," said JD.

The commander frowned. "You should be more careful, missy. This can be a hazardous area. Lots of dangerous people about."

Will had wrapped his arm around JD's waist, probably to keep her from lunging at Commander Taylor. She flinched but didn't try to take a step. The commander seemed to notice Will for the first time.

"What happened to you?" he asked, pointing to the bandage on Will's ear.

"I fell," said Will.

"You need to—"

"We need to move along," Frankie said, stepping in front of the commander. He stared into Taylor's puffy green eyes. Neither man's expression changed.

"Aw right, then. Roger and copy that," said Commander Taylor. "We are going to pursue the source of that gunfire on the mountain. Prolly some illegal huntin' goin' on. Safe travels. Squad! Prepare to move!"

Eyes straight ahead, Frankie and his group stepped past the line of men, who were standing casually like they were at a weekend barbecue. Last in the line, Danny turned toward the militiamen, who were watching them closely, and smiled. They walked in silence for several minutes.

When they were out of earshot, JD said, "Fucking assholes. Someone is going to get killed with them around."

"That is a possibility," said Frankie. "But not us. Not today."

32

CHOTO GOES LOOKING FOR RODRIGO

I t was afternoon when Choto drove himself to Cholla Bay in his BMW with the security team behind him in a second vehicle. He was fuming when he left the hacienda near Montezuma Palace, ready to storm the house and level everything in it. But as he drove, he began to relax. As he thought it through, he knew he had to take Rodrigo alive if he wanted the gold and silver. He was impatient to hear about Rodrigo's campsite. The three men he'd dispatched in anger that morning wouldn't find Vicente and Carlos in Arizona until later. He had yet to hear anything but coded signals from them. No new leads.

When they reached Cholla Bay, they passed a cement-shack guard post where a security man waved at them distractedly. Feet propped up on a desk, the guard in a gray uniform shirt appeared occupied by a football match on a tiny black-and-white TV. The entrance gave way to the subdivision, a rising hill of light-beige dunes with houses built on piles driven into the stable volcanic bedrock beneath. Originally settled by gringos as temporary weekend fishing shacks, the shelters began transforming into larger American-style residences after a Mexican developer built several block houses and subdivided the remaining properties into lots.

Choto's source had given him an address, a safe house where the police had stashed Rodrigo. The building he was seeking was on a truck-plowed sand street two blocks from the beach. A collection of new and old stuccoed houses fronted the road. Most had attached garages with room enough for multiple vehicles or a boat. The streets were narrow enough to make it difficult for Choto to park close to the house.

When he saw the building's location and layout, he knew he had to rethink how to extract Rodrigo from police custody. Two vehicles rolling up and stopping nearby would attract too much attention and would be seen from inside the house. *Might as well honk the horns and announce your presence over a loudspeaker.* It was clear to him why *policía* had chosen the multistory building as a safe house—it had good vantage points, and there was no way to approach it without being seen, even if the house had no TV cameras. But Choto assumed it was equipped with those anyway. They would have to stand off and surveil the area from a distance, see who came and went, and gauge the best time to grab the boy. It was not what he wanted, but there wasn't much choice.

The gathering clouds over the water added to his sour mood. Choto didn't like to wait for anything. But blasting their way into an unfamiliar house in a frontal attack risked creating a scene and unintended casualties. He and his men couldn't surprise the occupants inside without endangering the person he needed to question. No, he wanted to make sure Rodrigo was alive and talking. And soon. He feared the boy would confess to the cops where he'd hidden the gold and silver.

Choto banged on the BMW's steering wheel with his fists. "*Gacho, gacho,*" he growled. He grabbed his phone and called his crew behind him. "We're going to drive around the area and look for a place to set up watch on the *casa*. We will have to wait."

The two security guards behind him acknowledged his announcement. After driving the sandy road around the subdivision, he picked an open spot at a high point. On the hill near a cell phone tower was a partially hidden space with sight lines to the house and also to oncoming vehicles. They could tuck themselves behind a low concrete-block retaining wall and be mostly shielded from the house's direct line of sight.

Choto drew up to the wall and stopped. He shut off the engine, exited carefully, and walked around to the back. He popped the trunk and retrieved a go-kit in a travel bag. Among other items, it contained binoculars, extra ammunition, a few grams of cocaine, a burner phone, and a smaller, less flashy Glock. He carried his nickel-plated show gun tucked into his waist and a modified military M4 under his front seat. His two security men in the SUV pulled up behind and remained inside the vehicle, waiting for instructions.

Choto walked up to the SUV as the driver lowered the window. "I don't know how long we'll be here, but could be for an extended time," he said. "We'll watch whoever comes and goes. Keep eyes on the house at all times. If our little *cabrón* tries to leave, we will follow. We'll intercept him away from the area."

Unwrapping the straps of the binoculars, he returned to his car. Leaning against the trunk, he focused the optics on the house, checking for activity. They were parked about eighty or ninety meters away. On the right side of the house, a concrete stuccoed staircase led from the patio to the second floor and then the roof, which had a large banana-leaf *palapa* in the center. The left side of the house had a third story that opened toward the *palapa* and a view of the sea. On the ground, a short man wearing a large straw hat stood atop a ladder that leaned against the wooden overhang of the patio. He was adjusting something attached to the beam. Choto assumed it was a light or a camera. This activity signaled to him that the informant's tip was solid. He concluded that Rodrigo was in the house.

"*Chido.* Cool," he said under his breath. He tried looking through the sliding glass doors below the patio overhang, but the cloud's reflections on the glass blocked him from seeing inside. He would need a plan. There was no way to be certain how or when the police might try to move Rodrigo.

Choto had five *sicarios* in Arizona. *And still no word from them.* He could feel his anger rise. It left him a little shorthanded. He blamed the men for not getting the job done. He would deal with them later. But this was critical. *Quero mi tesoro.* He wanted that treasure. It was his property. He needed to secure it before his bosses found out.

He watched the man climb down the ladder, adjust the angle of his huge straw hat, and enter the house through the sliding glass door. Choto tried to look inside the house when the man opened the slider, but the room was too dark. He needed more information. He didn't know the layout of the house or how many people besides Rodrigo were inside.

Standing behind the trunk of his BMW, he motioned to his bodyguard in the passenger's seat of the SUV. "We'll take turns on watch," Choto said when the guard approached him. "Eyes on anything that moves." He handed him the binoculars.

The guard nodded and took up a position, resting the binoculars on the low wall to begin observing the house. The traffic through the gringo subdivision was almost nonexistent. Most vacationers and weekenders wouldn't show up until Friday.

Once more, Choto called a burner phone to contact Vicente and the team in Arizona, but there was no answer. He could send another coded radio message, but he wanted to talk to them. He fumed at the lack of response. *What could they be doing up there that could take so long?* He'd ordered them to check the campsite, look around, and report. Vicente and Carlos, whom he trusted most, had been at the site for more than twenty-four hours. *The second team should be there by now.*

Choto got back into the BMW and turned on the air conditioning. The gathering storm was bringing in some humidity. *Think.* He again suppressed his first impulse, which was to storm the house and grab the boy. *Patience,* he thought, removing a metal flask from the center console and swigging silver tequila. The alcohol burned as it ran down his throat, and the feeling relaxed him.

He picked up a notebook on the seat next to him and sketched out some ideas of how to intercept a vehicle with Rodrigo inside without injuring their captive. Several kilometers of plowed sand lined the road like snow drifts leading into Cholla. They could overtake a vehicle along that road and force it into the meter-high pile of sand along the side of the road. The bladed pile of accumulated sand on the road's shoulder would force the people inside a vehicle to exit onto the road, where they could be dealt with easily. Choto hoped they moved the *cabrón* soon.

If Rodrigo stayed put, they would surveil the people holding him and look for a chance to extract him there. It would take time, maybe more time or patience than Choto had left in his tank. There would come a time to act. Choto liked to have control and grew frustrated and angry when he did not. In this situation, he couldn't dictate the terms. Events would determine which way this went down.

The crew settled in for the day, switching the watch. After the man on the ladder went back inside, there was no more activity visible at the house. As the morning dragged on into the afternoon, Choto was getting hungry.

He got out of his car, taking the binoculars from his security man on watch, and approached the driver's window of the SUV. "There is a very good taco stand near Shack's Fifth Avenue. You know it, I'm sure," he said. "You two, go bring us some carne asada *burros con queso y un six de cheves*."

The driver nodded without a word, and the two men drove off down the hill overlooking the street. Choto watched the SUV through the optics as it left. His stomach rumbled in protest of the hour. He figured it would take at least forty minutes for them to go order and return with the food. He settled in. There was still no activity at the *casa*. Squinting through the lens, he saw a figure walking along the road past the houses. He followed it and focused the optics. He recognized a familiar gait. The hitched bravado of the walk, the squeaky-clean white Nikes—it was Chuy. *Unbelievable. Why is he walking down the street? Fuck me!*

Choto threw the binoculars on the adjacent seat, started the car, slammed it into reverse, and floored the BMW in first gear, the tires chewing sand as they bit the crusty packed road. He powered through a controlled slide around a curve and raced in front of the houses to catch up to his dealer. He expected the boy to run, providing Choto the definitive proof that Chuy was a *traidor*. But when he pulled up alongside the short young man, Chuy just smiled and waved.

"*Qué pedo, wey*? What's up? Get in," Choto said through clenched teeth after lowering the passenger window.

"*Hola.*" Chuy, his expression unchanged, opened the door and slid into the leather seat, handing the binoculars to Choto, who tossed them roughly onto the back seat. "I bought the *farmacia,*" Chuy said matter-of-factly. "Gracias for your guidance."

"Qué pasa? What are you doing here?" Choto asked, his pants crotch chafing against his silk underwear. He shifted into gear and began driving.

"I was going to talk to you. The police called me. They said an old amigo from school was in custody. They said he would only talk to me."

"Who's your friend?"

"His name is Rodrigo," said Chuy, studying Choto's face.

"And he is in a casa back there?" Choto asked.

"*Sí*," said Chuy, still smiling.

Choto couldn't tell if Chuy was playing dumb, but he was smart enough not to lie to Choto and raise his suspicions. Choto asked for loyalty and deference, but he also hated deceit. Choto watched Chuy neutrally as if examining an inanimate object.

"Why are they keeping your friend here and not at the station?" Choto kept his breathing measured.

"Avoid publicity, the cops said. They think he's the one passing *plata* around town. It has everyone stirred up. He did admit to spending it in *el centro*."

"Did he tell you where he got the *plata*?" Choto circled the streets of the subdivision toward the observation point.

"He wouldn't say. He did tell me there's a lot of it somewhere. And he knew where. Then he stopped talking. We just sat there for a while, and the cops gave up and told me to go."

"Where is your truck?

"It's around the corner. I didn't want to park in front. I don't hang out with cops."

"Are you busy?" Choto asked as he rounded a carved-out corner. It was a rhetorical question. "Let's go back."

Chuy shrugged. Choto drove back up the hill and stopped the car at his previous location. They sat inside with the air conditioning running and waited for the food. Choto aimed the binoculars through the windshield toward the house. It was *siesta* time and quiet. Choto's stomach was rumbling like a series of small earthquakes by the time the SUV rolled up the road and around the curve and settled behind the BMW. Choto retrieved the binoculars, quickly got out of the car, and handed them to the security men. In exchange, they gave him a brown bag full of burritos with a six-pack of *cerveza*.

Chuy watched in the side-view mirror. He took out his phone and sent a quick text message to Chief Ramirez. He jammed the cell phone back into his pocket before Choto opened the door again. The smell of grilled beef and chili and onions smacked him in the face when Choto, holding the *comida* high and balancing the cardboard package of Modelo lager, flopped into his seat.

"*Mira*, take this burrito," said Choto, drawing a tightly rolled white paper of meat-filled tortilla from the bag and handing it to Chuy. Balancing the bag of food on his lap, Choto opened the center console and picked up the silver flask inside. He took a deep pull on the flask and then silently held it up. Chuy declined, and Choto shrugged. "It's good stuff. Special silver reserve."

"*Un cheve, por favor*," said Chuy, pointing at the Modelo cans.

"How many are in the casa?" Choto asked, handing him a can of lager.

"Besides Rodrigo?" Chuy looked up at the car's ceiling, wondering whether he should tell the truth or overestimate the number and maybe deter Choto. "Uh, I saw five," he said, making a show of counting. "But there could be others I didn't see. La casa es muy grande." He spread his hands wide, cerveza in one and the carne asada burrito in the other to demonstrate how big the house was.

"Are they all cops?"

"Except the house owner, but he's an ex-cop. A gringo."

"Were they all armed?" asked Choto, taking a big bite of his burrito.

"*Sí*," said Chuy. "Two of the cops had military semiautomatic rifles and handguns."

"Have you seen the whole house?"

"No, Jefe. Rodrigo is in a bedroom on the second floor

with two cops standing over him. I saw the entrance and a living room, and then they took me upstairs to his bedroom. I saw several bedrooms on that floor." He was riffing now, just making things up. He'd been to the house twice and knew the layout pretty well, but he couldn't tell Choto that. The less Choto knew about the house, the safer it would be for everyone, especially himself.

Choto told Chuy that he considered storming the house, but if Chuy were telling the truth, he would need all his men, including the five in Arizona. The men on the mountain still hadn't been in contact. Chuy watched Jefe's anger grow. Choto attacked the brown bag on the console, yanked out another burrito, and after peeling away some of the white wrapper, munched on it, silently fuming.

"Rodrigo was wearing this *grande* T-shirt and shorts," said Chuy, trying to lighten Choto's mood. "Way too big for him." He smiled, hoping the image would register with his boss. But Choto was steaming in his anger marinated by the tequila, coke, and cerveza. He stared straight ahead.

They spent the rest of afternoon in silence and boredom with Choto fitfully nodding off. A few vehicles passed by the house on the way to another part of Cholla. There was still no activity at the house. Chuy was relieved by the lack of further outbursts from Choto. The cartel boss apparently accepted his story about why he'd suddenly appeared at the Sandman's *casa*.

The heavy storm clouds brought on the darkness earlier than scheduled. Traffic increased slightly, and a few more vehicles drove past the house. A light rain began to fall. Still sitting in the passenger seat, Chuy was on watch, looking through the binoculars. Droplets began beading on the windshield. He saw a white car with Arizona plates pull up to the house and stop.

"Jefe," said Chuy, tapping Choto's shoulder. Jefe was leaning back and lightly snoozing. "Activity!" Chuy's gaze focused on a blond woman wearing a dark-blue dress. She got out of the car and, ignoring the rain, strode purposefully toward the front door before disappearing from his view.

"What is it?" asked Choto, groggily coming to consciousness after the afternoon of food and alcohol.

"A visitor. A gringa," said Chuy, though he knew the woman was no longer visible.

"Let me see," said Choto, grabbing the binoculars from him.

Choto aimed the optics through the windshield at the car in the driveway. But the woman was out of his view. The car's windows were getting foggy, so Choto fumbled with the keys to start the engine while focused on the Arizona car. He said he was sure that when the woman left, she would take Rodrigo with her.

33

ERICKA COMES HOME

I t was dark, and a light rain was falling when Ericka walked to the front door of the family house in Cholla Bay where she'd spent many happy hours growing up. Finding it locked, she sorted through her set of keys below the outside lamp above the door. After going over her talking points all afternoon, she'd worked up the courage to tell her father about her orientation and sex life. Instead of calling him, she'd convinced herself to talk to him face-to-face, afraid her voice might reveal too much over the phone.

Nervously, she worked the house key into the lock and took a deep breath as she pushed open the door. Now was the time, and she didn't want to give herself the chance to back out. As she stepped into the dark foyer, she was so startled that she dropped her keys and purse and screamed. She stared directly into the barrels of two handguns several feet away.

"Ericka!" shouted her father and her lover in unison.

"Uh, Ericka's here," said Speed from behind them. Speed was supposed to be monitoring the outside cameras from the laptop in the den. His huge hat and wide eyes were all that could be seen peering into the foyer from the hallway.

"Thanks," said Sandman, lowering his weapon. "A little quicker next time, or we'll find you another nickname. I'm thinking Pegleg." Speed retreated quickly without comment. Sandman turned to Ericka. "What are you doing here?" He holstered the Glock and hugged her tightly. Ericka, shaking in his embrace, looked around her father's shoulder at Toni, who gave her a pained look.

"Not a good time," Toni said, dropping her arms.

"But we talked." Recovering a bit from the shock, Ericka asked, "What's going on?"

Sandman held her at arm's length. "What's wrong? Why are you here? Are you in trouble?"

"No," Ericka said, feeling both hurt and defiant.

"We're in the middle of something here. I'm sorry you didn't call," said Sandman. "We're on high alert."

Ericka's resolve to talk frankly to him crumbled, and she strained to ask, "What do you want me to do?"

"Let's all stand down and go into the den," said Toni, who waved her arms toward the other room. She hadn't told Ericka anything about using her father's house for an operation. But Ericka hadn't told Toni about her plan to discuss their sex lives that day with her father either.

When they entered the den, Speed was at the laptop, contritely demonstrating that he was alert and on task with the camera monitoring. Everyone sat down in the worn overstuffed leather chairs.

"Do you need something to drink?" Sandman asked his daughter.

"No. But I would like to know what you're all mixed up in. Especially since it involves pointing guns." Ericka's attention shifted quickly between her father and her lover. Putting the anxiety of her planned confession aside, she reverted to her default skepticism about her father's freelance activities in Mexico.

Toni looked toward the base of the interior staircase.

"We're all clear in here," she barked loudly. The police at the bottom assumed an at-ease posture but otherwise didn't move. She turned toward Ericka. "A young man is at risk. We believe the new Mexicali Cartel that has shown up in our area is looking for him."

"We're holding someone in protective custody," said Sandman.

"Here?" Ericka threw her hands in the air.

"I thought the station wasn't safe," Toni said. "We couldn't just lock him up in a jail cell, and your father offered to host him here at the house."

"Toni, why didn't you tell me?" Ericka asked, giving her a pleading look.

"Wait. Why would you think that Toni should tell you about this?" Sandman asked. "And how? You just got here."

Ericka could feel her face redden, and her anxiety instantly returned. Her mouth opened, but no sound came out. She refocused and tried again.

"It's okay, Ericka," said Toni, smiling softly. "You might as well tell him now."

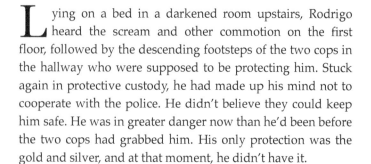

L ying on a bed in a darkened room upstairs, Rodrigo heard the scream and other commotion on the first floor, followed by the descending footsteps of the two cops in the hallway who were supposed to be protecting him. Stuck again in protective custody, he had made up his mind not to cooperate with the police. He didn't believe they could keep him safe. He was in greater danger now than he'd been before the two cops had grabbed him. His only protection was the gold and silver, and at that moment, he didn't have it.

He'd begged Chuy to help him, and he'd thought his friend was sympathetic. He reminded himself that even in school, Chuy could play all the angles. Chuy had apologized for bringing that woman police chief to him, but Rodrigo didn't trust him after that. A lot of gold and silver was at stake. His life was at stake. He worried that Choto's men would find where he'd buried the large sack of treasure. Going over it again and again, he tried to hold the exact burial location in his mind. With Choto's *sicarios* looking on, he thought he'd dug in the estuary in the right location. But the more he went over it, the less sure he was. A mark on the road at night was hard to find. He berated himself for relying on the odometer to measure the distance. Now he didn't even have access to his car. He needed to find the buried treasure before Choto did and then get to the mine where the rest was waiting. He would figure out how to dodge Choto's *sicarios* in Arizona. Only he knew where the mine shaft was.

The upstairs was as dark as the mine. Rodrigo didn't hear the two cops come back, so he got up from the bed and peeked into the hallway. No one was there. He couldn't feel their presence in the blackness. He could hear voices speaking English, both men's and women's, coming from the first floor. He walked carefully and deliberately past the archway of the enclosed, unlit stairwell. Rodrigo knew from his previous time at the house that a door led to an outside set of stairs on that level. In the ebony void, he just needed to find the door that opened to the outside, and he could leave. He placed his hands on the wall, searching for the end of the hallway, and slowly opened the door as quietly as he could manage. The muffled voices seemed like they were directly under him now. He sensed he was in another bedroom, larger than the one they'd put him in. He could barely make out the outlines of several doors inside the room. He felt along the edge of a large bed then put his hand out until he touched a door. He opened the first door and, from the echo, concluded it was a bathroom. He moved on to another door that faced the back of the house. He guessed this was it. The door was locked with a deadbolt. He very carefully flipped the lever to open it and then grabbed the knob below it and turned. His heart jumped. The door opened toward the inside of the room. He could hardly restrain himself. Inches at a time, he pulled it toward him, hoping the hinges wouldn't squeak or an alarm wouldn't sound. He heard the gentle rain falling on the other side. The door was quiet. Moist outside air entered the room, and as he opened it wider and looked outside, he saw that the stairs were lit and patio lights illuminated the entire courtyard. He ducked down, squatting to minimize his profile. If the cops were concerned about keeping out him of sight, Choto could be close. Choto was the last person he wanted to see.

He crept down one side of the stucco-wall stairs toward the ground, and when he reached the level of the top of the patio wall, he leapt up, rolled over on it, and jumped to the ground and into the night. He edged along the wall of a neighboring house and found the unlit street in front and, in the darkness and falling rain, anonymity. He walked along the crusty, bladed sand of the road and around a corner, where a lone pickup truck had parked. As he got closer, he recognized that it was Chuy's. He felt along the top of the driver's-side rear tire well and found a magnetic box with a car key. Chuy had told him the extra key had once saved his life.

And now it's saving mine. He started the truck and drove with the lights off toward Rico's Bar. He pulled up to the front parking area of the bar and waited, his heart pounding. Flood lamps lit the parking area and the entrance to the bar. No one had followed him. He could hear the juke box blaring from inside the bar even with the windows rolled up. He waited a couple of minutes. No police cars, no SUVs, no movement on the street. He started the truck again, turned around, clicked the lights on, and drove to the entrance of Cholla Bay and then down the road toward the rows of shops at Shack's Fifth Avenue *mercado.*

Inside the house, Sandman was stunned by his daughter's announcement. "Why didn't you say something earlier? Did you think I wouldn't understand?" His voice held a mixture of hurt and anger. He was frozen to his chair, and his body felt like it weighed a half a ton. "And you," he said, turning to look at his protégé. "Why didn't you say something? You've never made a secret that you're gay. Why would you hide a relationship with Ericka?"

"David, I didn't hide it," she said firmly, giving him a hard stare. She seldom used any form of his first name and never David. He heard it as a rebuke, and it felt like a stinging slap. "As I said to her, and I am telling you, it wasn't my story to reveal. It is hers. At her own time, in her own way. Which is what she did just now."

Sandman looked at Ericka, whose pale face had turned blotchy red from crying. Tears streamed down her cheeks. With her fingers, she tried to comb the stray blond hair from the sides of her face. The sight of his daughter in pain tore at his gut. He tried to get up to comfort her, but he couldn't make himself move. No one spoke. The sound of the rainwater dripping from the roof of the second floor filled the quiet room.

"Ericka, if I have ever done anything to make you feel like you couldn't come to me…" His voice trailed off into a long pause.

"This isn't about you," Toni said tersely, breaking the silence.

Speed, who was still at the laptop, looked startled. He accidentally nudged the computer and, sending his huge straw hat flying, grabbed at the laptop to prevent it falling to the floor.

Sandman saw that his daughter was emotionally spent after her confession. Toni was ready to pounce to Ericka's defense. He was more bewildered than anything by her news. He'd never really suspected. *Why didn't I know?*

"Even before Mom died, we weren't really seeing eye to eye," she said to her father. "After her death, I dealt with my grief without reaching out to you. You did the same. I couldn't even get you on the phone sometimes."

Sandman nodded. "I didn't handle it well. There are days when I still don't," he said, his voice softening. "We are more alike than I want to think about. But when I see you smile or do that gesture with your hands, I see pure Gloria. There's some pain as well as happiness in that."

Ericka moved to stand up. The action pulled Sandman out of his chair. He met her, and they embraced. "I am so sorry," he whispered in her ear. "What do you want to tell me about your relationship?" He drew back a bit to look at her face and smooth her hair.

"We're at the beginning, but we're off to a really awesome start," she said, looking over to Toni.

Toni smiled at her then glanced at Hector and Luis, who were still frozen in the near darkness of the base of the stairs, transfixed by the conversation.

"Why are you two standing around down here? You have other duties. Go," she barked. "*Andele!*"

Hector turned his wide body in a surprisingly quick move and waddled rapidly up the stairs. Luis, much thinner, couldn't compete for the space and had to wait for him to go up while enduring an extra dose of the chief's ire. Luis had just disappeared on the stairs when Hector wailed in a strained voice, "Jefe, Jefe, the boy is gone!"

The upstairs hall lights flipped on, violating Sandman's earlier directive to avoid attention or giving a lurking *sicario* something to shoot at. "*Apaga las luces!*" shouted Sandman. "Turn off the lights!"

The group searched upstairs for the boy, but their efforts were fruitless. They found that the door leading to the outside stairs was ajar.

"*Madre de Dios ayúdanos!*" Toni hissed.

Inside the BMW, Choto was still watching the car in the driveway through the binoculars. He saw the lights go on and then off again on the second floor of the house.

"*Mira*, it's some kind of signal." The windshield wipers scraped on slow intermittent, and the sun-dried rubber blades dragged loudly against the glass. The drops of rain became tiny rivulets that ran down the sides.

Choto had fixed his gaze on the car in the driveway and that object only, convinced that the Arizona *machina* was the center of whatever was going to happen. The car would take Rodrigo from the house, Choto said, and he was going to be watching and waiting when it happened.

"Motherfucker, what's going on?" Choto asked.

Chuy had an idea because he had witnessed Rodrigo's escape. But he said nothing to Patrón. A few minutes earlier, Chuy had been staring absentmindedly at the back of the house. Unconstrained by the limited field view of Choto's binoculars, Chuy had watched the door at the top of the stairs open while Choto was focused on the car in the front. Chuy knew where Rodrigo had been kept on the second floor—he'd been inside. He was sure that the figure he saw creeping low in the dark shadows along the wall bordering the stairs was Rodrigo. Chuy watched as the figure hesitated then hurled himself sideways like a high jumper and landed prone on the top of the wall surrounding the backyard. Choto's binoculars never strayed from the sight line of the car. Chuy had wanted to text Ramirez, but he couldn't risk it with Choto so close to him.

Where is he going? Chuy thought as he watched the figure. *How is he going to get out of Cholla without being discovered?* He could only sit in silent witness when the figure dropped silently to the sand outside the wall and disappeared into the dark night.

34

THE SICARIOS DISCUSS THEIR GOOD FORTUNE

"I don't think we should tell Patrón," said Ricky, sitting against a shaft wall inside the mine. "We must keep it. Divide it five ways."

Vicente stifled a sigh. Three men sat, legs splayed, on the floor, leaning back against the walls of the mine-shaft anteroom, whispering in near darkness about the bags of gold and silver stacked in the middle. Paco and Carlos lay prone at the narrow entrance. If they were following orders, they were watching and waiting for the two groups of armed hikers to move on. Vicente could hear them nudging and pushing each other like little children lying down in the back of a car on a long road trip.

"I'm not sure that is a good idea," he said to Ricky. He rubbed the stiffness in his thighs. "I've worked for Choto for years. Once he's on a course, you cannot get him to change. How are you going to tell him we failed to find anything?"

"It was a *lotteria* pick even for us to find his tracks," Ricky argued. "Only *gente loco* would believe that we could just go up the mountain and discover a treasure that no one else has seen for at least a hundred years."

"Rodrigo did." Vicente could feel his heart beat in his

chest. He imagined he could hear the quick *thump, thump, thump* of the others as well.

"*Sí*, but—"

"Did we not have a conversation earlier at the campfire about how irrational Jefe is?" Vicente interrupted. "If I remember it faithfully, it was *you* who brought up the subject of the *patrón's* mental condition." He heard some extra scuffling at the entrance. "Ayi, what's going on up there? *Cabróns*, stop it!"

"*Sí*, Señor Patron," said Carlos, exaggerating the pronunciation of the final word. "If this *gomero* doesn't quit farting, I'm going to plug his ass with a hollow point."

"*Vete a la chingada*—fuck off!" Paco said.

Vicente could hear the metal scrape of their rifles against the rocks. "*Basta!*" He really might have to kill Carlos someday.

Ricky was a dark shape slumped against the wall on the opposite side of the chamber, but Vicente knew that the man was staring into the darkness at the bags full of fantasies in their midst. Imagining. Thinking. Dreaming. Because Vicente was doing the same thing. It looked like it would be a fortune, even if it was split five ways. And liquid. Vicente liked liquid. More fungible and less traceable than cash. But he didn't see the possibilities that Ricky saw.

"What chance do you think that when the five of us return to Puerto Peñasco, we can keep this from Choto?" Vicente asked. "No one would say anything? No slip of the tongue? Nada?

"The riches would keep them quiet," said Ricky confidently, maybe to bolster himself.

"*Sí*, that is a lot of riches sitting there," said Alfonso, chiming in. "A lotta riches. I would be on my best behavior."

Vicente could hear the smile in Alfonso's voice across the dim chamber. The rock anteroom felt tight and was closing in on him. He could hear support timbers randomly cracking from the elevated temperature and humidity caused by the people in the room.

He sighed. "He will bring each of us, one at a time, out to the patio, probably during his *desayuno,* and in between bites of *huevos* and hits of cocaine, pepper us with questions about the search of Rodrigo's campsite. 'Where is it? What does it look like? Where did you go after you found the site? What other things happened? Why did it take you so long? No treasure?' 'Oh no, Patrón. We didn't see nothing. But we did bring back Rodrigo's backpack.'" He paused, waiting for Ricky to respond, but he heard only silence. "Now, think about the members of this crew, especially *dos niños luchadores* at the front. Do you think they can lie to Choto without him seeing through them?"

"We have time. We can work on our stories," said Ricky, considering Vicente's argument.

"Time? Maybe. And if we all say exactly the same things, wouldn't that be suspicious?"

"*Sí, pero…*"

"How much do you trust everyone here?" asked Vicente, struggling to remain calm. "We don't know each other. Carlos and I have been in Choto's employ for a long time. The three of you are new. If someone turns, or Choto doesn't believe even *one* of us, then we all wind up hanging upside down from an overpass, naked and headless."

The entire room was silent except for the sound of the shuffling of feet repositioning. And breathing. Lots of breathing. Even the wooden beams were breathing. Vicente coughed again from the dust they had disturbed. He thought he heard an earthen growl deep underground coming from one of the mine's drifts. He pushed down the feelings of paranoia. He felt himself sweating. They'd been sitting in the chamber for about forty minutes, the darkness cloaking their individual thoughts. The air wasn't moving. He wondered how long the five of them could sit there before the lack of fresh air forced them out. He wiped his forehead with his sleeve and hoped all this talk of running off with the treasure would stop. It was a painful way to wind up dead.

"I still want to think about it," said Alfonso after a time. "We don't have to decide now."

Vicente was going to bring up that they all had to agree or none of it could work, but he didn't want to cause more friction, so he kept silent. He heard an animal's faint howl and then a gunshot in the mine entry. It sounded like a detonation reverberating in the shaft. The three men inside stood up reflexively, Ricky bumping against a support beam.

"*Poca madre*! What was that?" Vicente shouted. He hit his head on the top of the short ceiling.

"Your partner is an idiot," shouted Paco. He and Carlos were rolling around the ground in the small opening of the mine shaft. "He shot at a coyote."

Vicente bowed his head, moved to the opening, and bent down to grab one of Carlos's legs. Carlos pushed the barrel of his rifle against Paco's neck with his left hand while trying to unholster his Glock. Vicente held a leg of each *luchador* and dragged both of them along the ground back to anteroom. Carlos kicked at Vicente, sending him sprawling awkwardly onto the bags of precious metal. Vicente felt a sharp pain in his back. He turned his head to see Ricky in faint light of the shaft entrance moving to separate the two men just as Carlos squeezed off a loud round from his handgun. Ricky grabbed at his shoulder, which sent him stumbling hard into a support beam. With a splintering snap, the ancient dried wood collapsed. Then a second beam fell. The rock seam behind it groaned, and the very air seemed to shake as the ceiling of the anteroom failed, triggering a rockslide on top of all five men, pinning them underneath.

Clouds of rock dust mixed with the stale air. Vicente felt the weight of the mountain on his chest. He struggled to suck a breath. It came in tiny gasps as if he was inhaling through a straw. The only sounds were rocks and cascading dirt and gravel settling in the now filled shaft. He heard a groan that might have come from himself, and then he lost consciousness.

≈

Commander Stuart Taylor led the file of slow-moving men of the National Patriot Militia lazily toward where he imagined the earlier gunfire had come from. He hadn't explained to the rank and file what they would do when they got there. He wasn't sure himself. He thought that they would investigate the area, look for any signs of suspicious activity, and report it to Border Patrol if they found anything. He would lead a cautious exploration. There was no need for anyone to get hurt. The ragtag militia was slowly working its way up the slope when they heard a rifle shot coming from a different area higher up the mountain. They stopped in their tracks, and most ducked instinctively. Then came the muffled rumble of a blast coming from deep inside the mountain.

"Column, halt," ordered Commander Taylor to his already crouching troops. Everyone was still. "Probably an explosion from a working mine. But we better investigate anyway." He turned the column toward the sound, and the group began bushwhacking its way reluctantly through the rough terrain upward.

≈

Vicente rose to consciousness from his own coughing and the anxiety of struggling for air. The dust irritated his lungs, and he couldn't find enough space for him to really breathe. Rocks pinned him in place. He couldn't move. There was no feeling in his hands or feet. He was sure he was paralyzed.

"Can anyone help?" he wheezed, but his voice was a whisper.

His ears rang with pain. He thought maybe they were bleeding. He struggled through the ringing to listen for the other men. It was quiet except for the mountain's slow rumbling and the settling of debris. All he could do was to lie helplessly under the rubble in the blackness and hope that someone might have heard the shots or the mine collapsing. *There are people on the mountain. Will they come? Can they find me if they do?* He felt himself drift off again. A few minutes later, his breathing stopped.

35

CHOTO HAS A NEW PLAN

The slow drizzle of the unseasonable rain depressed Choto. He handed the binoculars to Chuy and called the burner phone again, trying to reach the men in Arizona. The phone went to voicemail. Again. The three he'd sent that morning should have found Vicente on the mountain by now. He was sure of it. Vicente, his most experienced *sicario*, was reliable, and just dropping off the grid wasn't like him. He would have kept the others in line. Even if they were intercepted and arrested, any one of them should have been able to get a message back.

Especially if they were arrested. They would need lawyers and cash. Choto thought about cell phone reception. It was possible that they were in a dead zone, stranded on the mountain and unreachable. *But they should have found a way.*

Choto grew suspicious. He felt his groin tighten. Maybe they did find his treasure. *Did they decide to keep it?* He didn't think it likely, but he had to consider it. It was one reason why he'd sent in the second team. Five men couldn't keep a secret. *They don't have the brains among them to figure out a plan to disappear with my gold and silver. But where are they?*

He checked with his snitch at the US Customs and Border Protection to see if any had been arrested.

"No, Señor Choto," said the informant. "There is no word."

He tossed the burner phone over his shoulder into the back seat. "*Chingá!*" he shouted and pounded the steering wheel with his fists.

Chuy pretended to watch the car at the front of the house through the binoculars. Choto grabbed at the center console and retrieved his flask. He took a long pull and this time didn't offer any to Chuy.

"I think it's time to force the situation." Choto snapped open the door handle and climbed out of the driver's seat into the drizzle. "Stay inside!" he barked at Chuy from the other side of the door.

Chuy extended his right hand into his pocket, settling on his cell phone, hoping to get a chance to text Chief Ramirez. Choto gave a low whistle to the SUV, which was also running, and the two security guys reluctantly exited the SUV in the rain. Choto motioned for them to come toward him. He glanced back at Chuy and muttered something in low conversation that Chuy couldn't hear. Chuy didn't dare take out his phone and risk its lighted screen being seen.

After some back-and-forth, everyone nodded, and Choto shooed the two men back to the SUV. He climbed back in, his wet clothes rubbing noisily on the leather seats as he scooted across. He removed his nickel-plated show gun from his belt.

"Do you have a gun?" Choto asked.

"Uh, no. I hate them," said Chuy, trying to tamp down his nerves.

"Never mind, take my spare," Choto said, reaching down his wet right pant leg and retrieving a Smith & Wesson bobbed-hammer .38 from an ankle holster inside his boot. He held it up by his thumb and index finger like a delicate pair of women's panties.

Chuy squinted at it. The gun was like an alien object.

"Take it," commanded Choto. "They are easy to fire. Try not to hurt yourself with it." Choto's gravelly laugh was almost a cough.

Chuy gently wrapped his hand around the cylinder and took the gun.

"If you're going to be a big-time *patrón* someday, you will need to be able to use this."

But Chuy didn't want to be El Chapo—he wanted to be Kiki Cruz, a businessman. Respected. He didn't say any of that to Choto. He simply acknowledged Choto's gesture and kept his finger far away from the double-action trigger. He leaned back in the seat and stuffed it into his pants gangsta style.

"The blond gringa is going to try to take him with her when she leaves. She must be a cop. Choto can feel it. We have a nose for these things. The car out in the open, *es bueno*. We are going to take little Rui as they leave the house. You and me, we'll wait at the front door for them to open it. If he is with her, we'll force them into the car and take them both back to the Montezuma hacienda. If he isn't with her, we'll shove her back into the house, guns out, and take her hostage. The boys will climb the back stairs, surprise the cops protecting the little *cabrón,* and grab him. *Claro*?"

Dumbfounded, Chuy could only mumble a quick "'Kay."

But no, it wasn't at all clear. This wasn't how he'd pictured it. He was certain Rodrigo was the shadowy figure who'd vaulted the wall just a few minutes before, so he wouldn't be in the house. They would have to wait in the rain, grab the gringa—guns drawn—and push their way into the house, where anything could happen.

He didn't know who the gringa was, but if she was a cop, then there were five armed cops altogether, and he and Choto would be outgunned. He didn't think Ramirez would just surrender. *And Sandman?* The Sandman was a hard guy to figure, but Chuy was sure he would act rather than surrender to the two of them.

In his favor, both Ramirez and Sandman knew he was an informant and would understand that he was a reluctant participant in Choto's scheme. When Choto had pulled him off the road, he'd found a way to warn Ramirez by text, so the people inside the house knew they were being watched. *Will Choto be able to surprise them?*

His heart raced as Choto signaled for him to get out of the car. He tried not to focus on all the things that could go wrong. He was sure the other cops, Hector and Luis, would remember him. The *gringa* for sure didn't know him. A gun battle could have many casualties, including Chuy Ruiz.

They were going to walk in the rain on the sand-packed road that led past the house. He shrugged and opened the door. The rain beaded up on the BMW's paint job, tiny droplets on the car's body reflecting the distant light from surrounding houses. The desert ground was so parched that the landscape greedily sucked in the water, leaving wet sand caked to his white shoes. Once Chuy and Choto were outside, the two security men opened the doors to the SUV and got out. They stood by, and Chuy and Choto walked silently down the hill in the dark. The only sound was their feet crunching in the wet sand.

It was more misting than raining by that point, and he could feel cloudy atmosphere around him as they stepped carefully in the blackness. Chuy looked at the house with its small rear-patio lights glaring through the patchy fog and water dripping from the eaves. He doubted the security cameras would see much with the rain falling on the lens, obscuring the details. *How long will we have to stand outside the door and wait?* He didn't trust that Choto wouldn't just decide to burst through the door suddenly and let the chips fall. Jefe was fixated on getting his treasure.

The houses were spaced on quarter-acre lots along the

road, some with porch lights on, others dark. He assumed that Choto's security guards were moving into position behind the wall of the house. Choto had them on the phone through his Bluetooth earbuds.

As the two of them approached the casa, Choto signaled for him to move close to the building to avoid any cameras. Chuy could see the gringa's rain-spotted sedan under the foggy light in the short driveway. The misting rain ran down his temples after soaking his hair. He resisted the temptation to rub the water from his scalp.

Near the home's entrance, Choto grabbed his arm to get his attention and motioned with his shiny pistol, pointing up at the hastily strung camera on the small overhang at the entrance. Chuy gave a sign that he understood. Choto pointed at Chuy's waist, indicating that he should draw his weapon. Chuy nodded and felt for the Smith & Wesson. He removed it carefully from his belt. It felt small and inadequate in his hand. No matter—he had no intention of using it.

They took up alert positions on each side of the door. The handle to the large wooden door was on the right side, where Choto stationed himself, pistol at the ready. Chuy knew the door would open to the inside, the gringa would step outside, and Choto would take her before she knew what had happened. Choto wanted Chuy to back him up. Chuy could see that Jefe was amped up just by the way he stood poised next to the door like a formerly confined tiger set free to hunt. He wondered how much coke Choto had managed to ingest between *tequila* shots during the long wait. Choto violated the number-one rule his former boss, El Jefe, had taught him: never be your own best customer.

Standing near the lighted doorway, Choto tugged at his ample groin restricted by the patrón's tight trousers. So the *sicario* gossip was true—Choto possessed a *verga gigante*. He thought it odd to consider all that *chingadera* as he stood outside in the rain, waiting to abduct a gringa he didn't know.

Suddenly, he could hear a burst of activity inside. Muffled voices and footsteps. The door opened, and the blond gringa came out alone with an umbrella poking through the doorway first. As she expanded it, Choto put the revolver to her head, pitched the umbrella onto the sand, and pinned her arm against her back.

"Now," he said into his Bluetooth mic. The gringa gave a high-pitched scream that rang in Chuy's ears as Choto forced her back through the entrance. Chuy followed him after dropping his arm to his side, his Smith & Wesson pointed at the ground.

"*No te muevas!*—don't move! I have the gringa!" Choto entered the foyer. Chuy saw Ramirez and Sandman pointing their weapons, but Choto had leverage and position with the gringa in his grasp, squarely in front of him. "*Suelta la pistolas!* Everyone put down your weapons!" he growled. "I will shoot her."

Sandman looked directly at the man. He saw Chuy behind the man, armed but pointing his gun at the floor. He cradled his Glock, open palmed, for examination. "I'm laying it down," he said, bending his knees and setting it softly on the tile floor. He shot a quick glance at Ramirez, who was doing the same.

"I want the boy, Rodrigo. Give me what I want, and we will leave." Choto waved his gun from Sandman to Ramirez. Chuy made eye contact with Ramirez and gave her a look of resigned apology. "Where is he?"

"*No sé,*" said Ramirez. "He ran away a few minutes ago."

"I don't believe you."

"See for yourself." She had a daggerlike look of anger in her eyes that unnerved Chuy. He'd never seen that look from her before.

"Chuy, collect the guns," said Choto, looking away.

Hector and Luis, guns drawn, came down the stairs to the living room to see Choto holding the gringa hostage and waving his gun. They were standing in the hallway between the living room and Sandman's den. The gringa looked terrified and was breathing rapidly. "You two. Same. *Suelta sus armas!*"

"Do it," said Ramirez, still staring at the gunman holding the gringa. The men placed their service weapons on the floor.

"Chuy, get the *pistolas.*"

Chuy walked the short distance to bend down and grab the weapons and had to absorb Hector and Luis's disgusted gaze. He knew they recognized him from earlier interrogations about the death of his *wey* Omar.

Choto's two security men came down to join the group after entering from the outside stairs. "Jefe he isn't here," said one.

"Did you check the entire floor?"

"*Sí*, Patrón," said the other guard. "He has disappeared."

"How did he get out?" Choto asked no one in particular.

"He left the same way your men got inside," volunteered Hector.

Ramirez frowned at him. She, Sandman, Hector and Luis were standing in the foyer with their hands up, their eyes darting from one to the other, looking to figure out what would happen next.

"Let's go to this next room and sort it all out," said Choto, motioning toward the den. "*Vámonos!*"

Chuy knew Choto was having to ad lib, which was not his favorite thing, but Jefe was comfortable being in control. With guns pointed at them, Ramirez, Sandman, Hector, and Luis filed into the den.

"Line up on your knees! Hands behind!" Choto shouted, waving the gun at them.

The four kneeled in front of the leather couch against the

far wall of the den. He shoved the gringa toward them. "You too."

Her bare legs shaking beneath the narrow skirt of her blue dress, she wobbled to the four and knelt next to the chief. Chuy caught Ramirez trying to reassure her with a calming look. He looked at Sandman, who was fidgeting, probably just to distract Choto and his men.

"I can shoot you all now, or you can tell me where I can get some rope," Choto said.

"Garage," said Sandman, twisting his head and body around to look at Choto and glancing at the men holding them. The three men with pistols stood directly behind them. Chuy stood off to the side with his arm cradling their weapons, his gun in the other hand pointed at the floor. He saw Sandman look toward the desk.

"Chuy, go fetch the rope," said Choto.

"Sí, Jefe." Chuy laid the collected guns in a leather easy chair and left the room.

In the garage, he found some yellow nylon rope rolled up on a hook. He stood next to the parked police SUV, considering whether to run or call the policía, but one of the security men popped his head through the interior door.

"Jefe says now."

Chuy grabbed the coiled rope, flipped off the garage light, and followed the man back to the den. "Rope," said Chuy, raising it for emphasis.

"I don't suppose you are a knot-tying master?" asked Choto, who seemed to relax a little.

"Mi padre was, but fishing killed him, and I hate everything about it," Chuy said dismissively.

Choto ordered his two security men to tie the hands and feet of the hostages. The men holstered their pistols, and one took out a fishing knife to section the rope into pieces. The two began looping the rope, one at a time, around the wrists of the five people kneeling on the floor. They began on their left with Ericka then moved to the police chief. Hector and then Luis were next.

"Hurry up!" barked Choto.

Chuy stood on Choto's left and a step behind him. He swallowed hard to suppress a yelp after he caught a glimpse of Speed sneaking toward them, the laptop held high in both hands. In a quick but inaccurate motion, Speed brought the laptop down on Choto's head with all this strength. The computer glanced off the side of Choto's skull, whacked his right ear, and came down with enough force to thump his shoulder.

"Ayi!" Choto shouted in pain, stumbling a step forward jolted, his arm dangling at his side. His gun clattered to the tile floor.

Everyone turned and looked, the five who faced the sofa as well as the two security men who were kneeling, applying the rope restraints. Speed looked surprised that the man hadn't gone down. He flinched when Choto staggered, regained his footing, and spun around. Then Speed jerked the laptop over his head for another strike.

Raising the revolver in his hand, Chuy stepped between the two men and pointed the small bobbed-hammer gun at Choto's chest. He hoped Choto would back off, but Choto, just inches away, grabbed at the Smith & Wesson and stood nose to nose with Chuy, staring at him. But the flash of anger in his eyes disappeared when the gun discharged near Choto's heart.

The big man sagged toward Chuy, whose knees buckled. He tried to stabilize himself while holding up Choto. Chuy felt Speed clutch at him and stagger backward. The two lost their balance, pulling the dead weight of Choto on top of them.

Sandman, the only hostage not tied up, turned from his kneeling position and lunged toward Choto's gun, securing it in his right hand. Still on the floor, he rolled and aimed it at the two security men, who seemed stunned by the sudden change in circumstances.

"*No se mueva!*" he yelled. "Don't move!"

The two men froze.

He gathered himself to stand. "*Manos arriba*! Hands up!"

The one dropped his knife, and both men put their hands in the air.

Speed wriggled free of the pile to help Chuy out from under Choto's motionless body. They were both bloody, but Chuy was the only one who was breathing, and he was breathing hard. Chuy felt Speed push the gun out of the way and put his fingers in Choto's bleeding chest wound.

Ramirez got to her feet and began to work her way out of the rope. She picked up the security guard's knife to cut everyone loose as Sandman stood over the two men.

"Hector, get a dish towel from the kitchen, and help Señor Speed with the intruder."

She called for a police van. "Everyone okay?" she asked, taking inventory as she picked up her weapon from the leather chair.

Luis handcuffed Choto's security guards as they lay facedown on the floor. The gringa was still kneeling, sobbing into a sofa cushion.

"Where the hell did you come from?" Sandman asked Speed, who was still bent over Choto's body.

"I had to hit the can," Speed said, trying to sound nonchalant. He pointed with his free hand to the half bath near the stairs. "You gave me such a hard time about monitoring the cameras that I took the laptop with me. Just an FYI, the cameras weren't very useful in the rain. Not my fault."

Hector returned from the kitchen with a striped dish towel, and Speed allowed him to press it hard against Choto's chest to staunch the bleeding. Choto wasn't breathing. Hector kept the dish towel firmly against Choto's chest to stop the blood from draining.

"So then what happened?" asked Sandman, looking like he wanted to punch him and hug him at the same time.

"I was just sitting there when I heard the commotion. I was going to come out, but I heard all the yelling, so I thought I'd better sit tight." He looked a little nauseated. "I heard all the movement in here, and when I opened the door a crack and peeked in, everyone had their backs toward me. So I thought I would sneak up on everyone. Chuy was the only one who saw me, and he didn't make a peep."

In shock, Chuy sat on the floor next to Choto's body. "It just went off. I didn't try to fire the gun," he said absentmindedly. "I just wanted him to stop."

Standing over them, Ramirez patted Chuy's shoulder and checked the victim's carotid artery for a pulse. "He's gone," she said flatly.

36

THE MILITIA STUMBLES ONTO A PRIZE

The militia meandered through the brush, looking for whatever it was they were looking for. So far on their reconnaissance, the militiamen tramped up the mountain in one long lazy file. In the lead, Commander Taylor, sweating profusely despite the cooler weather, reached a ridgeline and a well-trodden path.

He raised an arm to halt his column. "Fall out, gentlemen. Take ten." They all gathered at the top of the hill and took a break for water and smokes. "After break, we'll separate into squads. Squad one, you take the trail that way," he said, pointing to his right. "Squad two, follow me, and we'll move in the opposite direction. We'll meet at this spot in one hour. One hour. Try not to disturb anything you find. If you do see something, call it in. We'll communicate on channel four and try to stick to military discipline on the radio."

Commander Taylor's squad went off in the direction of the last shots they'd heard. There were footprints in the dirt along the path, but it wasn't clear who had trodden there. After about fifteen minutes of fruitless searching, the radio squawked. "Squad two, this is squad one. Over."

"Squad two."

"Found a campsite. Abandoned. Over."

"Squad two. Squad one, what's your position? Over."

There was a pause. "Squad one, what's your position? Over."

"Well, Commander, we jes' down the path maybe a klick or so from your position. Russ, whaddya think? Maybe a little more, maybe less."

"Son, talk to me, and keep it military, can you? Over."

"Yeah, okay. Campfire's cold, sir. There's footprints in the dirt, but we've been walking around too. Could be some of ours. Do you want us to come back?"

Commander Taylor made a frustrated gesture toward the sky. He tried to speak calmly into the radio. "Squad one, are there some telltale signs or footprints or anything you can follow? Over."

"Uh, yeah. They lead back to where we came from. Uh, over."

Commander Taylor's squad was walking in the opposite direction from squad one. They moved slowly, careful to examine the trail and the surrounding areas in search of signs. "Squad one. Come back. Meet us on the trail. We haven't gone as far as you. Over."

"Ten-four, over and out."

Commander Taylor lowered the radio from his ear and shook his head. He would have to reexamine personnel assignments after this. But for the moment, he was determined to press ahead and reconnoiter the area. He needed to finish the investigation, report to Border Patrol and get his men down off the mountain safely. And it was getting later. The sun was already heading behind the peak to the west.

～

R odrigo thought he knew anxiety, but his heart raced more than it ever had before as he left Puerto Peñasco, driving Chuy's truck. He kept feeling someone was pursuing him, though he could not see anyone following. The *policía* protective custody had only set him up to be killed. If he got caught again by Choto's men, it would be a horrific end. He'd betrayed Choto twice. The cartel boss would torture him for sure. He didn't think he could hold out if that happened. No expectation of mercy—Choto would inflict a slow form of retribution on him even if he told the madman where the gold and silver were. He was sure to die an excruciating death. Rodrigo was in a full-blown panic. His temples pounded, and he couldn't get enough air into his lungs. He tried to slow his breathing, but he gasped frantically, as if he'd exhausted all the oxygen in the cab.

Wind blew light rain erratically across the truck's windows. He played with the windshield wipers, turning them on when the soft spray hit his field of vision and then off again as if he could exert some kind of control through that simple action. His neck and shoulders were tight, almost locked. He had to keep going. He didn't dare go back to the estuary for the buried sack of gold and silver. He had to make it to Arizona and the mountain. If he could get back to his treasure, he had a chance to escape.

Instead of his previous travels, he would head north to Sonoyta and take the main highway east to reach Sasabe and the tunnel to get across the border. He felt weary, but the adrenaline pumping through him kept him wide-awake. His eyes darted back and forth between the rearview mirror and side mirrors, looking for any suspicious vehicles that might approach. He was tense as a rubber band stretched almost to breaking.

But no one followed. He was too afraid to stop. Chuy's truck had a full tank, so he kept going. It was early morning and the rain had stopped when Rodrigo arrived in Sasabe. He took the keys and left the pickup on a narrow out-of-the-way street. He still wore the oversized T-shirt and ill-fitting shorts that he'd changed into after showering at the old cop's house. Walking toward the tunnel, he was glad he'd kept his own shoes, but the caked sand irritated his feet. The clothes had dried after his escape into the rain, and they sagged on his thin body, loose and uncomfortable. He bought water and snacks on the Sonora side, but he had no equipment other than a flashlight he'd taken from Chuy's truck. Stealing Chuy's pickup from Cholla Bay was another betrayal that left him feeling truly alone.

He walked to the warehouse that camouflaged the drug tunnel running under the border to Arizona. He found the underground opening and went through it slowly, careful to ensure that it was unoccupied. After exiting the opening in Arizona, he found his way into town and walked the streets of the US side, trying to blend in. The mountain was miles away, and he knew he would have to hike there. Two static Border Patrol checkpoints were obstacles he was able to dodge by staying in the countryside away from the road. Once he passed the checkpoints, he caught a ride from a rancher who got him closer to the mountain. It took all morning for him to reach the base of the trail.

He found the trailhead, but locating his former bushwhacked trail was difficult. It was kilometers from the main trailhead, and he hoped he wouldn't encounter other hikers. The sun moved behind the mountain. The shadows deepened in the afternoon light. Despite his lack of tools and preparation, he steeled himself to spend the night on the mountain. He'd do whatever it took to get his treasure.

He saw no one else on the hike up the trail. As he got closer to the mine adit, he quickened his pace. He ignored the beating his bare legs endured as they scraped against the cactus and were cut by the sharp edges of the desert grass. Instead, he focused on the search for the mine opening that would lead him to his treasure. His single-minded pursuit forced everything else from his consciousness. He forgot about Choto and the *policía*. Leaving Chuy's truck in Sasabe was a distant memory. The day wore on as he climbed, but he reached a ridge top he recognized as being near his old camp. He was close now.

He took a break and drank some of the water he'd brought. Shielding his eyes with his hand, he looked around the slope to orient himself. He knew he could retrace his steps to the mine opening from there.

"*Tranquilo,*" he said out loud to help himself remain calm. But it was difficult to contain his excitement, knowing he would soon be reunited with his gold and silver stashed in the mine shaft.

The sun was over the top of the mountain, and the shadows deepened. He found the subtle stone marker that he'd laid down from before that identified the path down to the shaft opening. He knew the way very well from there. He moved slowly and carefully to avoid the chance of another fall, but his pulse raced, pushing him along. He located the spot where the opening should have been. It was unrecognizable.

"It has to be here," he said to the hillside.

There was evidence of a rockslide. Rocks and dirt had fallen where he was sure the opening should have been. The shock of the discovery stunned him. He turned to the valley below and then examined the hillside. This had to be it. He checked the rock formations and the area near him. He recognized much of the scene below him, but the topography had changed. It was as if the earth itself had collapsed. Panic rose inside him. Frantically, he pushed dirt and smaller rocks aside with his, throwing handfuls away in every direction. Large rocks had fallen from higher on the mountain. At least, he'd thought so. But then he wasn't so sure.

He couldn't see an opening under all the debris. He

looked around the area again, trying to get his bearings. It was late afternoon and getting dark, so he decided to stop. He searched for fuel to make a fire and prepare for the night. He would try again in the morning. He climbed back up to the ridgeline and was surprised by a line of armed men about fifteen meters away, who saw him and pointed their weapons. He'd been so focused he hadn't heard them.

"Halt! Identify yourself," the man at the front of the file rasped through a megaphone. Rodrigo didn't understand what was said, especially since it was distorted electronically, but he got the meaning. A row of guns all aimed at him were lined up along the path behind the older fat man in front.

Armed only with a flashlight, he held his hands up in surrender. "Don't shoot, don't shoot," Rodrigo said in English. They weren't Border Patrol. They looked like some local vigilantes.

"I am Commander Taylor of the National Patriot Militia, Nevada Chapter. I repeat. Eye-dentify yourself." The young man's oversized shorts and T-shirt were not at all appropriate for hiking.

"*Cómo te llamas?*" one man shouted from the line.

"Rodrigo!" he responded. He had no idea who the National Patriot Militia was, but he did understand the word militia. *Some sort of private army.* He was chilled by the thought.

"Drop the flashlight!" Commander Taylor. "And turn around!"

Rodrigo was shaking and gave him a confused look. "I don't understand!"

"For Pete's sake, what's the *habla* I'm looking for, Keller?"

"Uh, *ponga las manos detrás de la espalda?*" another man—probably Keller—answered tentatively.

Rodrigo dropped the flashlight, turned around, and put his hands behind his head.

"What are you doing up here?" Commander Taylor asked, coming up behind Rodrigo.

Rodrigo didn't understand. "I want asylum," Rodrigo said in English. He thought if he asked for it, they would be more likely not to hurt him and return him to Mexico.

"Okay," said Commander Taylor. "Keller, get BP on the holler, and tell them we're bringing down a Mexican a-sy-lem seeker."

"Uh, will do."

Taylor looked at Rodrigo's filthy scratched up hands. "I wonder what you been doing up here, boy." He looked around.

"You don't look pre-paired for a day hike. Did you just cross the border?"

Rodrigo didn't understand.

"You don't look like a drug watcher."

Rodrigo did understand that part, but he feigned ignorance.

"Oh, for Pete's sake," said the fat man. He raised his hands in futility, the reaction Rodrigo had hoped for.

"Commander, CBP says to bring him down but try not to hurt him," said Keller, returning to the front of the file.

"Try not to hurt him?" Taylor snorted. "Why would we do any of that?" He motioned for the column to head down the mountain.

37

RAMIREZ HAS HER OWN PLAN

R amirez stared at the mess curled up in a ball in front of her. Tears had dried on Chuy's cheeks, but his eyes remained watery. He sat on a wooden chair in her office, still whimpering. She was sure that even though he was waist deep in the local drug scene, he'd never killed anyone before.

Choto was dead. He had a dish towel stuffed into the bloody hole in his chest and was rolled up in Sandman's rug. *Did Chuy intend to do it?* She didn't think so, but as the minutes passed, she wasn't so sure. Choto's death potentially solved a number of issues for Chuy.

After sorting out the scene, she drove him back to the station, just the two of them, to isolate him from everyone else. He sat in the passenger seat, trembling. She figured the consequences of what he'd done would close in on him during the ride. He said over and over that he never intended to use it, but the gun went off.

Sandman drove Speed and Ericka to the station in Ericka's rental. Hector and Luis transported the two *sicarios*, restrained in the second seat, and loaded Choto's rug-wrapped body, covered with a plastic tarp surrounding it, into the back of the police SUV. She told them to leave the body in the vehicle while they took the prisoners to the holding cells in another part of the station. She didn't believe the two *sicarios* had seen what happened or who'd caused the shooting.

She gave Chuy a bottle of water and told him to drink some. He was still shivering in his wet clothes after standing in the rain outside Sandman's front door. She sat down at the chief's desk across from him and tried to look sympathetic, but she was pulled in several directions. She really wanted to be with Ericka, who was crying on her father's shoulder in the main room of the station. Through her office window blinds, Ramirez could see the two of them sitting with each other.

But the first priority was duty. She had to concentrate on the problem in front of her. So many things had happened so fast. She wanted to settle the details from all perspectives and get a picture of how the home invasion had taken place. She was especially interested in Chuy's point of view. It wasn't clear in her mind.

When the shooting occurred, she, Ericka, Sandman, Hector, and Luis had all been facing the sofa, with their backs toward what happened. The two *sicarios*, tying them up, kneeled behind them. She remembered her own reaction, flinching when gunshot erupted and feeling surprised that she or one of the other hostages didn't fall. None of them saw directly what happened except Chuy and Speed and maybe Sandman. She wanted Chuy to start at the beginning and tell her how he had gotten hooked into the kidnapping plot after he left Sandman's house.

She reached across the desk to hand Chuy a tissue while looking into his eyes to get him to concentrate. "Chuy, I need you to focus on what happened while your memory is fresh. When you left Sandman's house, where did you go?"

Chuy wiped his eyes and tried to sit up in the chair. "I left the house to go back to my truck. I was walking on the road, and Choto drove up. Told me to get in."

"He must have been surprised to see you."

"*Sí*, he was suspicious at first. He wanted to know what I was doing there. I told him that Rodrigo asked for me—that I was the only one he would talk to. I said once Rodrigo quit talking, the police told me to go. He asked me if Rodrigo was still in the house. I lied and said I didn't know."

"So you got in his car. Where did you go?"

"He drove to that high hill above Sandman's house, where the cell tower is. There was an SUV with the other two guys in it. They were watching the house."

"You were on the hill with them, surveilling the house all that time?

"*Sí*," he said shivering. "I stayed in Choto's car. The others had left to fetch *comida*. Choto said he wanted burritos. When they returned, he got out of the car to get the food. That's when I texted you."

"Did you know that they were going to invade the house?"

"Not then. Choto wasn't sure if Rodrigo was still in the house. I didn't tell him the truth, so he was waiting for some clue."

"How did the plan to invade the casa happen?"

"Hours went by. It was getting dark, especially with the storm. Then the blond gringa drove up to the front of the house. Choto thought she was a cop or something. That was when he said he was sure that Rodrigo was in the house."

"Why?" Ramirez was surprised that Ericka had played an unwitting part.

"He thought she was there to pick him up. That's when he began planning to kidnap Rodrigo at the casa. After he thought about it, he decided that we would wait at the front of the house. The security men would watch the back of the house." Chuy was becoming more agitated as he related the story.

"What changed his mind?"

"He said he didn't want to lose him again. Rodrigo escaped once already. He said, if she came out with Rodrigo, then we would force them both into her car and take them away. If she didn't have him when she came out, we would grab her and push her back into the *casa* and force you to release him."

"Why didn't you alert me?"

His eyes pleaded. "I couldn't. I was never alone again."

"Okay, this 'plan' emerged on the spot." She wasn't sure she believed that, but she let it go for the moment. "Where did you get the gun?"

"His other pistol. Choto insisted I take it. He kept it in his boot. I knew Rodrigo wasn't inside the house," he said, changing the subject. He clearly didn't want to talk about the gun.

"How did you know he wasn't there?" she asked, surprised.

"Choto was looking through the binoculars at the *chica's* car in the driveway. It was still raining."

"And…?"

"I saw someone sneak out the door on the upper floor and go down the stairway in the rain. I knew it was him. No one else saw him go." He paused. "I did my best." His body began to heave again but without tears.

"Did you see where he went?"

"He disappeared in the dark, between Sandman's *casa* and the house next to it." He sniffled. "I saw him walking toward the road."

"Do you know where he would go?"

"To get his treasure, I guess. Back at the estuary or the Arizona mine. Where else could he go?" Chuy's face froze in panic for a moment. "I just remembered. My truck. It's in Cholla."

"We're almost through. We'll take you back to Cholla to get it. I know you're deeply upset by taking a life. Even if the life was a piece of shit like Choto. But, Chuy, you may have saved other lives."

"I don't think I can do this anymore. This… this informing."

Ramirez sighed. With all the things running through her mind, she couldn't have him backing out now. "You know the deal, Chuy. If you quit, I can't protect you from whatever you get mixed up in. Even if we dismiss the killing of Choto as self-defense, you just assaulted a woman. You were part of a plot to kidnap a police witness. Think about it. *Te chingas*."

She was distracted because outside her window, she could see through the open blinds into the room where Ericka and Sandman were talking earnestly, looking at each other intently, nodding, and hugging. Señor Speed was by himself in a chair nearby, talking animatedly on his cell phone, no doubt to his wife, Carol. He had a surprised look on his face as he talked, as if he realized he had done something both heroic and horrifying.

"But I…" Chuy said.

His delayed response brought Ramirez back to their conversation. He appeared whipsawed by her inconsistent reaction. First she'd praised him for intervening, and then she'd threatened him. The effect was intentional on her part.

"Chuy, it's time to grow up. You've made choices. You got into the drug business on your own. No one made you do it. After your friend's death, you offered to inform. Remember, I warned you at the time."

"I bought a *farmacia*. I'm trying to get out of the illegal drug business."

"You bought it with proceeds from your illegal drug sales." She hoped the comment would snap him back to the present reality and steel him. He needed to understand the position he was in and not do something rash or just smile and try to talk his way out of it. Tough love, Sandman called it. It did have the effect of pulling Chuy out of his spiraling shock. He wasn't a bad kid. He was likable and quick-witted and seemed to have a general—if somewhat misguided—sense of right and wrong. He wasn't a psychopath like most of the cartel leaders and *sicarios*. She couldn't imagine Chuy in his present state—sitting balled up in his chair, an emotional wreck—as a *sicario*.

Maybe Choto was trying to groom Chuy to be a hitman, but he wasn't physically aggressive enough. Or pliable enough. Ramirez trusted Chuy's cunning nature and instinct for survival.

"When the two of you grabbed Ericka and pushed her back into the casa, I saw that you didn't raise your gun."

"I didn't want to shoot anyone."

"Describe what happened when you shot Choto."

"The *gordo* one—the fat one you call Señor Speed—he came up behind us from somewhere else in the casa. He hit Choto on the head with a laptop. It bounced off. But it hit him on his shoulder, too, and Choto dropped his arm."

"Which shoulder?"

"The right one, the side that held the gun. I remember a loud whack. Then Choto spun around."

"Where were you standing?" she asked.

"I was on the left of Choto and a little behind him. So I saw Señor Speed hit Choto."

"Then what?"

"The next thing, I was the little guy between the two men, squeezed like the middle of a *torta*," he said.

"Show me."

Chuy stood up and pointed out where Choto and Speed had stood, in front and behind him. The reenactment seemed to calm him a little.

"How did you come to shoot Choto?"

He looked at her. The terror of the memory shone in his face. "Choto looked down at me. He is much taller. I felt him grab at the pistol in my hand.

"Which hand?"

The question slowed him down and caused him to think. "I guess his left hand, *derecho*. And it went off. The sound was really loud."

"Do you remember shooting him?"

"No, it just went off, I swear."

That's not what happened. It's a double-action pistol. You have to consciously pull the trigger. Maybe he can't admit it to himself. "Okay, Chuy." She opened the center drawer of her desk, drew out a form, and fished around inside for a pen. "I need you to write down everything you told me on this sheet of paper and sign it."

He stared at it like it was soaked in poison. He had a panicked look on his face.

"Don't worry. This is not going to court. I need to collect everyone's version of what happened. When I put it together, I'll find a way to fix this to protect you because you are an informant. Take your time, and wait here for me." She got up from the desk and walked to the door then glanced back at Chuy who, pen in hand, stared at the form.

She passed Hector and Luis at their desks. Hector was looking over the witness form that Speed had filled out.

"Did they say anything?" Ramirez asked, referring to the two men they'd taken into custody.

"Not much but *basta*," said Luis. "We know where their hacienda is. Could be a trap."

"It's a chance I'll take," she said. "If you know where it is, I'll need you two to help me with a reconstruction project there."

They nodded. Ramirez walked over to Ericka and Sandman. Ericka stood up and grabbed for her as if she were a life preserver. She'd calmed down after her father talked to her, but Ramirez could feel her tremble in her embrace.

"I don't know what happened," Ericka said as if she felt as though she were responsible.

"It's going to be okay,' said Ramirez, looking into her eyes.

"Don't worry, *mi amor*." After their hug, she held Ericka out from her body. "I need to talk to your father for a moment."

Sandman was still seated. Ramirez made a motion for him to follow her, and she led him away from the others.

"Even though the mayor was informed, this was all extracurricular *mierda*, so I need to find an alternative scenario that explains Choto's death, keeps Chuy's cover intact, and protects you and Ericka and Speed."

"Tall order," he said but signaled that he was on board.

She knew that what she was about to do would be unimaginable in the States. But in Mexico, institutions were fragile, the criminal justice system barely functioned at all, and real justice was a distant hope that frequently was pursued outside the regular channels.

"I'm imagining how to reconstruct this scene at Choto's beach hacienda. I need to know what you and Ericka saw during the incident. Por favor, write down for me everything you saw, especially the positions of the participants. Your insight will be important. I hate to ask, but can you take care of the cleanup of your casa? We will be very busy for a while."

"*No problema*. Do you need my help out there? I'm volunteering."

"We could use it, no doubt. But when you finish your thoughts, I'd like you to take care of Ericka and drop Chuy off at his truck in Cholla, if that's okay. After I collect everyone's statements, Hector and Luis and I are going pack up and then go out to gather whatever evidence we can find at Choto's. Then we'll create a new crime scene to explain Choto's death. Then I'll call in the drug task force. I don't expect them to look closely at the details at the hacienda. They'll be too busy elbowing us out of the way to take credit. It should work out fine for everybody."

∽

S andman returned to Ericka and Speed, who handed his cell phone to Sandman.

"*Mi esposa*," Speed said to him. "My wife would like a word."

"Carol," Sandman said off-handedly after accepting the phone.

"What the hell is going on?" asked Carol. "Speed just told me some crazy story about hitmen and a cartel boss, and how he's a hero. What have you two been doing?"

"Well, allowing for his usual hyperbole and exaggeration, what he told you is probably near the truth."

"He told me he's okay. Is that true? He said he's at the police station."

"I'm looking at him right now, and he appears normal. Normal for him."

"A year ago, you got him involved in a kidnapping back in the States, and now he's in the middle of a confrontation with Mexican drug lord. Trouble in one country isn't enough for you? You and I will talk."

"Carol, everything is fine. I'll bring him home soon."

"Soon," she said. It was a command.

38

RODRIGO ENCOUNTERS ROUGH JUSTICE

His hands zip-tied behind him, Rodrigo stumbled down the trail at the front of the file of ragtag militiamen. Walking several paces behind him, Commander Taylor clicked the trigger of his amplified bullhorn at odd intervals as if to remind Rodrigo of things he already knew—that these gringos were taking him to immigration and detention. He hoped it wouldn't be anything more than that. The random electronic *clack* that echoed off the hillside was intimidating. He felt his feet slip as he negotiated the loose dirt and rock on the downward slope of the path. When the trail disappeared, he was forced to bushwhack across shoulder-high creosote and shrubby mesquite without being able to use his arms to move the brush from his path. The sharp, stickery plants scratched and clawed at his already cut and bruised legs and arms.

He knew the men were trying to humiliate him, shoving him along when he slowed too much for their liking. He felt their collective hate against his back. He'd done nothing to them, but they viewed him as someone who didn't belong there and maybe as something other than human. He feared that they would decide he was too much trouble and just kill him. So Rodrigo submitted to their instructions. He struggled to control his emotions, concentrating on where he placed his feet in the dying light.

He felt a sharp pain in his back where Commander Taylor shoved him with the front edge of the metallic speaker. "Keep a move on!" Taylor shouted moments later into the bullhorn. "*Comprende*?"

"*Sí*," Rodrigo replied over his shoulder.

The column continued down the mountain as night fell. Rodrigo, unable to maintain balance with his arms tied, stumbled along a path of his own in the dark. Flashlights behind him illuminated the desert like torchlights signaling a night carnival. Rodrigo could see the pickup trucks ahead of him randomly parked at the edge of an open area as they neared the dirt trailhead at the base of the mountain.

"Let's halt right here!" Commander Taylor shouted through the bullhorn, turning to the column. Taylor offered him some bottled water, bringing it to his lips, and Rodrigo drank thirstily until he gagged and coughed.

"You'll probably accuse us of water torture, now," Taylor said derisively, minus the megaphone.

Rodrigo didn't answer. He was glad to have finished trooping through the brush. He looked down at his bare legs and, in the dim glow of flashlights, saw a mass of scrapes and cuts. He peered over his shoulders at his arms. They were just as beat-up as his legs. His hands were numb from the plastic ties on his wrists. Even if he couldn't feel them, he knew they were scratched and bleeding from pawing at the rubble of what he believed was the entrance to the mine shaft. Standing by the trailhead, he was afraid but so weary and tired that he was resigned to whatever these ignorant vigilantes were going to do to him.

His fear grew to terror when he saw several sets of headlights come up the dirt road from the highway. He couldn't run—they would just tackle and beat him. He had no energy to run anyway. As the headlights grew closer, he saw the reflection of the light bars above three white SUVS with green stripes on the side. *La migre*—US Customs and Border Protection—was coming. The lead SUV flicked its headlights, and the militia troops gathered in a lazy assembly. Two men in green Border Patrol uniforms got out and approached Commander Taylor.

He snapped to something resembling attention. "Commander Taylor, National Patriot Militia, Nevada Chapter."

The agent with Villaseñor written on a name tag across his breast pocket nodded. "You said you had an illegal here. That him?"

"Yes, sir," answered Commander Taylor. "A border jumper."

Villaseñor nodded again. "What's your name?" he asked, turning to Rodrigo. "*Cómo se llama?*"

Rodrigo was surprised by the officer's use of the formal version of the question. It put him slightly at ease. Maybe they weren't going to beat him.

"Rodrigo Sanchez Serrano. I would like to request asylum in the United States," he said in English. The cartel *sicarios* who'd trained him told him to memorize that phrase and repeat it if he got caught. They said it would give him some kind of protection. At worst, CBP would return him to Mexico, they said, probably sooner rather than later. That was where Rodrigo wanted to be anyway.

Agent Villaseñor gave a wry smile. "Of course you do. Got any ID? *Puedo ver su identificación?*"

The other agent, taller and Anglo, stood next to Villaseñor. He said something into the radio mic on his shoulder and folded his arms. The two SUVs behind their lead vehicle backed out.

"No, señor," Rodrigo said politely. He pointed to his

clothes, the ones he'd changed into after he showered at the old cop's *casa*. "It was stolen on the journey here."

"Okay," said Agent Villaseñor in the weary voice of someone who'd heard that story more times than he could count. "How did you get here?"

"A coyote, but he abandoned me. I got lost." Rodrigo was deliberately vague.

"We're going to take you in for processing." Villaseñor motioned to his partner to take custody of Rodrigo. They both put on latex gloves. Still speaking Spanish, he said, "We'll do your fingerprints, find out if you're in the system, and if you're lying about who you are, we'll add that to the charge of illegal entry into the country. Okay?"

"*Sí, señor.* I'm not lying."

Villaseñor pulled a pair of wire cutters from his belt and clipped Rodrigo's zip ties. Immediately, Rodrigo rubbed at his wrists, massaging the circulation back into his swollen hands.

Villaseñor looked down at Rodrigo's dirty shoes. "Take your shoelaces off. *Remueve su los cordones de los zapatos.*"

Rodrigo looked at his raw hands and the line on his wrists where the zip tie had cut into them. He bent down and complied then handed the laces to Villaseñor.

"*Ponga las manos detrás el cogote,*" Villaseñor said.

Rodrigo put his hands behind his neck. The two agents led Rodrigo back to the SUV. The Anglo pushed Rodrigo's head beneath the door frame as he placed him in the back seat. A metal cage separated Rodrigo from the front seats.

"It's a busy night. Thank you for your assistance, Commander," Villaseñor said, drawing out the word *Commander*. He climbed into the driver's side of the SUV.

Villaseñor radioed that he had one in transit. He turned the wheels of his SUV and accelerated, forcing the militia members to move out of the way and kicking up dirt on the road as he passed by the other BP vehicles. The second and then third vehicle pulled around and followed.

As the car moved away, Rodrigo could hear Commander Taylor calling his troops. "All right, mount up," Taylor said into the megaphone. "Time to head back to camp. Our work is done."

R odrigo sat quietly in the back seat of the SUV as it moved down the road. He looked around to keep track of what the agents were doing and where they were taking him. But his mind kept snapping back to the gold and silver in the mine shaft. He didn't have time to retrace his steps back to the original path from his old camp. Maybe he'd been in the wrong place. His path marker could have been moved. He wondered if Choto's men might be waiting for him at the camp. The gringos who'd captured him said there had been gunshots. He hadn't heard any. *Were they lying?* He trusted no one.

Don't think about the treasure. Think about what is happening to you right now.

Communications traffic on the dashboard radio cut in and out, coded and garbled with words he couldn't understand. The pair of agents, faces glowing in the reflected panel lights, had been polite but stern. He expected worse treatment at their hands. They sped down the dusty road toward the two-lane state highway that led to Interstate 19. The freeway connected Tucson to the north and Nogales to the south at the border. In between the two cities lay the large retirement community of Green Valley and the art town of Tubac, site of a Spanish presidio centuries before.

At the freeway interchange, the vehicles turned north toward Tucson. They traveled a few kilometers until they approached a static border checkpoint on the interstate just north of Tubac. Ahead was a large white fabric overhang covering the northbound lanes of the freeway. Lights on long poles flanked the lanes approaching the inspection station, casting harsh illumination down on the road. Orange cones marked a gradual slowdown in speed and funneled the traffic into a line approaching the overhang.

Closer in, an agent shepherded a Belgian Malinois between vehicles, and the dog actively sniffed the tires and undercarriage of trucks and cars as they crawled forward. Another agent stood at the left side of the lane, looked into the vehicles one at a time, and often wordlessly motioned them through.

The Border Patrol vehicles pulled out of the inspection line and drove toward a long trailer that sat along the right side of the checkpoint. They stopped about twenty-five feet from a van that was under close inspection.

Agent Villaseñor turned his head toward the metal screen separating their captive. "You'll wait here until the *autobus* arrives with the others. Then the *autobus* will take you to Nogales for processing. *Comprende*?"

Rodrigo nodded. The two agents got out of the vehicle, leaving him inside. He heard the door locks click as they walked toward the trailer. Rodrigo was alone with his thoughts and the intermittent squawking of the radio. He had no clear idea of where he was.

He knew that they'd traveled in the opposite direction of the city of Nogales that straddled the border. He knew there was a major Customs and Border Protection facility in Nogales. If that was where they were taking him, he could be back in Puerto Peñasco in a few hours or a day.

He was excited by the thought. He wondered how long the paperwork took to fill out. He just wanted to get it over with because he wasn't going to follow through on his asylum claim. He thought it would be quick. *They want Mexicans like me removed as fast as possible. Getting rid of us is standard procedure.* He saw the wisdom of the cartel *sicarios'* advice. It coincided with his plans. If he could get back to Puerto Peñasco, he could start over, dig up his bag of treasure in the estuary, and use it to fund his return to Arizona to recover the rest.

The time passed slowly as he sat in the car. He tried to count the minutes, but he couldn't concentrate. Fear began to overtake him. How long would they keep him, and where would they take him? Who else would he have to share lock down with? It couldn't be worse than a Mexican jail. He tried to distract himself. He could see some graffitied initials and names inked and scratched into the upholstery of those who'd come before him: *R-S, Renaldo, Choo-choo.* The tinted SUV windows filtered the garish checkpoint lights into twinkly eerie colors.

A white *autobus* with heavily screened windows pulled up alongside the SUV, stopped, and sat with the engine running. He could see an eagle seal within a circle on the side of it. The bus door remained closed. Diesel fumes from the exhaust began to filter into the SUV.

Villaseñor appeared beside Rodrigo's door, and it clicked open. The agent opened the door and stepped back for Rodrigo to exit. "Time to go," he said.

"Where am I going?"

"Nogales," said Agent Villaseñor. "You'll be processed there, and a decision will be made about what happens next."

The *autobus* doors flapped opened, and Rodrigo climbed the steps. In the dark, he stood next to the driver's seat, letting his eyes adjust. No one looked up at him after he appeared at the top of the steps except one curious small girl in a plaid dress, sitting in the front row. He looked down the aisle at the others sitting in bench seats—men, women, and a handful of *niños.* He could smell the sweat and desperation. More than a dozen people, weary and exhausted, stared straight ahead. They were dressed in rough rural clothes and soiled counterfeit T-shirts. They didn't look Mexican. He decided they came from farther south, maybe Chiapas or Honduras or Venezuela.

"*Siente se,*" said the driver. "Any open seat."

Rodrigo walked the length of the bus to the rear and took a seat in an empty row. The people he passed looked away or had their eyes closed. They were all on their way to somewhere they couldn't know or do anything about. Rodrigo comforted himself knowing that they were headed for Nogales, just this side of Mexico and closer to home. *Only a few hours more.* He knew he was different from the rest of them. He had something none of them possessed. Rodrigo had his treasure and the knowledge that only he could retrieve it.

39

THE SCENE IS SET

By the time Ramirez, Hector, and Luis finished processing the witnesses, it was sunrise. The ride was a half hour to the estate properties at Montezuma Palace, the site of Choto's custom-built hacienda. Ramirez spent most of the time on the phone with the mayor, updating him on the situation and her plan. The first priority was to protect all those involved from the potential blowback of Choto's death.

Mayor Bustamonte signed off on the general plan, but he wanted to get updates as she finished the *hacienda* search and set the grisly scene with Choto's body. He also wanted input into the decision of when the state and federal police would be called in to investigate the scene at the *hacienda* that the three of them were about to compose.

In the exclusive area of the Montezuma's luxury lots, only a few haciendas were built and even fewer occupied. Most lots were vacant land, though there were several with large homes under construction and a new upscale security hut, with the resort's logo spelled out along a white-cement stuccoed wall, that had been completed. Two uniformed guards stood near the hut trying to look professional and efficient. The sand was still wet from the unseasonal rain, and the ocean fog was lifting as the wind pushed out the humidity. When the police vehicle approached, one of the guards raised the weighted counterbalance of the long tubular metal gate striped with reflective yellow tape. The other guard waved them through without stopping them.

A two-story white hacienda stood with only two other houses among the ocean lots with stretches of vacant land. The house had a direct view of the open sea with its own beach front and an attached multicar garage at the end of a long concrete driveway. Behind and off to the right side of the hacienda was a tall boathouse large enough to accommodate an ocean sport-fishing boat in dry dock. Ramirez checked the area to make sure no one was around before they approached the front entrance, which was protected by a wall and gate.

She planned to enter the house, even if it meant breaking in, and create a scene that would appear to outside police investigators as if Choto had been surprised by intruders or possibly betrayed by his security people. Choto's body would be left in the living room with a weapon nearby. She, Hector, and Luis would artfully shoot up the area and obscure Choto's original chest wound from the small-caliber pistol that Chuy had fired.

"Glove up, you two," she said.

They all put on blue latex gloves and began to look around the casa's exterior for any sign of activity. Hector and Luis removed a tool kit from the back of the SUV, careful not to disturb the tarp-covered body next to it. They saw no sign of activity at the hacienda—no vehicles in front, no light on inside the house, and no resistance of any kind when the police SUV drove up. An HVAC whirring on the roof was the only sound in the humid air.

They checked the entrance for security equipment. If there was a home-security TV system, it was well camouflaged.

Luis said they should search the house for a server and collect whatever computers and hard drives might store surveillance footage.

They decided it would be best to cut power to the house before entering. Physically cutting the wires would be another indication of a planned attack, another nugget for the federal police to find. They traced the line and noticed that there was an electrical hookup for house and garage and a separate line that ran from the box to the ground under the extended driveway to the boathouse behind that faced the sea.

"Must be some ocean cruiser Choto has," said Hector to Luis, both staring at the power line.

"Probably thinks he can outrun the navy," said Luis. "I would like to see the rig he's got. We'll check it out after we've finished the main house."

Hector put on heavy electrical gloves over his latex ones and then grabbed a large pair of bolt cutters. With a loud grunt, he snapped the line coming from the electrical box to the house causing an arcing flash. The humming of the HVAC unit on top of the roof slowed and then went quiet. They waited to see if anyone from inside the house came out to check. They still heard no sign of activity.

Hector slammed the lockset with the heavy bold cutters and forced open the front door. The front wall hid the activity from the public street. Ramirez, who waited in the SUV while her two cops secured the outside, got out and checked again to see if anyone was about. Neither of the other two fully built estates on the cul-de-sac appeared occupied.

Ramirez walked to the front door, gun drawn, to back up Hector and Luis, who had just gone inside. The three of them methodically cleared the main floor of the house, going from room to room, covering each other, announcing "*Claro*" as they went. The rooms seemed enormous, but they were remarkably sparse of furniture. It looked like the occupant was temporarily camping out rather than living in the space.

Hector and Luis worked their way around to the large stone-countered kitchen on the right wing of the house, which was fully equipped and functional. Hector opened the refrigerator door. The inside was well stocked with food. They then moved to the large curved staircase that led up to a loft foyer and presumably the bedroom wings. Ramirez's cowboy boots clicked a little too loudly, she thought, on the terrazzo tile floor.

"First floor clear, Jefe," said Luis.

Ramirez nodded and motioned the two up the stairs. They reached the top and turned to the right wing. She followed and stayed in the upstairs foyer to confront whatever threats might appear from the opposite wing. She kept her gun pointed toward the long hallway that led to several bedrooms on the left side. Dim sunlight shone into the hallway from open doors. She saw nothing out of the ordinary.

Hector and Luis reappeared behind her. "Jefe, it's clear," said Luis quietly. "But there are some interesting things in the master bedroom to view later."

"I'll lead down this wing." She entered a large study that had a few cheap chairs and a desk with a large wooden armoire against the wall behind it. Hector and Luis followed in ready position. The room was unoccupied, but there were signs of activity. Another bedroom had bunk beds shoved against two walls. *Where his personal security guards stay*, she thought.

At the end of the hall a bedroom was being used as a kitchenette-dining area. There was a small refrigerator with a coffee maker on top, a card table, chairs, and metal garage shelves that were partially filled with canned goods and other food. A large, messy bathroom was accessed from the hallway as well as from another bedroom that had several sleeping bags piled haphazardly. It was an expensive home with custom fittings being used as a temporary shelter.

"It's clear on this side," she said, holstering her weapon. "We don't have much time. Choto has been dead for hours now. Let's do this."

The three of them walked down the staircase. "You two bring the body inside. I'll find the best setup." She waited at the entrance by the front door. "Careful moving the body."

"*Sí*, Jefe," Hector said.

They returned moments later, each holding an end of the rolled-up tarp. Over his shoulder, Hector also carried a bag of confiscated guns seized from past crimes. They laid the tarp-covered body down softly on the shiny beige terrazzo floor. Hector slipped his arm from the sling and handed the bag to Ramirez.

"I think he should face the front door as though he confronted a threat," she said, like a director arranging a movie set. "Unroll him carefully. Don't damage the body."

The two men pulled the plastic tarp slowly from around Choto's body and then unwrapped the rug that surrounding him. This was the first time she'd had a chance to closely examine the corpse. Sandman's dish towel, stuffed into the small hole in Choto's chest, was soaked with drying blood. She figured the bullet had hit Choto's heart. It explained why he'd died quickly.

The fast application of the towel had sealed much of the blood inside the body cavity. Rolling the body on its side, she saw an exit wound between the spine and the scapula. She would ask Sandman about the slug in his casa.

After they positioned the body on the floor, she drew an AR-15 from Hector's bag of guns. The weapon had been smuggled into the country from the US, a military rifle that was meant to inflict maximum damage on combatants to remove them from the fight either by death or injury. Because of the velocity and action of its fired rounds, the bullets ripped through the body to disable the enemy in even nonfatal wounds. Shooting the deceased Choto would disguise the gunshot wound, obscuring the original bullet hole.

"Hector, you and Luis pick up the body from its position and hold it upright under the arms," she said, snapping a magazine into the weapon. "I'm going step back a bit nearer the door."

She moved back into the entrance foyer and raised the weapon. Hector winced as they picked up the body and held it up. "Do you think I'll shoot you by mistake?" she asked.

"No, Jefe," Hector said. "You're an excellent marksman, I know. Beginnings of *rigor mortis.* He's a little stiff." Luis stood on the other side of the body and remained silent.

"No one likes this situation," she said, lowering the rifle. "I would prefer to play this straight up. But you know we can't trust the federal police. And the state cops are infiltrated by the cartels."

"*Sí*, we know," Hector said, giving her a disapproving look.

"As the mayor says, there are some cancers that will kill you if you don't cut them out and others you can't cure but learn to live with. I agree." She raised the AR-15 again. "This isn't what we want, but I need to protect everyone who was involved, including the two of you."

She took a deep breath and fired a round at the body's wound. It did more damage than she'd expected. Some blood spattered on floor and the two young cops. Choto's torso was ripped by the round passing through the body. His head jerked slightly from the impact. His lifeless eyes stared down at the floor.

"Place him on his back." They laid Choto on the stone floor. She fired another two rounds into the wall behind him. "Where's that fancy gun we took from him?" she asked.

Hector rummaged through the sling bag of weapons and

brought out the .357 that only a few hours earlier Choto had aimed at them. He held it up delicately so he wouldn't ruin Choto's fingerprints, which he saw on the shiny finish.

She took it from him carefully. "Now I'll stand here where Choto would have been if an intruder had come through the door."

When she aimed the pistol at the still-ajar front door, two figures in orange hazmat suits and respirator masks, holding rifles, burst into the foyer. Startled, she fired Choto's gun at the first figure through the entry. The figure dropped the weapon and fell to the floor with a lifeless clatter. The second figure turned and ran, retreating without firing. Ramirez chased the figure to the door.

The intruders surprised Hector and Luis, freezing them where they stood. Then they drew their guns and approached the person in the entry. They heard several rounds exchanged outside. Luis kicked the rifle away from the body, and Hector bent over it to lift a bloody industrial respirator from the head. It was the face of a young Mexican man, no more than twenty years old. Hector felt the man's neck for a pulse and didn't find one. The man had been shot in the head above the eyes. Hector saw blood leaking into the hazmat suit. The wound's placement confirmed Hector's judgment that Ramirez, even under pressure, was a very good shot.

"I have another one out here," Ramirez called from outside. "Luis, help me bring him inside the house."

It had all happened so fast that Luis hadn't followed her as backup. He went outside, expecting her to chastise him. Instead, he found Ramirez smiling in relief and standing over the second hazmat figure lying in the long concrete driveway that curved toward the boathouse. They dragged the body across the concrete and into the entranceway of the casa.

"Careful where you touch him. We don't know what they were mixing up out there," she said. "Don't touch any part of your body with your gloves."

When she and Luis pulled and shoved the body inside, Hector gathered himself to his full standing posture, groaned in pain, and grabbed at his back. It had been a long twenty-four hours with no sleep, much excitement, and a number of dead bodies. Everyone's nerves and patience were exhausted.

They arranged the bodies so it might appear that the two hazmat-dressed men had attacked the boss and Choto's fancy gun had killed both of them. She placed it on the floor near his right hand. She took one of the rifles from the hazmat-suited guys and fired a couple more rounds from the doorway into the wall. She then placed the weapon near one of the bodies and confiscated the other unfired rifle. Competent crime-scene investigators would see through the ruse but only if they were motivated to look.

The three of them stood in the entranceway and examined their work. It was as good as they had time to do. "Hector, I apologize for snapping at you earlier," Ramirez said. "We are all tired and drained."

"I understand. Too many people to worry about," Hector said. "I know you were upset about the *chica*."

Luis shot him a warning look.

"*Sí*, I was." Her attention shifted from Hector's reaction to Luis and turned to face them both. "It's okay. We're not hiding anything."

"*Sí*, Jefe. I noticed the way you looked at her." Hector still felt concerned about whether they were allowed to talk about it.

She looked at him and burst out laughing. "Let's collect whatever loose papers there are from Choto's room, then we'll check the boathouse."

The three of them moved quickly up the stairs and back into the study. They rifled through the drawers of Choto's desk, scooping up whatever was there. Ramirez saw two chunks of precious metal, each resting on a pile of papers. She grabbed the gold and silver and put them in her pocket. Inside the armoire, they found a locked safe.

"Leave it for the *federales*," Ramirez said. She and Luis heaped a stack of papers onto the outstretched arms of Hector, who teetered down the stairs and put them in the trunk of the SUV.

The midmorning sun was behind them when they approached the tall boathouse. Overhead metal doors covered either end. Function was in the design. A boat trailer would back the vessel into the boathouse from the driveway. The door at the other end allowed it to exit the boathouse and be launched into the sea. A side door to the boathouse was locked, and Luis used the heavy bolt cutters from the equipment bag to whack off the substantial handle.

Opening the door, they found no boat. Instead, a multitable professional chemistry lab was set up at the far end of the overhead door closest to the sea. Large plastic bottles and several boxes of chemicals were stored on the floor on one side. A few boxes had chemical names taped on the outside: *benzylfentanyl* and *4-anilinopiperidine*. At the other end, industrial shelves were stacked with tightly wrapped plastic bags of white powder.

"I know what's in those kilo packages, so we should leave," said Ramirez. "Those two wore hazmat suits for a reason."

"It is fentanyl," said Luis.

She nodded.

Luis knew that even a small amount of pure fentanyl could cause an overdose, and unlike the well-equipped federal drug police, Puerto Peñasco cops didn't routinely carry Narcan with them. They backed out the door slowly and deliberately.

Ramirez stripped off her latex gloves. "Let's get a refuse bag for this stuff," she said, wagging the gloves in front of her. "It's time to call in the federal police and watch the show."

40

RODRIGO GETS THROUGH TO CHUY

"Chuy, I need your help," Rodrigo said into a rented cell phone. He heard a derisive snort on the other end of the phone. "Don't hang up!"

"Where's my truck?" growled Chuy.

Rodrigo had been afraid Chuy wouldn't answer the call from a strange phone number appearing on his cell. But Chuy was really his last hope.

"I -I left it in Sasabe," he said. "*Lo siento.* I had to leave it, you know?"

"Sasabe? You abandoned my new truck on the street of a border town? Then you call me to ask for help?"

He could feel Chuy's anger through the connection. Chuy would know that the truck was a lost cause by that point, without a doubt stolen from the street where Rodrigo had parked it and stripped for parts at some border chop shop. "I don't have time to explain. I borrowed this phone to call you."

"Where are you?" Chuy's speech was clipped.

"Juárez," said Rodrigo. "At the bus station."

"What are you doing in Juárez? That's almost *pinche* Texas."

"The gringo ICE brought me here. I got caught in Arizona, you know, and I asked for asylum."

"Why did you ask for asylum? You don't care about gringo land."

"Jefe's men told me if I got caught, I should ask. They said I would get better treatment."

"And they took you to Juárez? Was that better treatment?"

Rodrigo absorbed Chuy's venting like a boxer taking body blows. "No. It was horrible."

"Why should I help you? I want my truck."

Rodrigo was wrapped in a sweatshirt he'd gotten from the shelter where he stayed. "I have no money. I'm desperate, hanging around here, begging for food."

There was silence on other end.

"Half. I'll give you half," Rodrigo pleaded.

"What?"

With his hand, Rodrigo cupped the cell phone near his mouth for privacy. "I'll give you half the gold and silver that I buried in Puerto Peñasco."

"Gold? There's gold too?"

Rodrigo didn't think Chuy believed him, but he hoped dangling the offer of treasure in front of him would get his attention. "You helped me. You deserve half the money, you know."

Chuy had earned it, trying to help him. Rodrigo hoped he wouldn't ask for more. With that kind of money, Chuy could buy a new truck and have money left over for his *farmacia* business.

Rodrigo looked around the crowded bus station. He had little time left to speak. "Por favor, you're the only one I can turn to for help."

"Juárez is a long way. Maybe I could wire you money for a bus ticket."

"Por favor, don't do that! There are bad people around here. Serious bad people. I'm afraid I'll be robbed if I go to a *cambio.* It happens all the time. Por favor. Come and get me. In person. I'll give you half. You have my word."

"The word of a truck thief," Chuy retorted, but his tone had softened.

Rodrigo knew he was thinking about it. "Por favor, Chuy." He hoped that by now the police in Puerto Peñasco had lost interest in him, but he was afraid to ask about it.

"Okay. I'll come. Be at the bus station this time tomorrow. Okay?"

"*Sí,* gracias," said Rodrigo. "Muchas gracias."

It had been two weeks of hell for Rodrigo. He'd been transported by bus to the Customs and Border Protection station in Nogales, photographed, had his fingerprints taken, and then locked in a caged holding area with more than twenty others who, like him, had been picked up or had approached agents to request asylum. His legs were scabbed and sore from the forced trip down the mountain, shoved along by the militia. He still wore the clothes he'd had on when he escaped from the old cop's *casa*—a large T-shirt and a pair of too-big athletic shorts from the Sandman. He had his own shoes but with no laces. The clothes were enough for the outside weather, but the detention centers were cold and the floors hard and maybe as bad as a Mexican jail after all.

The men were kept separately in the large cinder block room, sitting and sleeping on the hard concrete floor with Mylar blankets and no real bedding. The lights inside the cage were on twenty-four hours a day. And it was cold—they ran the refrigerated air compressors constantly. The women and children were kept in another part of the facility. The noise of unseen children coughing and whimpering echoed against the hard bare walls. Through the night, he could hear metal doors scraping and closing and agents walking the floors. The smell of disinfectant cleaners that permeated the air nauseated him. Sleep was impossible. He was sore, exhausted, and anxious. He forced himself to think about the waiting treasure that he'd buried on the coast. When he returned to Puerto Peñasco, he and Chuy would dig it up. Even if he gave half of it to Chuy, there would be plenty of money for him to start over. After he'd recovered physically, he would make his way back to the mine shaft and retrieve the rest of it. With enough time and the right provisions, he was sure he would find the cave entrance. He'd leave all this pain and suffering behind. *Just concentrate, keep to yourself, be alert, and and trust no one.*

After several days in an ICE detention center, he met with a pro bono lawyer for a very short time. Then Rodrigo was whisked before an administrator who sat behind a table in a large white tent. As he'd been taught by the cartel, he insisted that his life was in danger in Mexico, so he needed to stay in the United States. He was given a piece of paper with a date to appear for an asylum hearing. He was told he would have to wait in Mexico until his hearing to assess his case. Then Immigration and Customs Enforcement put him on another bus, and he was taken to El Paso to a different holding area that was no better than the first.

Days passed before agents transferred him across the border, where he was left on his own. He went to a migrant shelter to sleep and sometimes eat a meal, but he spent most of the time panhandling at the nearby bus station, dodging what he thought were cartel lookouts, hoping to beg enough money for a ticket. The shelter was jammed with people, most of them from farther south, who'd fled their homes to try to get into the United States. Anguish and despair were etched on their dark faces. The children were listless, trying to hold on to some kind of contact with a parent—a look or a touch. Some of the people who'd given up everything to be there gave up again and just wanted to go back—to what, no one seemed sure.

The bus station was overcrowded no matter what hour of the day or night it was. There were many people—men, women with small children—all doing what he was doing. And he could not raise enough money. After hanging out and watching what others did, he found a man who loaned his cell phone to migrants for a price. Rodrigo took the few *pesos* he'd stashed in his shoe, grateful for the opportunity, and handed them to the fast-talking man. It was all the money he'd begged, but no matter. He'd reached Chuy, and his high school friend was coming to get him.

Rodrigo would steer clear of Choto when he returned. The police might still be looking for him, but he was getting good at avoiding the *policía*. The call had energized him—a surge of adrenaline flowed through his exhausted body. He mingled with the crowd at the migrant center, undaunted by the smoky cooking fires, the crate-and-blanket shelters that families had created while they waited for their hearings scheduled for months in the future. He would spend a watchful night wrapped in his sweatshirt, propped against a chain-link fence. *Tomorrow, I'll be going home, where a fortune in gold and silver wait for me, buried in the estuary.* It was a treasure those around him could not even imagine. He could scarcely believe it himself.

41

MAYOR BUSTAMONTE IS IN A CELEBRATORY MOOD

"I called you here to celebrate our city's escape from potential drug violence and to look ahead to our future." Mayor Bustamonte was effusive and animated, raising a thick blue shot glass and toasting everyone with *tequila*.

In his mind, they'd all—unlike Choto—dodged several bullets. First, the precious metal had shown up unexpectedly in town and the public was in an uproar, convinced that someone had discovered a new silver deposit and the government was covering it up. Some people were ready to go out into the desert and dig up the countryside, looking for it. He admitted to himself that the sudden appearance of the telenovela stars, arranged by his father, had been a clever bit of sleight of hand. Their arrival had changed the subject and, together with his vague explanations of a liquor promotion and a telenovela production, dissipated the rising *plata* fever. Chuy had reported that Rodrigo's treasure, if it had ever existed, was gone.

Second, his law enforcement team had prevented a new cartel, the Mexicalis, from establishing itself in Puerto Peñasco. Several *sicarios* were killed, a few had been rounded up by the Marines, and others had presumably fled back to their scorpion holes. The loss of life was unfortunate, but these were murderous creatures. He was pleased that Chief Ramirez had handled the encounter with restraint.

Third, they'd sidestepped the jurisdictional issues with the drug task force and the federal authorities. As he and Ramirez expected, the Marine Special Forces took credit for the scene at Choto's hacienda after the chief requested that they "investigate." The military spent most of a day parading their fentanyl bust in front of the Sonoran press, granting interviews, and describing their heroic efforts to the television cameras that came from the state capital, Hermosillo. The *federales* didn't look closely at the crime scene, just as Chief Ramirez had predicted, accepting at face value what was presented to them. The real story of Choto's death at the Sandman's casa remained hidden. His government had weathered the storm. Drug enforcement had gotten their PR opportunity.

So the mayor had three excellent reasons to celebrate. To demonstrate his gratitude, he rented out the top-floor bar of El Pulpo Restaurant for a celebration lunch. The old restaurant was a local landmark. The three-story building sat on a pie-shaped lot created by the intersection of two angled streets near the *malecón*. The restaurant had remained in the same family since it opened. It began as a one-story café, and as more American tourists came, it expanded. Like many of the older buildings in the downtown area, the restaurant had been built over time with seemingly haphazard indecision as though the owners kept changing their minds during the construction.

The mayor invited Chief Ramirez, the Sandman, Speed and Carol Duncan, and Sandman's daughter Ericka. Chief Ramirez had reported to him that Chuy was out of town, retrieving Rodrigo. It was the first time the group of people had been together since the shooting, and there were hugs.

Except for Chuy, Hector, and Luis, they were the only ones who knew the truth of what had happened at Sandman's casa.

El Pulpo's third-story bar featured large windows that looked out over the town with an unobstructed view of the deep-blue water of the Sea of Cortez. Every surface of the square room—the walls, the tables, and the bar itself—was covered in various colors of Talavera tiles, with vivid blues, greens, yellows, and terra-cotta set in randomly patterned squares. Bright-striped red, white, and green serapes hung from the walls, artfully draped in curved shapes. The walls were also decorated with shiny cutout tin ornaments of stars, mirrors, and picture frames, the last of which displayed posters and photographs of famous Mexican actors and actresses. The restaurant's memorabilia represented the accumulation of many years.

The mayor had presented the owners with posters from the recent visit of the telenovela actors, signed by Gilberto Javier Romero, Barbara Miranda, and Sandra Perez, who added a fire-engine-red lipstick kiss to her signature. The bar was such a landmark that visitors seated for lunch or dinner on the first floor would take turns trudging up the two flights of narrow stairs just to record selfies in the bar. From the wear and tear of the constant stream of tourists and its proximity to the sea, El Pulpo Restaurant had developed the comfortable patina of a very old building.

The six diners sat at a large table in the middle of the room with the other tables and chairs stacked to the side. Waiters brought dishes on large oval aluminum trays from the first-floor kitchen up the narrow enclosed staircase, a task they navigated with graceful, practiced ease.

"*Bienvenido*. Welcome, and thank you all for coming," the

mayor said, toasting with *tequila*. He gave a wide grin. His tourist development plans for the town remained on track. "We are here because of the heroic actions of one of our expat *amigos*, Speed Duncan, who saved us from the horror of a mass murder." He raised his glass while Speed beamed. Speed looked as if was sitting on a cloud of contentment. "The citizens of Puerto Peñasco thank you." The mayor toasted Speed again and then presented him with a commemorative Thank You plaque.

"To Speed," said Sandman with his glass held upward as Speed soaked up the attention like a sea sponge.

"I'm so glad no one else got hurt," said Ericka. She sat next to Chief Ramirez, who put her arm around her, a gesture not unnoticed by the rest of the group.

"And to the one everyone calls the Sandman," the mayor said, turning toward the old cop. "We value your advice."

The mayor was laying it on thick, Sandman thought, but he accepted the Mexican formality. He raised his glass in recognition. "We're just trying to connect the dots, but we now believe that Rodrigo lied about the large cache of gold and silver. Whatever his reason, it was a dumb and dangerous move."

"From the chunks we found in Choto's study, it looks like Rodrigo may have created the story to sell Choto on the idea of a phony Arizona mine," said Ramirez. "Rodrigo told us he was trying to end his involvement in the cartels."

"It must have taken all the money he ever made to convert it into enough metal to fool Choto," said Sandman.

The mayor's effusive praise of Speed's actions disarming Choto triggered Sandman's memory of a recent conversation. A few days earlier, he'd heard a hard knock on his door. Before he could answer, Carol burst into the entry, holding up a bottle of single-malt Scotch.

"We need to talk." She breezed past him, wearing a sturdy Mexican beach dress, her blond ponytail swinging.

She strode directly to the den, and by the time Sandman followed, she was holding a cocktail glass to the light, checking his less-than-pristine bar with a suspicious eye. He made a face, so she poured a couple of fingers of eighteen-year-old Glenfiddich into two glasses.

"Carol, I'm sorry about the whole thing," he said, anticipating her anger as she handed him one of the glasses.

She plopped down in one of the overstuffed leather chairs, prompting him to take a seat. "Yeah well, he isn't," she said, sipping from the glass. "He's been walking on air ever since."

"It was not part of anyone's plan, but in the final analysis, he didn't hesitate."

"It's that word *final* that concerns me," Carol said, leaning forward. Her green eyes, wrinkled at the corners, stared at him.

He owed both Carol and Speed more than he could ever repay. After Gloria's death, he'd just shut down. Gloria had been his life, and her passing became one too many deaths for him to endure. He couldn't function. During that time, Carol and Speed had picked up the slack and taken care of everything—making arrangements for Gloria's funeral, consoling Ericka, and even cleaning his house.

"He hasn't told me about it in any detail," she said expectantly.

"Ramirez took his statement, but what I know is we—me, the chief, Ericka, the other two cops, Hector and Luis—were all kneeling, facing the front of that couch." He pointed at the sofa against the wall on her left. "Chuy, Choto, and two of his men were here," he said, indicating the floor nearby them. He skipped the part about Choto bursting into the *casa*.

"And they had guns pointed at you?"

"Yes."

"And where was Speed?"

"Speed was in the bathroom—you know, this one next to the kitchen," he said, nodding in the opposite direction. Her shoulders were tense, so he took a sip of the Scotch, hoping she would follow suit. "He had a laptop with him, monitoring the security cameras that he just installed."

"From the bathroom." She nodded. "So then what happened?"

"Carol, this sounds like an interrogation."

"Because it is—with refreshments," she said flatly. She took another sip.

"Okay. According to Ramirez, Speed said he sneaked up behind Choto and struck him with the laptop, knocking his gun to the floor. Chuy confirmed it. Chuy says when Choto turned around, he stepped between Speed and Choto. Chuy was holding a gun. Choto grabbed it, and he was shot. I reached for Choto's revolver, and it was all over."

"So my little mailman really did save the day."

Sandman nodded solemnly. "He did. He had our backs."

She leaned back in the seat.

"Carol—"

"What in the hell am I going to do with the two of you?" she said, interrupting him. Air hissed from her mouth. *Hell* was about as profane as her vocabulary ever got.

"Carol, I'm not looking for trouble."

"No, but it sure as hell seems to find you. Even at home. And Speed's right there.

"I'll always keep an eye on him."

"Do me a favor." She drained the rest of her glass and placed it on the bar table. "Just remember you have a daughter, and we—Speed and I—have kids and grandkids." They stood up, and she walked over to him and hugged him hard. "Don't make me limit your playdates," she'd said in his ear. "Keep the Scotch, just in case, but I don't want to repeat this conversation."

And then she'd left.

At the celebratory luncheon, Carol asked Chief Ramirez,

"Buried treasure and lost mines. Did you find a treasure map?"

"There was a map," Ramirez said. "But not from Rodrigo. Some enterprising street vendors on the *malecón* created one to sell to tourists. They claimed it was a joke."

The mayor interjected, "It caused a stir among the vendors. I brought the telenovela actors to town to distract the local citizens, replacing one shimmering image with another. It worked. Everyone forgot about the maps and the treasure."

"We confiscated them," Ramirez said. "If Rodrigo made his own, I assume it was in Choto's safe. We left that for the *federales*. No one has admitted to finding it."

"Where are Hector and Luis? And Chuy?" Ericka asked.

"They're working," said Ramirez. "We couldn't allow Chuy to come. He remains a confidential informant. Anyway, he said he is fetching Rodrigo from Juárez."

"How did Rodrigo wind up there?"

"He returned to Arizona after he snuck out of the house," Sandman said. "Border Patrol picked him up near Arivaca. He was running from Choto. He couldn't know that Choto was dead, and the cartel cell had dissolved."

"Chuy said after Rodrigo asked for asylum, ICE sent him to Juárez to wait for a court hearing," said Ramirez. "He had no money and called Chuy to bring him back."

"We're seeing that in a lot of asylum cases in Phoenix," Ericka said. "People, even US citizens who couldn't prove their citizenship right away, got sent to Mexico. What will you do with him when Chuy brings him back?"

"Nothing." Ramirez shrugged. "We have no interest in him anymore. His story has fallen apart. He's on his own. Chuy said he wants to help him. Of course, this is Chuy. He could be working some sort of angle."

"Maybe he'll give him a job at his *farmacia*," said Sandman. "There's some irony—Chuy owning a drugstore."

"We have our eye on Chuy," said the mayor. "But we do owe him. He, too, helped with this case."

Sandman wanted to say something but tipped back his glass of *tequila* instead.

42

A PRESENCE FROM CHUY'S PAST RETURNS

"There is someone to see you," said one of the Sotos' teenage daughters, who worked the counter sometimes at Chuy's *farmacia*.

Catalina Soto had knocked on the open door of Chuy Ruiz's office, where he was working to set up an Internet connection for his newly purchased drugstore. He'd settled into a routine at the *farmacia*, creating a small office in a back room of the store and taking over the bookkeeping. This was in addition to his regular duties of running his drug crew in the clubs, offering ecstasy, marijuana, and sometimes cocaine to tourists. With Choto gone, his product supply had become a bit erratic. Between the store and the drug business, it was a lot to keep straight, and he'd been unfocused since Choto's death.

Just as Chuy had promised, the Sotos ran the retail-customer side of the *farmacia* as before. Their two teenage daughters helped out. Nothing for them had changed very much. They came to work each day, happy that they no longer had to worry about the profitability of store. They didn't have to pay off the cartels—Chuy took care of all that.

They enjoyed the interactions with their longtime customers and the tourists who came into the store to fill their prescriptions from US doctors.

"Who is it?" he asked, distracted by his task.

"He didn't say," Catalina said, smoothing her dark-brown hair with a hand. She usually flirted with him, smiling at him in the sweet way she had, but this time she just sounded confused. "He said you don't know him but you used to work for someone he knew."

"I'll be right there," he said, frustrated by the login setup of the Wi-Fi he'd just installed.

Chuy didn't focus on who it could be. He'd met and worked with so many people in his short time as an entrepreneur. He'd sold time-shares to gringos until the resort learned that he was underaged and made him stop. He sold grass to tourists just because they asked and he knew people. He tried continuing with the time-shares through an older front man, and it was the older man who convinced him that it was easier and more profitable to drop the sales hassles with the suits at Montezuma Resort International and go full-time into recreational retail drug sales. The man had become his supplier, and Chuy's business had taken off. The man was El Jefe.

Chuy came to the front of the store, where a short, well-dressed Mexican man with close-cropped hair, light-tinted sunglasses, and a thin mustache was examining a box of cough medicine on one of the display shelves. Chuy also noticed a large man in a dark suit at the door of the shop, staring straight ahead impassively. The man was planted near the entrance like an Armani-clad desert palm tree. He didn't recognize the two, but the vibe he got from them was very familiar and unnerving.

"Can I help you?" he asked.

The man didn't look up from his intense inspection of the

medicine's package but said, "Hola, Chuy Ruiz. I am the one they call El Patrón."

"Wha…?" Chuy felt a sudden wave of coldness.

"You worked for my lieutenant, El Jefe." He turned to face Chuy. "You remember him, don't you?"

Chuy was frozen where he stood. "*Sí, sí*, of course," he stammered. "He spoke of you."

The man gave a slight nod. Everything about him was restrained, as though a greater gesture would be a needless waste of energy. "There was a temporary setback, but I have returned to restore things." His thin lips smiled below his pencil mustache, and he looked again at the cough medication.

Chuy couldn't make his mouth work. The name El Patrón was spoken in hushed whispers. Even the fearless El Jefe had been afraid of him. Chuy's former boss had always attacked, never surrendered.

"In the plaza, we've seen law enforcement conduct two cartel ambushes one after another. *Uno*, El Jefe's *grupo*. Now our rival Mexicali *putas*. Choto is dead, *muerto*. You survived both of them." The cold tone of his voice was no different from how it would sound if he was reading aloud the ingredient list of the cough medication. El Patrón looked up again from the package, his eyes piercing the tinted sunglasses and holding Chuy's gaze. "You must be one very lucky *chico*. *Con suerte, no*? Or a very clever one. *Muy listo*." He softly hissed the word.

"*Sí, suertudo*. I've been blessed."

"No, I believe clever." The empty coldness in the man's voice was chilling. "You own this store, *correcto*?" He waved his hands at the walls in a gesture that seemed more grandiose than it was.

Chuy sneaked a glance at the man at the door, who hadn't reacted or moved. The dark suit stared impassively straight ahead. "*Si*, it was a rare opportunity."

"And your other business opportunities—you continue to pursue them as well." It wasn't a question.

"*Sí*, as before."

El Patrón gave another nearly imperceptible nod. "I think you will be very useful to me, Chuy Ruiz. We'll talk again." He held up the box of cough medication. "I'll take this."

"*Sí*, of course," Chuy replied.

El Patrón turned toward the exit. The other man moved to open the door, and after looking out to the *camino*, he held it for El Patrón as the cartel boss left. It was like the door to an open freezer closing.

"Who was that man?" asked Catalina, who had been hiding around the corner of the tall display behind the counter.

"He was correct—I didn't know him," Chuy said quietly as he brushed past her, returning to his office.

"But he seemed to know you," she said loudly after him.

"You shouldn't listen to other people's conversations," he said, returning from the office. "I'm going to go out for a while" He looked at his cell phone. "I'll deal with the Wi-Fi later."

Outside, he texted the emergency signal to meet with Chief Ramirez, got in his new truck, and checking to see if he was followed, rushed off to their rendezvous place by the beach. Waiting for Chief Ramirez to roll up in her police SUV, he paced the sand anxiously back and forth at the site of the abandoned hotel construction. After several minutes, she popped out of the cab, smiling, and rearranged her cowboy hat.

"Hola, Chuy. We aren't seeing enough of each other? What's the emergency?"

"Th-Th-the store. El Patrón came in. He just walked in. He said he's back."

"That's good news."

"How can that be good news? He knows who I am."

"Of course he knows who you are. You were one of El Jefe's *chicos*."

Chuy didn't hide his panic.

"Chuy, think about it. First, it means your cover isn't blown. He might be wary, but he doesn't believe you were involved in taking out El Jefe or Choto. If he did, you would have disappeared by now."

Chuy was shocked by the thought.

"Second, he probably trusts you to some degree. Otherwise, he wouldn't risk meeting you in person."

Chuy acknowledged that much.

"He must have plans for you," Ramirez said.

"He said that he would come again."

"This puts you right in the middle of whatever is coming."

She let that hang in the air. Ramirez had a way of giving him uncomfortable truths that he didn't want to hear. He'd wanted a way out—to be legitimate. Now she was confirming his doubts that he would be able to do it. El Patrón's visit to his *farmacia* was in-his-face evidence of that. It had begun to sink in. He had to play the hand he'd been dealt, not the one he wanted to have. Reinventing himself would mean witness protection. He was sure the Mexican government wasn't going to grant him that. And he didn't think he was made for it anyway.

"You'll have more value to us as an informant. We are all indebted to you for saving us from Choto. Puerto Peñasco will owe you, as well, for this important work."

Chuy noted the overt flattery, but it had a positive effect on his mood anyway. He let it wash over him like a comfortable warm bath. On the way to the meeting, he'd begun thinking about what El Patrón might want from him— money laundering through the *farmacia* receipts for sure, but he wondered if El Patrón would use the *farmacia's* legitimate drug distribution as a cover to move illegal drugs like heroin and fentanyl. He really didn't want it to go that way.

He noticed Ramirez staring at him. "It will be difficult working with him, I know," she said. "But the truth is, you may not have another choice."

43

THE POST-PASQUA WING DING

By the time JD and Will arrived at Doc Savage's house, the party was already in motion. The sun hung brightly in the west over the eaves of the home. It was their first invite to the annual Post-Pasqua Wing Ding that Doc and his wife, Suzanne, had begun a couple of decades before. Over time, it had transformed from a small gathering into an open, multiethnic party with his Tohono O'odham neighbors bringing food, Hispanic friends arriving with traditional Sonoran dishes, and students and staff from the university coming for the beer and discussions. Musicians of every genre began showing up, their styles ranging from classical guitar to bluegrass, mariachi, and traditional native music.

The Post-Pasqua Wing Ding had a life of its own. Even after Suzanne's death, Doc had said it had to go on. A part of her lived on through the tradition. Instead of Suzanne doing all the arranging, volunteers showed up a couple of days in advance to string lights in the large ramada north of the house, set up tables and chairs in the surrounding desert, and lay in wood for the *chimineas* and grills to ward off the nighttime chill and barbecue the meat.

Will looked for a parking spot among the pickup trucks

and cars parked along the long dirt road. At the front of the house, the driveway became a horseshoe turn that doubled back to the access road after it swept past the brick-lined entrance. Wisps of gray mesquite smoke rose upward above the land's mature vegetation, which had grown high enough to obscure the house from the access road. The surrounding grounds were thick with prickly pear cactus still swollen from earlier rains, stickery strands of budding ocotillo, palo verde trees with early yellow blossoms, mesquite ready to push out their feathery leaves, barrel cactus, and brittle bush among the rocks and hardpan desert.

As they passed the driveway's curve, JD saw the Sand Papagos' light-green van, topped with its large-horned speaker, parked near the walkway. The peaked-roof Arizona ranch house was surrounded by an eight-foot veranda. Knots of people, most in casual dress, stood around the outside of the house, but JD spotted a couple of mariachis in broad ornate sombreros and *traje de charro* outlined with shiny steel-headed studs. The conversation level in the yard, audible from inside the car, had reached a sociable din. The sweet smell of mesquite smoke entered the car.

Will found a place next to an armless saguaro cactus about twenty feet high. JD retrieved the covered pan of green corn tamales they'd wedged between dishcloths in the back seat of Will's Ford Escape. She and Will had spent the previous evening preparing her family's recipe—working the masa, mixing the filling, and wrapping the corn husks to create the delicious little masterpieces they now carried into Doc's house. They walked to the gate, dodged a line of people drinking beer in plastic cups who were standing along the brick walkway, and entered through the front door.

Inside the house, JD saw a large long-haired Native American man sitting in a chair near a fireplace in the far corner of the main room, playing classical guitar. People holding drinks milled around or sat on the sofa and chairs and listened raptly. JD nodded toward two city council members speaking quietly in a corner. She stopped to listen to the musician, transfixed. The guitarist's braided hair draped behind his shoulders and his hands danced along the guitar frets, his eyes shut in concentration. It was a virtuoso concert happening in the ranch house's great room.

The warm tamales reminded JD to keep moving, though she regretted leaving the sonorous music behind. With Will trailing her, she moved toward the small kitchen on the right. A short, round Hispanic woman checking the oven motioned for them to continue through the kitchen to the screened-in veranda room to a long table covered in bright oilcloth. The fiesta table was full of clay casserole dishes, pans of spicy stews, baskets of tortillas, and bread. A Hispanic man in a faded denim shirt walked through the door from the outside, carrying a large bowl of colorful fruit salad. She recognized him as Chef Jerome, the owner of one of the top restaurants in Tucson.

"It's a simple salad," he said. "Just six ingredients, but they go together nicely." It looked delicious as he placed it on a table full of salads.

"I had to use frozen corn for the tamales," JD said apologetically, "but they came out pretty well."

"Here, put it here." A gray-haired *abuela* pointed to an open spot she'd cleared near the center of the table. "Mmm, *muy sabrosa*," she said after inhaling.

JD and Will carefully placed the large pan of tamales as directed.

"Gracias. *Donde esta* Doc?" asked JD.

"He's out at the truck grill," the *abuela* said, nodding toward the screen door where Chef Jerome had entered. JD and Will went outside through the door to the north end of the property. They saw Doc standing behind a '54 Chevy pickup painted in rust-colored primer. It looked like it might be capable of running. He was tending a large smoky barbecue grill perched the length of the truck's tailgate. The sweet smell of beef and mesquite rose from the sizzling meat. Doc's inflated cast was wrapped over a pair of Levi's. He hobbled a bit pushing around the strips of beef.

"Hola." Doc moved some pieces of carne asada around the grill with a pair of barbecue tongs. He grabbed a bottle of Negra Modelo, shook it with his thumb on the top, and then shot the stream of beer over the beef. "It's been marinating overnight in all kinds of stuff, but I think the beer gives it a christening," he said, still facing the grill. "Fitting for the time of year."

"*This* is a party," said JD.

"Thanks for inviting us," Will added.

"How's the ear, Van Gogh?" asked Doc.

"Still a bit tender, but it's healing," said Will.

"I know you've been doing this for a while, but how did all this get started?" JD asked.

"It was Suzanne's idea a few years after we moved out here near the reservation. We attended a Yaqui Easter ceremony at *Pasqua*. It's a very moving Passion Play that the Yaquis have been performing for hundreds of years. The entire village has a role."

"I've heard of it, but I've never had the chance to see one."

"They welcome visitors, but you can't record the performance or take notes. The Yaquis are relatively new to Tucson, if like me, you consider the 1800s 'new.' But they've lived in Sonora for centuries. The Mexican army killed many Yaquis in a program of government genocide, and some of the rest fled north, where they were safer. Once here, they built several small villages in the Tucson area and revived a some of their traditions, including the *Pasqua* they learned from the Jesuits in the early seventeenth century."

JD smiled. Doc was enjoying the day and the audience.

"The play itself is very structured with different groups in the village all taking part, but the outcome isn't," he continued. "To many Yaquis, the ceremony is a serious struggle between good and evil. The preparations take weeks, and the play itself can last days. It's always exhausting for the participants. After we were invited to see one, Suzanne decided that the villagers needed a break—to celebrate the celebration. So we invited a few Yaquis we knew to the house. Invited some *pascolas*—ceremonial hosts—first. You can't have a fiesta without *pascolas* attending—the hosts are called *pakolam* in Yaqui. And once you invite them, everyone thinks they're invited, too, so more Yaqui came. We asked our O'odham neighbors out here of course. Musicians wanted to play. You saw Conrad Elkins, the Yaqui classical guitarist. He happens to be home from a major tour. Mariachi Corazon is around here someplace." He waved the barbecue tongs like a pointer.

"When Suzanne died, I thought the whole thing might end. But my neighbors wouldn't hear of it. Now friends do most of the preparation and setup. I just provide the beer, the house, and the meat." Using the tongs, Doc moved the carne asada from the grill onto a cutting board, where it continued to sizzle. He then picked up a large knife and fork and began cutting the flat slabs of meat into small strips and smaller bite-sized pieces. "You know why we eat this? The Jesuit missionary Kino brought cattle here a little before 1700. He also introduced winter wheat, a new food crop, to the area. And now we have flour tortillas. Beef burritos."

He signaled a young O'odham boy, who was waiting nearby, to take the large platter of carne asada inside. "Don't drop it!" he called out after the boy, who walked the plate carefully toward the food area. "And if you do, don't tell anyone."

The boy laughed over his shoulder as he balanced the platter of meat.

"You must be feeling pretty good," JD said.

"Gettin' there. I can stand, and I can walk without a crutch until the leg gets tired. Should be back on the trail soon." He threw another slab of beef on the grill.

Frankie and Tim Antone pulled a cart of full of amplifiers and electronic cables past them.

"Frankie." JD ran up to hug him.

Will and Tim shook hands. "Love the battle scar," Tim said to Will. "I did a good job on the patch."

"When are you guys playing?"

"As soon as we get hooked up," Tim answered. "Hey, Buzzard Man, did you pay your electric bill this month?"

"Marines," Doc scoffed.

"We just finished the new album," Tim said. "We'll be playing some of the new tunes for the party. There's some rap, Indian Country style, in the set."

Doc rolled his eyes.

"Doc is upset because he had to upgrade this old shack for the parties," said Frankie. "We kept blowing out his ancient circuits every time we played. By *ancient*, I mean Thomas Edison installed the wiring."

"Power out here at the edge of the rez is problematic. It took forever to get it done," Doc said.

"We're grateful you used your white privilege for the good of the community," Frankie said, smirking.

The *abuelas* came out of the door of the screened in porch to announce that the food table was ready. A line of people at the screen door formed almost immediately. A giant stack of paper plates sat on a table before the large food table, and guests passed them around to each other while they waited to fill them. The table was loaded end to end with pans and dishes of enchiladas, carne asada, fry bread, beans, rice, salads, desserts, baskets of corn and flour tortillas and a dozen or more bottles of *tequila*, iced tea, and lemonade on a side table. Mariachi Corazon, trumpets, violins, and guitars played out on the front veranda while people of every size, shape, and age filled their plates and moved through the line.

And people kept arriving. JD couldn't count them all. She and Will took seats outside at one of the folding tables in the front yard as the mariachis played "La Bikina." Several people danced in the open dirt road among the parked cars. As dusk came, strings of overhead lights, added for the special day, illuminated the yard. Conversation and laughter punctuated the music.

When the mariachis finished, the six members of the Sand Papago flipped on the amps and filled the air with two-step *waila,* and, as Tim had promised, pushed the boundary with some ancient O'odham-poetry-inspired lyrics. Will and JD agreed, stomachs full, that they would never forget the experience.

After midnight, the crowd thinned a bit and a couple of bluegrass musicians were lazily picking old tunes on the front porch when Doc appeared at their table with his aluminum crutch.

"Saw your story on the dangers of old mines shafts," he said to JD. "Good piece. That had to do with those rumors of silver turning up in Mexico, didn't it? I saw that Rocky Point story too."

"It got my interest. It turned out there wasn't much to the Puerto Peñasco silver story. Just a few isolated pieces of silver turned up. But it got everyone excited."

"It's as I told you. Except for a few years in Tombstone, people here probably made more money selling bogus treasure maps to rubes and marks than they ever did actually mining silver."

44

RODRIGO'S TREASURE

"*P endejo*, hold the light steady," Rodrigo ordered.

The night was pitch-black with not even a sliver of a moon. The two men had been standing in ankle-deep mud for hours, and Chuy was bored. His feet were cold and wet, and his white Nike's were a mess. The two flashlights were heavy, and he was drawing little patterns on the ground with the beams to amuse himself.

"Are you loco?" Rodrigo hissed. "Trying to let everyone know we're here?"

Rodrigo was like a machine. He kept shoveling, digging a meter-deep hole in the wet, sandy loam. This was the third estuary site they'd visited that night, looking for the spot where Rodrigo buried his treasure. He could see the mud on Rodrigo's face in the dim illumination of the flashlights. They'd taken separate vehicles to the highway, and Chuy had met him at dusk.

"We've been working for hours," Chuy said, climbing up from the hole, although he wasn't doing the digging.

Rodrigo had kept a low profile since Chuy picked him up from Juárez, avoiding being seen in daylight or darkness. Chuy looked at him, trying to gauge how much Rodrigo might have figured out. The trip from Ciudad Juárez had been like a pressure relief valve for Rodrigo. He talked and talked. He apologized over and over for leaving Chuy's truck in Sasabe, where it had vanished by the time anyone knew it was there. Chuy let him talk, hoping that Rodrigo would tell him where the treasure was.

Chuy hadn't told him that Choto was dead and the cartel cell had collapsed. He did tell Rodrigo the cops weren't looking for him anymore, which didn't seem to affect him. Chuy's mind was on his club business. With the spring-break period in Rocky Point near its end, college kids from California, New Mexico, and Arizona were in town with money to spend, looking for ways to forget about school. There was work to be done with a more immediate financial payoff than driving up and down the Caborca highway in the dark, looking for tire marks on the road, would offer. Rodrigo had said the marks pointed to where he turned off the highway, dug a hole, and put who-knew-what into the ground.

"You get half, remember?" Rodrigo grunted. "But I'm doing all the work."

"Half of nothing is still nothing. You sure this is it?"

"The rain last month changed the way the ground looks. It's here."

Chuy heard doubt creeping into Rodrigo's voice. But his friend kept digging. He wasn't convinced anymore. Despite Rodrigo's stories, he hadn't seen any treasure except for a couple of pieces of melted silver.

"I don't mean this spot," Chuy said. "You were alone on the mountain a long time. You were captured by *sicarios* and *la migra*. I know what it's like to be a prisoner. The stress, it can be overwhelming. Are you sure what you saw—"

"You saw it! I've told you the story over and over. *Eres un marro*, a cheap bastard. You even shortchanged me on the *plata's* value." He shoved the spade into the ground like a spear.

Chuy ignored the slight. He figured he'd kept up his side of the bargain. "You showed me a few chunks of *plata* in a little pouch. I never saw any great pile of gold and silver."

"You think I'm making the whole thing up. *Son unas mamadas!* Fuck off, Chuy! You don't want to help? Leave."

"I didn't say I wouldn't help. Who is it that has helped you ever since you came back to town, even after you stole my truck? Who drove you back from Ciudad Juárez? The entire way, all you could talk about was the silver and gold. I understand your dreams of wealth. *Claro*. But could you… I mean, on the mountain, without company, long days alone, could you have just imagined it?"

"Why do you think Choto wants to grab me? He knows it's real."

"He snatched you because you left your post in Arizona. You ran away from the job. He couldn't let you get away with that. That's not how the cartels operate."

"He questioned me about the treasure. He believed me. It's the only reason I'm still alive.

"He told me," Chuy said, unconvinced. "You know he's loco. Did he see it?"

"No. I told you. I buried it before his men caught me."

"So the only one who saw the lost treasure—all these canvas bolsas of *plata* and *oro*—is you."

"Go ask Choto. He knows. I changed some of the *plata* at a *cambio* booth in Caborca. It was one of Choto's places. That's how they caught me."

"A few hundred *pesos*. You told me. We've looked for that buried treasure every night for days. You say it's right here. Where? You went back to Arizona, you couldn't find it, and now you can't find the rest you say you buried here. Somewhere in this area, you say. Why can't we find it?" Chuy was impatient. He was convinced this wasn't leading anywhere. *Time is money.*

"It's here. I know it. I just have find the right spot from the road. But you don't believe me," Rodrigo said incredulously.

"I believe that you believe it."

Rodrigo looked like he had been punched in the gut. "Ask Choto. He knows."

Chuy let that hang in the air for a long moment. "I didn't tell you before, but Choto is dead."

Rodrigo staggered and propped himself on his shovel. "What?"

"You escaped from the Sandman's casa, the old cop's house, in the rain."

"*Sí.* I told you that." He clung tight to the handle of the *pala* stuck in the soil.

"We—Choto and some of his men—were staking out the place. When it got dark, I saw you leave down the stairway. The others didn't see you, and I didn't say anything. That's when you stole my truck."

"You saw me. You were outside the house?" In Chuy's flashlight, his face registered shock. "You didn't tell me that."

"Choto picked me up after I left you at Sandman's house. He wanted you back. He was going to grab you there. He forced us to attack a blond woman who came to the house. We assaulted her when she tried to leave. When we pushed her inside, he realized you were gone. There was a scuffle, and he was killed."

"At the house? Who killed him? I bet it was that old cop. He has a bad look. But why didn't you tell me before?"

"I can't talk about it. They have sworn me to secrecy. I've told you more than I should."

"Who are *they*? The *policía*?"

"Everyone. Choto's body was found later at his hacienda. How do you think that happened?"

"I've been looking over my shoulder ever since I came back for someone who was already dead."

"Rodrigo, you still need to be careful. There are other things going on." Chuy was thinking of his unsettling encounter with El Patron. "We need to stop this. I've got other places that I need to be."

"Go ahead, leave," Rodrigo spat. He steadied himself and massaged his arms. "I'm going to find it whether you help me or not. Don't worry. You'll get your cut."

"I have to go," Chuy said. "Call me later to tell me you're okay."

He compared Rodrigo's journey with his own. They'd both passed through the crucible of hell and had been caught up in the cartels. He, like Rodrigo, had been captured by the cartel and had become the focus of the intense *policía* interest. And like Rodrigo, he got entangled in the machinery of the border and US Homeland Security. Chuy knew that he'd survived because he had amigos *y conexiones politicas*. But unlike Rodrigo, he'd had something to offer: information, something the powerful valued.

Chuy walked the grassy stretch of the estuary to his truck, pointing his flashlight toward the ground and wiping his muddy Nikes on the sawgrass along the way. It was getting late, and he still had work to do. At the truck's door, he turned back to look at the dim light of the single flashlight he'd left behind for Rodrigo a hundred meters off the road. He could make out the silhouette of his friend, still striving, still turning sand. He envied him in a way. Rather than bargaining with *los poderosos*, Rodrigo managed to survive on faith. He was sure of what he knew, even if he couldn't prove it to others and no one believed him. That sureness sustained him as he dug in the sand, alone in the feeble light of a single flashlight. More than gold and silver, maybe that was Rodrigo's treasure.

AUTHOR'S NOTE

RODRIGO'S TREASURE is a work of fiction, but it's based on historical fact. As Will Teagarden found, the **Arizona Mine Inspector's Office** estimates there are one hundred thousand abandoned mines in Arizona. According to the office, most were dug by "…small-time prospector(s) who worked a site for a few weeks or months until the mine played-out or the financial backing ran-out. Then they moved on, leaving unprotected hazards for later generations to find."

Nothing in RODRIGO'S TREASURE endorses entering abandoned mines and adits—quite the opposite. Arizonans from Tombstone to Gleeson have died, disappeared, or been injured in accidental falls from the ill-advised exploration of unsecured mines.

In Arizona, many abandoned mines are on public property overseen by the Bureau of Land Management, national forests, or inside National Parks. Others are within the boundaries of private property. Efforts by the state to identify and safeguard them have been hit or miss, so the locations of most old mines aren't known.

Exploring Arizona's amazing places is a big part of why many of us live here. But as Professor Creighton Savage said, if you're looking for gold or silver—the safest bet is to try a jewelry store.

A PREVIEW OF SPECIAL DELIVERY

The Margaret Mayfield Memorial Book Club in the retirement community of Green Valley, Arizona helps members of other book clubs around the country—buying cheap prescription drugs for those with chronic illnesses across the border in Nogales, Sonora.

At a checkpoint north of the border, US Border Patrol busts the club president and her husband, confiscating their drugs. It's illegal to import prescription drugs for anyone other than yourself.

Trying a different tack, Amanda and Jerry Tuttle vacation in Rocky Point, Mexico, where they are funneled to a local dealer and budding drugstore magnate Chuy Ruiz. Chuy can get them anything they need and more than they want.

Who knew book clubbing could be dangerous?

IN THE NEXT SONORAN BORDERLANDS MYSTERY:
SPECIAL DELIVERY

Rain was always welcome in the desert. The gathering monsoon clouds to the south hadn't yet chased the afternoon sun beaming down on Amanda and Jerry Tuttle. The couple had waited in a long line of people at the Dennis DeConcini port of entry in Nogales after a leisurely lunch at a Sonoran restaurant.

The second-floor restaurant was a local landmark that had been built into the side of a hill. Jerry had had his usual combination plate, and Amanda had enjoyed a freshly prepared red snapper with a salad and fresh guacamole. Her iced tea and his Bohemia cerveza hit the spot. All served by impeccably dressed waiters who fussed over them like they were the First Couple of Mexico.

Before joining the line, they had picked up their medical prescriptions and a few small curios in town. At the counter inside the customs house, an agent had briefly checked their purchases and waved them through to the US side and their parked SUV. Jerry's diabetes-swollen feet bothered him by the time they reached their vehicle, but otherwise, they were great spirits for the drive back home to Green Valley.

Dark afternoon clouds roiled in the south, preparing to

follow them across the border for a potential thunderstorm. Amanda drove north on Interstate 19 past Rio Rico and then past the ruins of the Tumacacori Mission east of the freeway. By the time they reached the artist colony of Tubac, Jerry had begun nodding off in his passenger seat, long strands of his thinning gray hair askew on the headrest. He was snoring by the time she slowed for the line of vehicles moving toward the US Border Patrol checkpoint just north of the former Spanish presidio.

The checkpoint, about twenty-five miles north of the border, had been established as a temporary inland inspection station years ago. Jerry had opined that like a lot of government, once it had been created, it would never go away. The traffic stop was part of a routine that everyone coming north on the freeway endured.

Vehicles inched slowly in lines that passed under a large white fabric canopy straddling the northbound freeway lanes. A long gray US Border Patrol trailer sat along the east side of the road. Jerry was roused from sleep by the start-and stop motion of their vehicle.

In and out of the canopy's shade, a drug-sniffing dog and its handler weaved among the lines of cars and trucks. The leashed Malinois nosed beneath the undercarriage and wheel wells of the car in front of them and then quickly moved on to the next vehicle. The dog sniffed around their SUV briefly before gamboling to an area between two vehicles.

One by one, the vehicles approached a green-uniformed agent standing to the side of the line who checked the occupants briefly and then motioned for the vehicle to move on. A Border Patrol van and several cars were parked next to the gray wooden trailer.

As she had many times before, Amanda lowered the tinted driver's window when she reached the agent. Road noise rushed into the cabin from the southbound traffic on the other side of the divided highway.

A young man with short hair looked into the SUV. "Where'd you come from?" the agent asked calmly. The question punctured the pleasant, day-trip bubble that had surrounded them.

"Uh, we were in Nogales," Amanda said.

"Did you cross the border? Buy anything?" the agent asked. His face was impassive—she couldn't read it.

"We had lunch," Jerry said, now roused from the passenger side. "And I picked up my prescriptions," he held up a white paper bag. "I declared it at the port of entry."

Amanda felt the hot moist monsoon air entering through the open window. "That's right. They checked."

She saw the agent motion with his arm above the roof line, signaling to some other BP agents who sat in the shade of the canopy near the trailers. "Ma'am, I'm going to ask you to pull over to the side there," he said, pointing to an open parking area in the sun.

Flustered, Amanda said, "Well go ahead."

"What?"

"If you're going to ask, then just ask." She waited for the agent to say something.

"Pull over to that parking area, please," the agent said more forcefully.

She raised the window and, after checking the other lanes, pulled the SUV to the side.

"Good one, babe," said Jerry.

"Huh, what?" Her hands trembled. She gripped the steering wheel tighter and stared at her manicured nails. Then she and Jerry waited. *Jerry must think I was mocking the agent.*

She heard tapping on the window and lowered it again.

"Please step out of the vehicle," said a short, Latina woman with black hair pulled into a bun. Her latex-gloved hands rested on the utility belt at the waist of her uniform. Two male agents, also wearing gloves, stood behind her.

"Bring your purse and any documents when you exit." She stepped back to let Amanda open the door.

Amanda saw that the dash's digital thermometer registered 105 F degrees. *F degrees is right*, she thought. She turned toward Jerry—his face screwed up in anger. He pawed through the glove box for the vehicle registration and insurance card. After grabbing an envelope with the documents, he opened his door. The SUV's warning indicator chirped that the door was ajar.

"Ma'am, please turn the vehicle off," said the female BP agent. Amanda killed the engine and the chirping stopped. She opened her door.

"I need the two of you to stand in front of that trailer over there, next to the sign." The agent pointed at a round sign mounted on the side of the gray, wood-paneled trailer about twenty feet from where Amanda parked. The sign featured a gold outlined map of the United States on a black background with the words U.S. BORDER PATROL in bold letters.

"We're American citizens. You can't just search our car," Jerry growled.

"Sir, under Eight USC Thirteen, Fifty-Seven, we are permitted to conduct vehicle searches without a warrant within a reasonable distance from the border." The agent curtly rattled off the statute.

"That's not right," Jerry protested, but he moved away from the SUV.

"Sir, leave the white bag inside the vehicle."

Amanda thought Jerry might say something back to the agent as he retreated back to the SUV with the bag, but he stayed silent. She noted that they were told to go stand in the direct afternoon sun.

The female agent opened the driver's side door, reached under the dash, and popped the hood in front. The hatch in back began to rise. The two male agents looked through the wrapped curio package in the back of the SUV. The female agent walked to the front of the SUV and checked the engine compartment.

Amanda shuddered as fear gripped her chest. Jerry's face was red, his lips pursed. He had put his hand up as a visor to shield his eyes from the sun. She knew he was trying to tamp down his anger—so was she.

"Agent Hernandez, got something," said one of the agents.

"Bring it here," said the female agent. She collected a half unwrapped brown paper package from him. "Keep looking," she said to the other agent.

By that time, she had looked through the small white bag of prescription meds that Jerry left on the passenger seat. Amanda gulped air in short bursts, trying not to show Jerry or the agents how anxious she was.

The other agent lifted the panel that covered the spare tire. He unscrewed the tire jack and pulled the spare out of the car. With his gloved hands, he felt along the rim for any sign of more drugs. Finding nothing, he rolled the tire a few feet and let it flop to the pavement like a unstable spinning top. He tapped up inside the wheel wells, searching for a false compartment.

Amanda perspired heavily in the heat. She knew that continuing the search was a waste of time—there wasn't anything else to be found. She saw Jerry moving from one foot to the other to keep the circulation in his feet. *Poor Jerry. He was fuming.*

"Remove the door panels," said Agent Hernandez.

Amanda's heart sank. She took a tissue from her purse and wiped the sweat from her neck and forehead. The other agents retrieved a power drill and a jimmy bar from a metal table on wheels nearby. They opened all four doors and began removing the retaining clips from the door panels.

"Could I get some water?" Jerry wheezed, pointing to a

water bottle on the ground that agents had removed from the side door.

"Sure," said Agent Hernandez. "Riley would you bring them that water? Also some stools."

Agent Riley picked up the water bottle and handed it to Jerry. Then he retrieved two short metal-shop stools from the area next to the trailer. Jerry nodded to him. Amanda was glad he could sit down.

They hunkered on the low stools, and Amanda grabbed Jerry's hand. "Are you okay?" she asked.

Jerry nodded, but said, "not so well" under his breath.

He wasn't going to give the Border Patrol the satisfaction of admitting his distress. Jerry the rebel. She knew he needed those meds.

Agent Hernandez approached, standing over them, feet apart, like a boxer. Amanda thought, *what? We might leap up from the stools and attack her?*

"I'd like to see your IDs, please," Hernandez said.

A little late to start down the politeness path. Amanda saw Jerry hunched forward, his breathing was labored beneath his loose yellow oxford shirt. She fumbled in her purse for her driver's license with the enhanced star that allowed her to cross the border. Agent Hernandez looked at her ID, returned it to her, and looked down into the purse. "Could you hold it open wider, please?"

Amanda stared up at her from the stool, the sun shining in her eyes above the agent's shoulder. "We were in Nogales. The customs people checked us at the port of entry," she said.

"Yes, ma'am," said Agent Hernandez. Still holding the packaged meds in one hand, she pushed aside the contents of Amanda's purse with her other gloved hand. More tissues, two kinds of lipstick, blush, mascara, a comb, reading glasses, and some receipts.

"Okay, now you, sir," Agent Hernandez said, sidestepping to Jerry.

Amanda looked over her shoulder at Jerry. His elbows were on his knees, pants cuffs inches above his ankles. Poor Jerry. He refused to wear shorts even during the summer months. He didn't like the way the blue veins in his legs and ankles looked.

He held his ID toward her. Agent Hernandez looked it over carefully and returned it. "Do you have a prescription for these?" she asked, holding the white bag in Jerry's face.

"Yes," he muttered. Amanda saw him try to rebalance himself on the stool. There was a grit in his voice. "I have type-2 diabetes and I need these medications to live."

The agent tucked the white bag under her arm and pulled a small cardboard box from the brown paper package. "What about these, sir? Is your name Jonathan Pritchard?"

"I was picking those up for a friend who couldn't come with us today,"Jerry rasped.

Agent Hernandez picked another box from inside the package wrapping, held it up to look at the writing on it.

"Is Susan Albright another friend?"

"We were just picking up some extra prescriptions," Amanda said, butting into the exchange.

"This drug isn't for diabetes. It says it's to treat psoriasis. Do you have psoriasis, sir?" Hernandez asked, ignoring Amanda.

"We were trying to be helpful," said Jerry, who struggled to keep his balance leaning over the tiny stool. Sweat dripped from his temples to the ground.

"Okay. You are permitted to bring FDA-approved prescription medications back into the United States for your personal use, but only a limited supply."

Jerry nodded, taking another swig from the water bottle, and looked away from her.

"Because the efficacy and purity of these drugs cannot be guaranteed, we recommend that you only obtain medicines from legal sources in the US. Since your ID says that you reside in Green Valley, I assume you probably know this."

Neither Amanda nor Jerry said anything.

"Okay," said Agent Hernandez. "I'm going to return the meds for which you, Mr. Tuttle, have a prescription, but I'm seizing the rest. They're not under your name, and you did not declare them at the border. They're considered contraband." After examining all the contents, she handed him the white bag. "And if the agents find anything hidden in the vehicle, we will have another conversation."

She walked toward the gray trailer with the brown bag and disappeared inside, presumably to report her discovery, Amanda thought.

She helped Jerry walk over to the shade to wait for Border Patrol to return their vehicle to them. Watching the agents work on the SUV, they said very little to each other, afraid that their conversation might be overheard and invite more intrusive questions. The agents spent another forty-five minutes looking through the SUV before replacing the air filter, spare tire and door panels.

Concerned for her husband, she watched him for any signs of an episode.

"I'll be all right," he said. "I just need to drink some more water."

The Nogales medical shopping trip was an activity of the Margaret Mayfield Memorial Book Club, a Green Valley organization, founded several years prior to the pandemic by its namesake. Prior to Margaret's death, Amanda had talked to her about helping a book club in Ohio.

After one of their regular meetings at the Green Valley rec center, Amanda casually mentioned to Margaret that Jerry had had problems getting his diabetes drugs. She had told Margaret about their Nogales connection. Amanda's book club friends back home in Columbus had learned about it.

The spiraling price of insulin and other diabetes medications had hurt its club members as well.

Amanda knew the problems of prescription drug prices. She and Jerry had ventured south to Nogales, Sonora to buy Jerry's type-2 diabetes medicine where it was much cheaper. He was on two different ones, a cheap generic and a second expensive one, that he took by injection. It hadn't been easy to control his blood sugar level, and his doctor was considering putting him on a third drug that cost even more.

"Jerry and I make the trip every month," she had told Margaret. "It would be easy to fill a couple more scripts while we're down there. We have a good relationship with the *farmacia*, so it wouldn't be a problem."

"Are you sure?" she remembered Margaret asking. Her mentor had liked the idea, but she had warned Amanda and Jerry that they might be signing up for a greater commitment than they realized.

"It'll be fine," Amanda had told her. "The Columbus folks can spring for a yummy lunch while we're on the Mexican side." On their first trip, they'd collected a couple of doctors' prescriptions from the club, just like a regular drug store, and presented them all to their Mexican *farmacia*.

The Mexican druggist was happy to fill them. She was the first to warn them that carrying prescription drugs for others through the DeConcini border crossing was illegal under US law. "I can fill them for you, but if customs finds them, they will confiscate them."

"Rosa, you won't get in any trouble?" Amanda asked.

"*No problema por mi*," the young woman said with a shrug. "But if you choose not to declare the meds, and they find them, CBP will take these meant for others and maybe yours," she said, pointing at the package on her counter.

They stood in the long lines of Mexicans to cross the border to shop on the Arizona side, along with US medical tourists reentering from appointments. Foot traffic was usually brisk at the border crossing.

Jerry had always declared his own prescriptions at customs. They'd disguised the few other medications inside Amanda's purse in a side pocket or sometimes had mixed them in with some other purchases in a shopping bolsa. They dressed as tourists which was what they were. They looked like Ohio.

Sometimes, after she'd threaded the long line that snaked along the main street to enter the customs house, an agent asked her to open her purse. Other times, she and Jerry bought a few small items at one of the remaining curio stalls and requested that the clerk wrap them tightly in newspapers. After a nice lunch, they'd rewrap the curios with the prescription meds tucked inside.

Their cover story was that if the other medications were discovered, they would claim the extra doses were for Jerry, and they'd simply forgot to declare them. And if there were too many, well, we're sorry—an innocent mistake. We've just moved here from Columbus, and we didn't know the rules. Plead ignorance. It would work out just fine.

And for months, it had been fine. The rhythm of their monthly drives south to the border became a smooth routine. They were careful to always park on the American side and walk into Mexico.

Once, an agent had asked them to unwrap one of the purchases, and an anxious Amanda thought she would pass out. Then Jerry feigned dizziness and pleaded physical disability due to his diabetes. They had stood in the line a long time, he told the agents, his feet were swollen, showing them his engorged ankles. The agents had told them to move on.

This time, the roadside checkpoint was different. This time, they'd been discovered and the drugs confiscated.

"We're not doing anything wrong, are we Jerry?" she

asked, arranging herself in the driver's seat after agents returned their SUV.

"If helping people get the medications they need to stay alive is wrong, then I guess we're doing something wrong."

"It feels strange to be hiding things from the authorities."

"The rules are unfair. They're skewed toward drug companies and profits. People are hurting."

"Jerry, I know the reasons. I came up with some of them," she said, trying to calm herself. "It's unsettling. I wish I felt more like a rebel and less like a criminal."

"I feel like a pirate," Jerry said with a smirk. "I even have the walk goin' on." He tapped a swollen leg. "In the states, we pay for everybody else's medicine. The rest of the world gets 'em cheaper."

"It could have been worse," she said, her voice wavering. "They could have taken your medication as well."

Jerry nodded, fastening his seatbelt for the ride home.

The checkpoint north of Tubac was a nuisance, and local residents had complained about it for years. Every election season, people would bring it up at Congressional town halls.

Tempers had sometimes flared. They would ask, why was it there? Shouldn't the Border Patrol be patrolling the border? Some angry residents would wave pages of the CBP's own statistics showing that the checkpoint didn't really stop drugs or even many migrants. They had complained about the lack of response from Customs and Border Protection to their questions.

It didn't matter which political party was in power, Amanda learned, the number of agents at the checkpoint seemed to grow and the mobile trailers and equipment became less mobile and more permanent.

After Amanda had offered to fill scripts, she'd learned quickly that the border crossing was only half the equation. She hadn't thought through the issues with the other half—getting the medications to the book clubs whose members had requested help. She'd thought it'd be easy to pack the medications among the books they regularly traded through the mail. It hadn't been a burden, and they looked forward to the lovely free lunch provided by the Ohioans.

But after awhile, through the magic communications web of book clubs, she'd gotten requests from clubs in other states. Soon, she'd felt like she was running a mail order pharmacy rather than a book club. Taking and filling orders took up more and more time. Once she'd started, she couldn't say no. She knew how much people depended on them—people just like themselves but didn't happen to live near the border. People were just trying to live their lives and stay healthy after surviving a long scary pandemic.

Other members of Book Club also had medical issues, and Amanda had recruited a few to help her and Jerry with the trips across the border. Keeping track of the medication requests became Jerry's new job. The number of requested drugs expanded beyond diabetes to other expensive medications for Crohn's and arthritis.

Some requests were for drugs that Mexico didn't sell, so they'd had to turn them down, disappointing people. She and Jerry had been forced to add a "delivery charge" because scheduling and postage added up. And depending on the medication, special packing was required.

Not to mention the mental toll it was taking on her. She had always played by the rules. All the years she taught school, she required her fifth grade students to play fair, admit when you did something wrong, and try to make it right. But in trying to make things right—getting people the medical help they needed, some of them desperate, she felt she was doing something wrong.

It wasn't immoral, but it was illegal. The situation was unjust. She told herself she was helping navigate a broken system, or at least making it work to ease the suffering of others. *That had to be good a good thing, right?*

Jerry, however, was all in. He looked forward to chances to flaut the medical guidelines. He had lived with his diabetes for years. He'd found that traipsing through the ever-changing obstacles of the health care and insurance system was a challenge for his bad ankles. It had been a constant source of annoyance and irritation. So he'd embraced any opportunities to thumb his nose at Big Pharma.

Amanda worried about his activism, but she shared his anger and frustration. It had been a big health-care transition from Ohio to Arizona—picking new doctors and getting his medications adjusted. And the costs had become a major headache. Learning about medical tourism to Mexico was a lifeline for him. They both just wanted to help others now. The checkpoint bust was a blow.

ABOUT THE AUTHOR

A recovering journalist and freelancer, as well as a
long-time university public information administrator,
Vern Lamplot has lived in southern Arizona for decades.
Before retiring, he was executive director of the
non-profit organization that is restoring historic San
Xavier Mission on the Tohono O'odham nation near
Tucson. Now he writes the Sonoran Borderlands
mysteries full time.

Thank you for reading RODRIGO'S TREASURE.

I hope you enjoy the other books in Sonoran Borderlands
series: A LINE IN THE SAND and the upcoming SPECIAL
DELIVERY

Readers like you keep independent publishing alive. Reviews
are the life blood of independent writers. Please consider
writing a short review of the book on Amazon or other reader
interest sites. email: VernWrites@earthlink.net Please visit my
Website: www.vernlamplot.com. Join my newsletter to stay in
touch.